BLAZE

BY

Teresa Gabelman

The Protectors Series

BLAZE

Copyright 2017 Teresa Gabelman

All rights reserved. The right of Teresa Gabelman to be identified as the author of this work has been asserted in accordance with the Copyright, Designs and Patents Act 1988. This is a work of fiction and any resemblance between the characters and persons living or dead is purely coincidental.

Gabelman, Teresa (2017-2-21). Blaze (THE PROTECTORS SERIES)

Editor: Hot Tree Editing

Photo: www.istock.com

Cover Art: IndieDigitalPublishing.com

Chapter 1

Blaze rushed back to the compound, his face emotionless, but his body full of pent-up energy that needed release, and soon. It had taken Katrina two days to fully heal; it was even touch and go for a minute, which shouldn't have happened when a full-blooded vampire fed from another full blood with an ancient lineage. She should have healed within an hour at the most, but that hadn't happened. And Slade, who could pretty much figure out anything medical, was at a loss as to why.

For two days after Katrina had been found beaten and bloody on the steps of the VC compound, Blaze had only left her side for moments at a time to replenish his own blood as she took his. He had brought her a companion, Sager, the German Shepherd she had saved and had been going to get from the vet when she was attacked. Since she had started healing, though slowly, he was set on finding out who had dared attack her. She said she couldn't remember anything, and with the beating she had taken, he believed her.

Hitting in the code for the door, Blaze walked into the compound and headed for Sloan's office. The shit going down hadn't given him time to even comprehend he was once again a fucking VC Warrior. Jesus, what the fuck was he thinking? The doc had texted him to come back to the compound ASAP. Thinking it was about Katrina, Blaze had texted back but got no reply, which pissed him the hell off.

"What's going on?" Blaze tried to keep his cool as he walked into Sloan's office. He needed to stay calmer where Katrina was concerned, but that was getting harder to do.

"Okay, Adam." Sloan ignored Blaze. "We're all here."

Adam nodded and walked from the back where he had been standing next to Jill and Steve. He stopped in front of Sloan's desk and in the middle of the Warriors. "We have a problem, a big problem."

"What the fuck is new?" Jared sighed with a shake of his head. "We always have a big problem." The Warriors murmured in agreement, then waited for Adam to continue.

"After Katrina was attacked and not healing quickly, I read her." Adam glanced at Blaze, then shifted his eyes quickly away. "I only did it because something wasn't adding up, and with Slade being concerned about her not healing, I wanted to see if she knew anything."

"And?" Blaze growled, not liking that Adam knew more about Katrina than he did.

"And she knows a lot," Adam replied, then frowned. "And this information could most definitely put us and those in our circle in danger."

"Circle, meaning?" Sid spoke up, his usual comedic attitude taking a back seat.

"Meaning, our mates and anyone associated with us." Adam glanced at Becky, Sloan's mate, who was listening intently at her desk. "And she knows exactly who beat her. She got away by calling on animals to attack her attackers."

"Who?" All Blaze heard was she knew who'd attacked her. She had lied to him when he'd asked. His anger was palpable. He felt the heat of his body soar and had to tighten his hands into fists to keep from blasting the room with angry fire.

"Spit it the fuck out," Sid growled, glaring at Adam. "What does she know, or better yet, who do we need to kill?"

"I would rather she have the chance to come clean and tell you," Adam replied, then cringed when every Warrior there except for Blaze starting cursing at him. Blaze didn't have to curse him; his glare said it all. "Hey, this fucking thing I can do really sucks. I don't like being able to pry into anyone's thoughts without them knowing. So, I don't think it's unfair of me to give the person a chance to come clean themselves. There's no immediate threat, and she's probably fucking scared to death. Knowing what I know now, I can't blame her. I would do the same for any one of you, and she *is* a Warrior in training, for now."

Hearing Adam say that Katrina was probably scared changed his focus from anger to protective mode in a flash.

"Go get her." Sloan nodded toward Steve and Jill.

Watching them both leave to get Katrina, Blaze glanced back at Adam, who was staring at him. "What?"

"Nothing." Adam shook his head, looking quickly away.

"You reading me, boy?" Blaze growled, his darkening eyes narrowing.

"No, it's just—" Adam stopped when Steve and Jill reentered with Katrina following.

Blaze looked away from Adam to watch Katrina stop inside the door, her eyes searching everyone before landing on him. Sager was right by her side, alert as if ready to defend her if necessary. Her hand automatically went to the dog's head as if seeking comfort and, for a split second, Blaze felt a jealousy toward the dog that pissed him off. His feelings for this woman were getting out of control, and he needed to do something about that before he totally fucked up both of their lives.

******

Katrina headed toward Sloan's office not realizing she was being summoned. She wanted to be cleared to start training again and had been told by Slade that Sloan had the last word.

"Hey." She smiled as Jill and Steve headed down the hallway toward her. Her smile faded seeing the look on their faces. "What?"

"Sloan wants to see you." Jill glanced away, looking down at Sager. She petted the German Shepherd on the head before rubbing her ears, an action that calmed the overexcited pup.

"Oh, ah, okay." Katrina's eyes landed on Steve, who couldn't seem to look her in the eye. "Why?"

When Jill and Steve shot each other glances, she knew something was up and dread filled her soul. They knew. Somehow they knew. Her mind raced as she stood there, her eyes going to the ground, a habit she used so many times in her life to hide her fear.

"Listen, I probably shouldn't say anything," Steve started, gaining Katrina's attention, "and I'll probably get my ass kicked...."

"Probably? I'd say definitely." Jill snorted, pulling her hand away from Sager. "Adam knows something, about you." Jill took the initiative and told Katrina.

"But he won't say until you're there," Steve, who never wanted to be left out, added. "He wants to give you a chance to tell whatever it is you need to tell."

Katrina felt physically ill. Everything blurred as fear replaced all rational thought from her mind. This couldn't be happening. She had been more than careful. Right now, she needed to calm down and figure this out, fast. If the Warriors knew who she was, everything would be ruined.

"What do you need to tell us?" Steve hedged, leaning toward her, one eyebrow raised.

"Nothing," Katrina said automatically, then glanced at Jill before looking back at Steve. "How good is Adam's skill?"

Steve leaned back, eyeing Katrina for a minute. "Let's just say, if you have a secret you don't want shared, you're fucked."

"Whatever it is, you're a Warrior in training." Jill jumped in with the same thing Adam had said, no doubt in reaction to the fear Katrina couldn't hide. "Come on before they come looking for us. Just be honest, Katrina, and everything will work out fine."

Katrina let Jill lead her down the hallway, but she didn't miss the concerned look on Steve's face before he turned away. As if knowing her turmoil, Sager stuck close to her leg as she walked toward what she knew was going to be her end of the line with the Warriors.

Taking a deep breath, she followed Jill and Steve into Sloan's office. Her eyes automatically went to Blaze before falling back to the ground.

"Katrina." Sloan's voice was deep and full of authority, quickly pulling her gaze from the ground to him.

"Yes." Her voice cracked, her breathing coming in short, fast pants and yet, she kept her eyes glued to him. She needed to be careful. She didn't know exactly what they knew; she couldn't blow this. Her life depended on the next few minutes.

"Is there something you need to tell us?" Sloan didn't beat around the bush about anything. It was something Katrina has learned quickly. He was in-your-face blunt, and she had found that trait honorable until this moment.

"No," she replied, her monotone lie ringing throughout the room, echoing in her head because she knew they knew she was lying.

"I know, Katrina." Adam stepped up with a frown. "And if you don't tell them, I will. I didn't mean to pry, but when you weren't healing, I wanted to help Slade help you and well, I know everything."

"That's rude." Katrina's eyes narrowed toward Adam, unhappy he had pried into her personal thoughts. Remembering where she was, she curbed her attitude and looked toward the ground again.

"So is keeping what you have been keeping from the Warriors," Adam shot back, but his voice wasn't angry, just edged with concern. "As well as dangerous."

"Well, if somebody doesn't say anything in the next second, I'm kicking Adam's ass," Sid said on a growl, standing from the chair in front of Sloan's desk. "If my mate is in danger, I want to know, and I want to know now."

Katrina jumped when Sid moved, her eyes shooting up from the floor.

"Katrina," Adam warned, his head tilting toward her. "Tell or I will."

"Katrina, this isn't a game." Sloan's tone rose, but only slightly.

"I know that." Katrina frowned, her eyes glancing toward Blaze, whose level stare gave nothing away as to what he was thinking. "Believe me, I know that better than anyone," she added, looking away from Blaze.

Sloan sighed. "Katrina, whatever it is, we need to know. You are going to be a Warrior. So far, all I know about you is Jill brought you in from the half-breed camp we successfully shut down."

This was it; the secret she had kept buried so deep was about to be exposed, and she was deathly afraid. Her life and the lives of those in this room were about to be put on the line, a line she had crossed knowing the risks. She wasn't naïve. She knew these Warriors were the best, but they followed the law from what she could tell, and where she came from, there was no law.

"This is bigger than you, and they can keep you safe," Adam encouraged, but it fell short.

"Safe from what?" Blaze finally spoke, stepping forward.

Swallowing back her fear, a legitimate fear that had plagued her since she was old enough to understand the world she had lived in, she looked Sloan straight in the eye. Maybe if she just told them about how she was changed, without giving many facts, they would be satisfied with that. Glancing at all the Warriors with a quick sweep of her eyes, she quickly looked past Blaze, whose body was poised as if he were ready to explode. His angry glare and downturned lips indicated he was pissed, and it was directed toward her.

"I was changed with a group of people," Katrina started, her eyes quickly flicking toward Adam's warning glare. "Someone in the group is the one who formulated what they gave us."

"This someone"—Sloan cocked his eyebrow at her, letting her know he knew she was keeping information from them—"that you know made an injectable that turned you and a group of people into half-breeds."

"Yes." Katrina gave a nod, but then remained silent. She knew that she wasn't going to get away with just that, but she wasn't ready to volunteer information.

"And who is that someone?" Sloan continued.

"His name is…" She didn't know his real name. "…Bones."

"Excuse me?" Sloan tilted his head, his eyes assessing her. "Who the fuck is Bones."

Katrina licked her dry lips, hesitating to say anything because once she did, it would all be over. "He's... just—"

Sloan slammed his hand on his desk, making her jump. "Adam?"

Her head snapped toward Adam, silently begging him not to say anything. He gave her a brief look of sympathy before it was replaced with business as usual.

"Bones is the name of a... patched member." Adam kept his eyes from her and on Sloan.

"Patched member?" Steve snorted. "What the fuck is he, a Boy Scout?"

No one said anything, but they all stared at her. Until that very moment, she had never understood what people meant when they said the silence in the room was deafening. It was so silent the roaring in her ears grew to deafening levels. God, she was going to pass out, even weaved slightly. Blaze reached out to steady her, then backed away as if touching her disgusted him. At least that was what she saw, and it silently broke her heart. Because as soon as they heard everything, none of them would want to have anything to do with her.

"Which gang?" Sloan didn't ask Adam, but her.

She hesitated, her mind going from shutting down, from passing out, to frantically thinking of a lie they would believe. She couldn't stand the thought of losing her place with the VC. As small of a part she had in their lives, it was a part she had wanted all her life. To feel involved with something good.

The growl had her answering quickly. "The Iron Drakes." Katrina didn't even look at anyone as those words she had held close to her fell out of her mouth. Yes, literally fell out of her mouth as if it were the only way they would form.

"Holy shit!" Steve finally got on board.

"And what are the Iron Drakes to you?" Sloan asked, again bypassing Adam, obviously wanting to hear it from her.

"I can't be sent back there." Katrina didn't even try to hide her terror. The thought that once they knew, they would toss her back into that life had her stomach rolling with nauseating fear. If she had been thinking clearer, she would have realized that wouldn't be something they would do, but even the smallest hint that it could be a possibility had her fighting against the irrational fear. "I will kill myself before I ever—"

"No one is sending you anywhere, Katrina," Sloan assured her, but his tone was harsh. "What are your ties with the Iron Drakes?"

"I'm Katrina Drake." Her hand, which had been rubbing Sager's ear, tightened, making the pup whine. She quickly removed her hand. "Samuel Drake, president of the Iron

Drakes, is my father." Bile pushed at the back of her throat as soon as those words escaped.

Cursing filled the room, but she ignored it until she heard Jill.

"You told me you were kicked out by your parents after you were turned," Jill questioned, her tone only curious, not accusing.

"I lied," Katrina responded automatically. "And I'm sorry, but…." Katrina knew she needed to come clean. They knew her dark secret so she might as well let it all out and get it over with. They would find everything out eventually so she might as well as be the one they found out from.

"But what?" this from Blaze, and she couldn't even make eye contact with him.

"I didn't know I was Samuel Drake's daughter until I was around seven. My mother told me my real father had died and I never questioned it." Katrina sighed, aware that trying to explain this mess wasn't going to be easy. Nothing about her life was easy. "From what I was told, my mother ran from the MC right after I was born before my father became president. We ended up in California where she married a man who was a piece of shit with a decent job."

"So how did you end back up with the Iron Drakes?" Blaze asked.

"My stepfather was a bastard who beat my mom and threatened to do the same to me once I got older." Katrina frowned, her memories of those years clouding her thoughts. "The first time he ever hit me, my mom came to my school about a week later and pulled me out. We headed toward the airport, got on a plane and ended up back here."

"And Samuel Drake just opened his arms and let your mother back into the club?" Sloan said, his tone indicating he felt there were holes in her story.

"I was seven years old, but I wasn't stupid," Katrina replied, knowing there was no way they could understand what her life had been like, so she tried to keep her cool. "On the plane my mom explained to me that my real father was still alive and that she was going to go back to him, that he would keep us safe. I didn't know anything about the MC, their rules, or their fucked-up way of life. All I heard was that my real dad was alive and he would protect us from my bastard of a stepfather."

"Jesus." She heard Blaze sigh, but ignored him.

"Waiting for us at the airport was a man I'd never seen before with an older boy who looked a lot like me waiting. He turned out to be my brother. My father wasn't what I pictured. His hair was long, his beard longer, but all I really saw was a big man who could make my stepfather pay for what he'd done like some hero." Katrina laughed, shaking her head. "But even at seven I knew something wasn't right when my mother walked up to him. The hug he gave her wasn't loving like I'd imagined it would be, not even friendly. Now I know what it was, what we'd walked back into. Now I know the hell my mother went through just to keep me safe. Except what she really did was leave one bastard to go back to another who was even worse."

Katrina glanced at Becky who looked confused. Even Jill looked at her with a narrowed look.

"You wondering why?" she asked Becky, then looked at Jill again. "Don't waste your time because I've asked that question myself over and over again. I even asked my mother, but the only thing she could say was that she had no choice. I guess my mom knew she couldn't just start over in California without my stepfather's money. Before meeting him, we were living hand to mouth. We had nothing. She made the choice of calling my father who was now Iron Drakes' president. Traded a bastard for the devil. Makes no sense, and believe me I've tried to make sense of it. Maybe in her own right, she loved Samuel Drake."

"Why didn't she take your brother?" Slade asked, his eyes tight with distrust.

"I'm not really sure except for the fact that my mom knew that Samuel Drake was close to becoming president of the club and my brother was being groomed for a position next to our father. It's a different lifestyle, hell, world, that's the only explanation I was ever given," Katrina replied, not knowing what else to say.

"And your stepfather didn't try to stop any of this?" Jill asked, her eyes sad as they stared at her.

"Not that I know of. And honestly it wouldn't have mattered. Once my mom called Samuel Drake, our lives were set in motion. Even though Mom deserted the MC, she wanted to return. My father, now president, allowed it. I can't even imagine what she had to go through, and it was never spoken about, but I heard whispers of what she endured to be accepted back into the MC, back into my father's life."

Katrina really tried not to cry, but dammit, what her mother had done was for her and that knowledge killed her. Aware of the horrors her mother endured by leaving the MC and then begging to go back was something she wished would leave her memory forever, but she knew that would never happen because she had to remember what a monster her father was; it was the only thing keeping her alive.

"The day I really opened my eyes was about three weeks later when my father came into my room and slammed a newspaper on my bed." Katrina bit the inside of her cheek to keep control of her emotions before continuing. "It was a Californian newspaper reporting that a man by the name of Justin Donnely was found brutally murdered."

"Your stepfather," Sloan said matter-of-factly.

"My stepfather." Katrina nodded. "He then picked up the paper, read the article proudly before patting me on the head and telling me that I would never have to worry about him again. He left me the paper, then walked out the door. I guess in some fucked up way that was how my dad took care of me. Showed me he cared."

"In all honestly, Katrina, I believe you and yet, I know outlaw MCs and for your mom to be allowed back just doesn't add up," Sid said, then threw his hands up before Blaze could say anything. "I'm not saying she's lying. I'm just saying it doesn't add up."

"Samuel Drake likes to make examples of people. My mother was no exception." Katrina didn't even flinch at Sid's words. She expected it. "She once held a position over the women in the club and my father was not even president then, but that all changed. She was treated like a whore, a deserter, but she tried to hide all that from me. Her life was forever chained to the MC because of me. I now understand a little better why she finally came back to the life." Katrina shrugged and gave a heavy sigh. "Waiting for the MC life to catch up with you is exhausting and… scary," she admitted.

"Is there anything else?" Sloan asked, his eyes searching hers as if trying to see if she was lying or holding back information.

"No, that's pretty much it." Katrina glanced at Adam again. "Ask Adam if you don't believe me."

"It's all true." Adam added, "But she did hold something back."

Katrina frowned. "No, I didn't."

"Yes, you did." Adam glared at her, anger dripping from his tone. "You held back that your father will go to the ends of the earth to find you and bring you to MC justice, because no one deserts the Iron Drakes once, let alone twice."

Katrina didn't want to show her fear because she did know the consequences, saw it first hand. It had been scarred into her soul. Adam was right and had managed to push past all the other crap swarming her mind. Then again, the thought of getting caught rarely left her thoughts.

Chapter 2

Blaze knew he looked as shocked as everyone else. Even though he wasn't from this area, he knew exactly who the Iron Drakes were; it was the Warriors' business to know about gang activity in the area, whether vampire or human. What he didn't know was why Katrina had been lying to them about who she was. Seeing the undeniable fear on her face clued him in on part of why she had lied. Once you were part of most motorcycle gangs, you never left unless in a body bag or you just plain disappeared. She was born into the outlaw club, which indicated not only to him but everyone else that she belonged to that club, no ifs, ands, or buts about it. At least to the Iron Drakes way of thinking. His way of thinking was way different, and he'd be damned if she ever went back there.

Cursing filled the air as everyone let what she'd just said sink in.

"And you felt it was in your best interest to lie to us?" Sloan cocked his eyebrow.

Katrina's head snapped up. "I never lied to anyone because no one ever asked who I was."

"Your last name is not Beach," Sloan pointed out, his glare softening slightly.

"And that is not a lie," Katrina countered. "My last name is Beach. I took my mother's last name, which is what most outlaw MC presidents do with their kids, so another competing MC doesn't use them as pawns."

"Motorcycle club." Steve leaned toward Becky, who wore a confused look.

"I know," Becky whispered back to Steve, then gave Katrina a sad smile.

"Wait outside." Sloan dismissed her with a nod of his head. "Becky, go with her."

"I know what you're thinking, and you're wrong." Katrina headed for the door. "I'm not a plant."

Blaze watched her go and knew she was avoiding looking at him. As soon as the door shut, he looked at Adam. "Is what she said true?"

"What, about not being a plant?" Adam asked, sitting down after Katrina left. "Yeah, it's true. She's been on the run since after she was turned. She has no loyalty to them."

"Son of a bitch, this is a fucked-up mess." Sloan rubbed his hand over his face. "I mean, can we seriously not get a fucking break?"

"Actually"—Adam wore a lopsided grin—"she just may be the break we needed."

"And how the fuck is that?" Sloan dropped his hand from the bridge of his nose to glare at Adam. "Other than minor gun running and small-time drugs, which are local police issues, the Iron Drakes have been no problem to us. They keep to themselves and stay the fuck out of our way. Now we have the president's daughter, who's a runaway even if she is of age. We all know it's different rules in the MC. I don't have fucking time for a damn war with a local club that's going to be a pain in my fucking ass."

"Yeah, well it seems they've been flying real low on the radar, because they've gone from small crime to our crime. Meaning Crimson Rush, trafficking, as in humans, and the list goes on." Adam nodded toward the door Katrina disappeared through. "And that girl knows everything."

Blaze cursed, but held his ground waiting to see what Sloan's reaction was going to be. He needed to keep his cool, this time literally. He felt his protective rage rearing its ugly head, but held it back, for now.

Adam stood and walked out of the room. Blaze saw from his vantage point Adam walk up to Katrina before turning around and coming back into the room, shutting the door behind him. Before the door shut completely, Blaze's gaze met Katrina's terrified golden stare.

"Sorry, had to make sure." Adam sat back down with a sigh. "This damn power is confusing as hell sometimes, but father dearest knows exactly who his daughter is playing with because as I said before, it was her father's guys who attacked her."

"Get her back in here, now!" Sloan cursed. Blaze reacted first.

Opening the door, he gave her and Becky a nod and then stepped back as they came back in. This time Blaze stood closer to Katrina, the damn dog wedging itself between them. Blaze glanced down at the dog, who was gazing up at him. With a nod from him, he stood his ground beside Katrina.

"I want to know every fucking thing about the Iron Drakes. I don't give a shit if it takes a week, I want every detail. I want to know what Samuel Drake eats, what he drinks, and even when he takes a piss." Sloan growled the words, towering over her. "And you are going to tell me. You understand?"

Katrina nodded without saying a word. Sloan didn't move.

Focusing on Katrina, Blaze noticed she had started to shake. "She understands, Sloan." He kept his tone level, but not his attitude. "Now back the fuck off."

Sloan's head snapped toward Blaze, his eyes narrowing, but before he could say anything, his phone rang. With one last glare at Blaze, he checked his phone. "Slade, go ahead and ask her whatever you need. I have to take this call."

Blaze watched Sloan head toward the door, reaching out to

squeeze Becky's hand before he left. Becky's worried eyes went back to Katrina, and Blaze was glad that Katrina seemed to have a friend in Sloan's mate.

"Katrina, what do you know about what was given to you?" Slade began, his voice calm but his eyes intense, indicating this was serious business.

Even though Blaze was not touching her, he felt her tremors as if she were in his arms. That connection to her worried him, but he pushed it aside. He'd deal with that shit later; for now, he was just as anxious to hear what she had to say as everyone else.

"Bones is the go-to guy for injuries. He's not a real doctor, but he knows enough to set broken bones and stuff." Katrina began slowly, as if searching for the right words. "I don't know how it started, but I know my father always wanted to be the biggest and best MC in the area."

"What does that have to do with half-breeds?" Sid broke in with a shake of his head. "We know every fucking MC around wants to be the biggest and the baddest. That's nothing new."

She flinched at Sid's remark, which pissed Blaze off. "Shut the fuck up and let her finish," Blaze shot at Sid.

"But none of them went to the extremes as Samuel Drake." Katrina frowned at Sid. "He found a way to change all his patched members into half-breeds, making them the most powerful MC not only in the tristate, but the surrounding areas, and he controlled it all. When I took off, he was making deals with other MCs to change them."

"But you just said he wanted to be the biggest and baddest around. How is changing other clubs going to accomplish that?" Damon, who had been silent until then, asked.

"Samuel Drake will do anything for money." Katrina's voice was low, to the point she sounded weak. "Money in the MC world is power. They also pledged their allegiance."

It wasn't until that very moment Blaze realized what kind of world this young, beautiful woman had been subjected to. His mind reeled, his anger soaring to a new level.

Sloan had come in hearing this, his frown deepening. "I have our source at the police station sending me the files on the Iron Drakes."

"And that is how you were changed?" Slade asked, his focus still intense.

"Yes." Katrina nodded, her hands fidgeting until Sager put his head against Katrina's leg, giving Katrina something to touch. "Bones, from what I understood, started injecting prospects with something. A lot of them died at first, but then it started to work. I don't know what it was, but I know Bones had a setup that he made the stuff in. Soon the whole club was changed and then...."

Blaze stepped a little closer to Katrina, the turmoil in her voice pulling him in. He knew his eyes were swirling red fire because Sloan kept looking at him, giving him a warning glare.

"Then what?" Sloan asked, his eyes going back to Katrina. "You are safe here, Katrina. Nothing is going to happen to you, but we have to know."

Katrina swallowed and nodded. "Bones, under my father's order, started to inject the women. My mom tried to escape, but she was caught. She wanted me and my brother to go with her. My brother told our father what she was up to. Once Samuel Drake found out my mother planned on leaving him again, her fate was sealed.""

"How old is your brother and where is he?" Sloan looked away from his computer to look at her, waiting for her answer.

"He's twenty-seven, and he's still there," Katrina replied, anger curling her lip in disgust.

Blaze watched as a lone red tear leaked from the corner of her eye, but she wiped it away angrily. Almost everyone in the room knew exactly what they did with snitches, but what they heard next confirmed to them exactly what they were dealing with.

"After my mother was passed around to every patched member as well as prospects, she was tortured and then murdered. I was made to watch what they did to her. The bastard kept her alive long enough to watch me turn, to prove to her and everyone else he was the one with the power." With another angry swipe, Katrina smeared the blood tear across her cheek, into her hair. "I have no loyalty to any of them, especially Samuel Drake or my brother. I didn't know my mother's plans until she was caught. She had went to my brother for help to get us out, which was a grave mistake. Before she died Samuel Drake made sure that my mother knew I would live and that I would belong to Breaker, his second in-in-command?"

"Who the fuck is, Breaker?" Blaze didn't catch himself in time, and the dangerous growl escaped his throat. Fuck if that would ever happen. Not in this lifetime and not while he walked the earth. Motherfucker was good as dead. No way in hell would Katrina belong to anyone.

"As soon as I could, I escaped, which wasn't easy because every prospect was in charge of watching me." Katrina ignored Blaze's question.

"What's a prospect?" Becky asked, staring at Katrina, a sadness shadowing her face.

"A prospect in the MC is someone who wants to be a patched member. They're at the mercy of all patched members and will do anything they are told—kill, rape, you name it. A patched member is the only one who can wear the colors of the club," Katrina replied, then frowned at Becky. "Don't feel sorry for me."

"I don't feel sorry for you," Becky quickly replied. "I feel sorry for your circumstance, which was out of your control. There's a big difference. I think you're a very strong woman."

Katrina only nodded but didn't say anything else. Blaze agreed 100 percent with Becky. They probably hadn't even scraped the surface of what Katrina had been through, living the life of a daughter to the president of a fucking outlaw motorcycle club. There were legit MCs that did wonderful work for children, veterans, etcetera, but not the Iron Drakes.

Sloan turned his monitor around so everyone could see. "This is your father?"

"That's Samuel Drake." Katrina nodded, and Blaze saw hatred darken her eyes.

Within an hour, Katrina had gone through all the file pictures of each member of the Iron Drakes, naming who they were and what purpose they served in the club. Each member that passed the monitor, the more she seemed to wither away. Blaze stood close to her, waiting, but she stood strong until the last picture was shown.

"That's Breaker." Katrina's voice shook. "His first name is Isaac, but I don't know his last name."

"Why do they call him Breaker?" Steve asked, staring at the picture.

"He's good at breaking things" was all Katrina said, her voice shaking slightly.

Standing directly behind her, Blaze noticed the crooked pinky finger on her left hand, which held her weight as she leaned on the desk to see the computer screen. She curled it up under her hand as she spoke. Blaze mumbled a curse as he returned his glare to the picture on the monitor, burning the image into his brain. He knew without a doubt he was staring at a dead motherfucker.

The room was silent for only a second. Sloan turned the monitor back and stood. "Suit up." He looked around, his gaze skipping Becky and Katrina. "We ride in half an hour."

Blaze waited back with Katrina who just stood with her head down before looking up. "I can draw you a map of their clubhouse and where everything is." Her voice shook. "It's big with a lot of hidden areas. I know where their spotters are and where they hide during their watch."

"That would be of great help, Katrina." Sloan slid her paper and a pen. He reached out and lifted her face to his. "I know what happens to people who go against MCs and I promise you, you are under our protection. Nothing will happen to you."

A sudden urge to break Sloan's arm flashed through Blaze's mind, but was gone when Sloan pulled it away from Katrina's face. Jesus, he needed to get a grip and fucking fast.

Once she was done, she handed Sloan the papers. Blaze had watched her draw them with notes. It was a precise map that anyone getting ready to raid would love to have.

"Am I allowed to continue to train?" Katrina asked, her eyes shifting away from Sloan, unsure of herself. Blaze could read her like a fucking book, and he wanted to shake her and tell her she was good enough.

"Slade has released you?" he asked, but looked toward Blaze who nodded. "Then I see no reason why you can't."

"Thank you." She turned to leave but stopped. "I know you guys are good at what you do, but you have morals. The Iron Drakes don't. Be careful."

Sloan actually grinned. "Blaze, it seems our façade has been working. We have morals."

Blaze snorted but didn't smile.

"If things go down, I'll do my best to protect your brother," Sloan added before she could leave. "Which one is he, you didn't point him out?"

"I don't have a brother." Katrina opened the door. "The day my mother was brutally raped and murdered I lost whatever family I ever thought I had."

Blaze watched the door close behind her, and his eyes went to Sloan. "You know this MC well?"

"Yeah." Sloan glanced to where Becky had gone back to her desk and lowered his voice. "It's going to get bloody."

With a nod, Blaze walked out to get prepared, and he knew the first motherfucker who was going to spill blood.

Chapter 3

Katrina stood in the shadows waiting. Sager sat quickly beside her. As soon as Blaze disappeared down the hallway, she snuck toward Sloan's office with Sager creeping right along behind her.

"What are you doing?" Both Katrina and Sager jumped straight up in the air.

She spun, her hand slamming to her throat where a scream was lodged. "You scared me."

"Good." Blaze cocked his eyebrow. "What are you and that damn dog sneaking around for?"

"His name is Sager, not damn dog," Katrina corrected him absently, her eyes not meeting his. She really didn't want to have this confrontation with Blaze or explain why she had been waiting in the shadows for him to leave.

"Look at me," he ordered, taking a step toward her. When she did, he crossed his arms over his massive chest. "What are you going back to Sloan's office for?"

"I… ah… I remembered something," Katrina said, her eyes flickering away from his intense stare.

"What?" Blaze stared down at her instead of turning around

and leaving, which she had hoped he'd do.

"Samuel Drake has a unique power." Katrina licked her lips nervously. She had learned that the hard way. "He can control moods as well as manipulate thoughts, but you can block, and he can't do anything."

"I'll let everyone know, but we are always blocked," Blaze replied with his "always business" attitude.

Katrina nodded and then glanced at Sloan's door before turning to walk away. "Just be careful," she whispered, but knew he heard her.

"You lied to me." He stopped her, turning her back around to face him. "You knew exactly who attacked you."

"I didn't want to bring trouble here," Katrina replied, her lip trembling. "I'm sorry."

Before Blaze could say anything, Sloan came out of his office with Becky following him.

"You ready?" Sloan asked, his eyes going between Katrina and Blaze.

Katrina looked up at Blaze, who was still staring at her. He was so handsome, and his touch warmed the coldness she always felt. She would give anything for him to take her into his arms, but she knew that would never happen. When his touch left her, so did the warmth.

"I'm ready." Blaze nodded, finally looking away from her.

"I should go with you," Katrina said, her stomach clenching at the thought of walking into that hell again. "I know where everything is. I know how they operate, but I don't know if I can physically walk in there again." Katrina had never felt more like a failure than she did at that moment. "Not very Warrior-like."

"Actually, it's very Warrior-like," Sloan replied, his eyes narrowing. "It's smart to know when to step back."

"Just, please, be careful," Katrina urged, her worried eyes landing on Becky, then Sloan. "They live by no rules."

"In certain situations, neither do we," Sloan replied, then bent down and kissed Becky before leaving.

Katrina quickly glanced away from their show of affection, everything in her body wanting what they had, but she could only wish for something like that in her own life. Blaze only gave her a nod before following Sloan out the door.

Soon, all the Warriors were heading out the door as the mates stood in the entryway watching them leave.

"How about a movie and a drink?" Tessa suggested, her eyes still on the door that Jared had just disappeared through.

"I think tonight we're going to need a few drinks, strong drinks," Nicole replied, a worried frown marring her features.

"I'm sorry," Katrina said to the group of women. "They were never to find out."

"Honey, this is what our men do." Lana wrapped her arm around Katrina's shoulders. "And they are damn good at it."

The women nodded in agreement as they made their way to the game room where the Warriors and their mates usually enjoyed some downtime. Even with their kind words, the feeling of doom wouldn't leave her.

******

Blaze followed on his bike, his focus on what had to be done and Sloan's warning to him to not burn the fucking place to the ground without specific orders. Yeah, well, he made no promises. Heat pounded his body, wanting release, and it wouldn't take much to release it. Just one fucking word about Katrina and shit would get real, fast.

Pulling into a Park N' Ride behind everyone, Blaze stepped off his bike and waited for instructions, hoping he could follow through with them. He was a fucking Warrior now and needed to play by the rules. Well, was supposed to play by the rules. He didn't play fair, never had, so he guessed it was up to the fuckers he was about to play with whether they died tonight by Sloan's orders or his own.

"We're about a block away," Sloan said as soon as everyone

gathered around. "Steve, you're going to go in first."

"What?" Sid and Jared said at the same time, while everyone else stared at Sloan as if he'd lost his mind.

"Yeah." Steve eyed Sloan surprised. "What?"

"You wanted a power, you got a power, and now you get to use that fucking power," Sloan growled. "You think you can do that without fucking up?"

Steve thought for a moment. "Absolutely."

"Good, because if you fuck this up, it's your ass." Sloan eyed him.

"Ya know, I'm so glad this job comes with low stress levels," Steve mumbled, sticking his hands in his back pockets. "I'd sure hate to shit my pants."

Sloan pulled out a paper and handed it to Steve. "Disappear."

"Okay." Steve took the paper and started walking away looking down at the sheet of paper.

"You want to kick his ass or want me to do it?" Jared sighed, shaking his head.

Steve turned, glancing around. "He said disappear." Steve tossed his hands up in the air. "I'm disappearing. Why kick my ass for that? I'm sure I'll do something worse than that before the night's over."

"Amen to that shit." Sid nodded with a cock of his eyebrow.

"Let me go." Blaze was done with the Steve Show. This shit was too important to fuck up, not to mention he was ready to get his hands on someone.

Sloan ignored him, his glare never leaving Steve. "Are you that stupid, son?"

"Depends on who you ask," Steve mumbled again, then stood quietly for a minute as if in deep thought. His eyes popped open as his mouth formed a perfect circle of understanding. "You meant disappear as in my power disappear, not walk away disappear."

Jill stepped next to Steve and smacked him upside the head, but leaned close to him with a whispered, "He wants to see if the paper disappears with you. Get your shit together."

Blaze rolled his eyes and watched as Steve disappeared, but the paper didn't. He knew the paper he held was the notes that Katrina had given Sloan on the Drakes' compound.

"Is it gone?" Steve asked, waving the paper around, making it look like it was just blowing in the breeze.

"No," Sloan replied, taking the paper as Steve reappeared. "All I want you to do is get in and give us a count on how many are there. Look for scouts that we need to worry about and their location."

"No problem." Steve nodded, waiting for more orders.

"It better not be." Sloan glanced up from the paper then passed it to Blaze. "You have fifteen minutes. If you aren't back here to report by then, we're coming in."

"I'll be back." Steve gave him a nod before turning around. "Do I get a raise if I pull this off?"

"No, you'll get to live," Blaze answered for Sloan, ready to beat somebody's ass. If it was Steve's, then so be it. He didn't know what the hell was going on, but he wanted answers to who Katrina really was. Why it mattered so much to him, he didn't know. Yes, he did, but he refused to admit anything other than looking out for her. End of fucking story.

"Oh, great," Steve called out as he headed toward his first real orders with his new powers. "You know this should be a happy time for me. Thanks for fucking that up with threats of my looming death, Blaze. Appreciate it, bro."

Blaze didn't reply, but he did look toward Adam. "You reading him?"

A grin split across Adam's face. "Like a book." Adam glanced at him. "And you really don't want to know how he feels about you at the moment."

Chapter 4

"Fucking fire boy, being all badass," Steve said under his breath as soon as he knew he was far enough away that the big bastard couldn't overhear him. "You'll get to live." He mocked Blaze's deep voice as he continued down the street.

Knowing he was close, Steve disappeared. They all may think he was just a fuckup, but Steve was damn serious about what he did. He just liked having fun and yeah, sometimes he had major brain farts, but who the fuck didn't? Well, Sloan probably never had a brain fart in his life, but the rest of them had, so screw them.

Seeing the entrance that Katrina described, Steve stopped and studied his surroundings. No one was around that he could see. Stepping out into the street, he crept toward the gate then stopped. What the fuck was he doing? Nobody could see him. He started walking again, this time normally, and noticed the place looked deserted. He tried the gate, finding it unlocked, and then slipped in. If anyone was watching, they were probably shitting themselves thinking they were having a paranormal experience, seeing the gate open on its own. Steve chuckled to himself. He couldn't wait to start fucking with people.

Once inside, he waited, but no alarms were shouted. Making his way deeper inside, he noticed a large house that had seen better days, along with two garages and a large fire pit in the middle of a huge concrete slab. A noise had him looking back toward the house. With one last look around, he walked toward the house. Finding the door open, he walked inside.

The stench of sweat, sex, vomit, and cigarette smoke filled his senses. He immediately found two men sitting at a table playing cards, smoldering cigarettes hanging from their mouths. Across the room was another man, this one with his bare ass facing him. Steve looked around, knowing that they were the only ones in the room. He headed toward the bare-assed guy, who wore a vest with a prospect patch sewed on the back. Steve noticed shapely legs wrapped around the man's waist—well, not exactly wrapped. They hung limply while the man held them as he pumped his hips.

Anger hit Steve as he rounded the couch to see a girl passed out as the asshole repeatedly rammed inside her. His eyes left the girl as he looked up at the man, then around the room again. Without thought, he let his anger fly and punched the man square in the face, knocking him back and off the woman.

"What the fuck!" The man jumped up as fast as he hit the ground, pulling his pants up while he gazed around, confused, with a look of fright on his face. Once he had his pants fastened, he glared toward his buddies at the table who were staring at him.

"What the hell is your problem?" one of them asked, the cigarette still dangling from his lips, his cards held up as he glared at them.

"Somebody fucking hit me." The guy Steve had hammered touched his jaw.

"What? Did Jenny have enough of your little dick?" The other one guffawed, then broke out in a deep, racking cough.

"Fuck you!" The prospect rubbed his jaw as he looked around wide-eyed. "Someone fucking hit me, and it wasn't Jenny. She's passed out cold."

"You are a sick fuck." The first guy stood, shaking his head as he looked over the couch. "She's going to be pissed when she wakes up because no way in hell would she let you touch her."

Disgust rolled in Steve's gut. He knew he'd fucked up, but no way in hell could he just stand there while this bastard had his way with an unconscious female.

"Like I give a shit," the prospect spat, still looking dazed and confused. "I want to know who fucking hit me."

"You're an idiot." The guy walked back to the table and sat down, shaking his head.

Steve nodded in agreement, then glanced at the two men who were back to playing cards, dismissing everything the dumbass said. Figuring to fuck with the guy further, Steve reached over and grabbed a throw blanket and placed it over the girl.

The guy actually yelped as he stumbled backward, banging into the wall. "Holy shit!" he shouted, his voice shaking with fear. "Did you see that? Did you fucking see that?"

"Pollard, shut the fuck up," one of the men growled, not even looking his way. "Stay off the dope, man."

"The goddamn blanket just floated in the fucking air, man." Pollard looked over at them but pointed to the couch. "Floated!"

Steve chuckled just loud enough the asshole heard him. Damn, this shit was fun. He could stay here all night and fuck with this asshole, but he needed to get back before the Warriors came running in full force, blowing shit up. Not able to help himself, he walked close enough to the idiot who remained staring wide-eyed at the blanket draped over the girl's naked body and flicked him hard on the earlobe.

The large grin Steve wore at the man's girly scream faded quickly as he saw who stood in the doorway. Shit was about to get real.

******

Katrina sat watching the movie without seeing a thing. She had no clue what the movie was, who starred in it, or what was even going on around her. All she could think about was the Warriors walking into the unknown. She hadn't given them enough information. She knew they were grown badass men, but the Drakes were no joke. Finally pulling her blank stare away from the television, she looked at the women who surrounded her. If anything happened to any of those men, it would be her fault. These were her friends now, her family, yet she'd let them go without giving them all the information. But why? She was afraid of what they would think of her once they knew exactly what her life had once been. This was her fight, not theirs, and there she sat watching a movie.

Nicole glanced her way, giving her a small smile. Katrina tried to smile back, but failed miserably. She stood quickly, drawing everyone's attention.

"Are you okay?" Tessa, who was lounging next to her, sat up.

"Yeah, just think I'll head to my room," she lied, hoping they didn't press because she didn't want to lie any more than she had to. She hated to lie because she was damn good at it, had been taught to be good at it. Mentally she told Sager to stay, which the pup did. "If you don't care, I'll let Sager stay here so he's not cooped up in my room. I'll come back to let him out in a little bit."

Pam was on the floor with Sager and Daniel. Daniel loved playing with the pup and Sager was loving the attention.

"Go ahead and rest. We'll take care of him." Pam laughed when Sager licked Daniel on the nose.

"Thanks," Katrina replied. Then without looking at anyone

else, she quickly slipped out. Once out of sight, she ran to her room. Quickly she changed into jeans and a long-sleeved shirt. She didn't have a coat, but she'd be okay. She didn't really get cold anymore, at least not like she had when she was human.

Peeking her head out of her room, she made sure no one was around, then headed out one of the many doors toward the garage. The crisp November air seemed to crackle around her as she hurried toward the garage. Her eyes slid toward the cameras that were watching her every move, but she knew no one was manning them. The Warriors were gone for the moment, so the place was on lockdown. No one could get in, but they could get out.

Reaching into her back pocket, she pulled out her lock picks as she reached the garage door. Glancing up, she saw the alarm system and frowned. Dammit, she hoped this worked. It usually did, but with the Warriors' setup, she wasn't too confident. She was going to have to work fast, but one thing her piece-of-shit daddy taught her was how to pick a lock and disarm an alarm system. Her eyes once again found the camera pointing straight at her, and guilt washed over her, but she had to do this.

Kneeling, she got to work on manipulating the components of the lock, and within seconds, the lock clicked. She grabbed the piece of thin metal that had never let her down and slipped it between the two magnets that would set the alarm off. With a deep breath, she slowly opened the door, keeping the metal in place as she slipped in and then closed the door, removing the metal strip. The alarm began its warning beeps, and without thought, she used her fist and smashed it. She should have known the Warriors' alarm wouldn't work like the other alarms she had disarmed. She knew that the only alarm that would sound was the one on the computers that no one was sitting in front of. She had spent a day in their control room learning everything there was to know about the security of the Warrior compound. There were no cops who would show up, because what the hell could the cops do that the Warriors couldn't to an intruder? She actually felt a smile slip across her lips remembering Jared saying those exact words. And yes, the guilt weighing her down by using that information for breaking into their garage was unbearable.

Walking over, she hit the button to open one of the garage doors, then went on the hunt. Seeing a Harley Sportster ready to go, she hurried that way. She'd ridden many bikes in her life and never found one fit for her size, but she made do. There was nothing better than the freedom of riding. Excitement to finally ride overrode the fear and guilt of what she was doing. Pushing the bike out of the garage, down the drive of the compound and onto the street, she wasted no time hopping on and starting it up.

The power from sitting with the energy of the bike between her legs had her smiling, the guilt and fear of what she was doing disappearing for a split second. With no thought other than taking off, she did just that, and had never felt freer in her life, even though she was heading toward the hell she had tried so hard to run away from.

Enjoying the ride more than she should, she began to focus on what was to come. Knowing she couldn't just show up without backup, because honestly, she didn't know the Warriors' plans—she hadn't been involved in that—she called out to friends, confident that they would show for her.

The closer she got, the more focused she became. The mind games, the evil intentions were about to start, and she had to not only be mentally ready, but physically prepared. Samuel Drake may be her father, but she was nothing to him but a pawn he had used and would continue to use if she fell into the madness of the Iron Drakes again.

Sensing her call to friends had been answered, she slowed as she rode up to the Iron Drakes' clubhouse. The gate was open, so with a deep breath, she rode right through them. Six large, mean-looking coyotes stood in the shadows waiting for her, their eyes glowing briefly in the darkness. She didn't have to see them to know they were there; she felt them. What she did look for was the activity that was always going on at the Drakes' clubhouse, yet she found none. Instantly she knew that her father had deserted and moved to a different location, which he only did when he felt any kind of heat. And she also knew without a doubt the Warriors were the heat he was worried about.

Pride swirled through her body, but just as fast as it arrived, it disappeared, replaced by dread of what she had done. It was as if he still had power over her life. *Break this law, disengage with these people, do as I say and ask no questions because I am the law here.* It was as if he were standing over her shoulder directing her like a puppet.

Climbing off the bike, her hands shook, and her knees felt weak, making her stumble. She knew without a doubt that after what she'd just pulled, she would never be trusted. Leaning her head back, she sighed as she looked at the sky and wondered if she would ever get a fair break in life. Yeah, she deserved a moment of self-pity, but that soon came to an end.

Her body became alert as she heard a noise to her left. Snapping her head down, she looked that way. She figured the Warriors had been there and gone by now, seeing that no one was there, but maybe that wasn't the case. She cast a look toward the coyotes; they fell in step with her, and as one, they headed toward the main house, which was covered with overgrown bushes. Once she was around the front, she saw light, heard cursing, and her stomach cramped. She knew that voice, and she absolutely hated this house. The memories threatened to overtake her, but she pushed them back. She was stronger than the memories. She had to be stronger.

Slowly, she climbed the stairs and stood in the open doorway unnoticed. Her eyes went from the bastard Pollard, one of her father's prospects and one of the men who had beaten her weeks ago, to the unmoving figure completely naked with her legs hanging over the arm of the nasty couch. Anger so strong hit her, making her hands ball into fists. Before she could act, she watched, amazed, as a stained throw blanket floated from one end of the couch, traveled up in the air and slowly floated down to cover the naked female. Instantly she knew that she wasn't alone. Steve was with her as well as the low growling companions who surrounded her.

Pollard screamed at the sight of the blanket floating in midair, making Katrina smile, no humor involved, only satisfaction that the bastard felt some of the fear he bestowed on others.

The coyotes grew restless, their nails clipping on the hardwood floor as they pranced in place. Katrina glanced to the other two in the room, who she didn't know. One was looking straight at her.

"Who the fuck are you?" He stood, his eyes going from her to the coyotes.

She didn't answer, just swung her gaze back to Pollard, who had turned toward her. His eyes narrowed. Reaching deep for the confidence she needed, she took a step into the room and then another, the coyotes in step with her. Her eyes went from Pollard's thin, ugly face to see Jenny lying unconscious. Her stomach rolled as disgust, thick and hot, rose to her throat, but she pushed the bile back.

"Only way you can get a girl, Pollard?" Katrina snapped, not knowing where Steve was, but knew he was there. That and the coyotes gave her courage; it was exactly what she needed. The Iron Drakes could sniff out weakness, and once they did, it was pretty much over for the one who dared show anything other than confidence in their presence.

"Well, Kat, I never thought you were stupid enough to show up here." Pollard sneered, one corner of his lips curving up into a cruel smile.

God, she hated to be called that, but she didn't even flinch.

"But your father did." Pollard sniffed, then wiped his nose, a clear habit of a coke addict. He snorted more coke than anyone she had ever seen. It was all he cared about and all he worked for, the next snort of white powder.

"That's her?" The man who remained standing stared at her, his eyes roaming up and down, making her sick to her stomach. "Damn, man. I thought she'd be… ugly as fuck. I mean, Drake is an ugly son of a bitch."

"I'll make sure he knows you think that. But her momma was a beautiful piece of ass." Pollard laughed, his eyes also raking down her body before his evil stare met hers. "And a good fuck."

His words hit her and anger exploded throughout her body. Her lips pulled back, exposing her fangs as the pounding in her ears beat a raging tempo. The coyotes reacted to her emotions and lowered their heads, ready to pounce, but Pollard was quick. He pulled a gun, aiming it at the closest coyote.

"You call that fucker back, or I'll blow its head off," he

ordered, his eyes shifting to her then back to the threat.

Her only answer was to step in front of the coyote. "Go ahead and shoot." When he quickly looked away from her, she laughed. "But that's not your orders, is it? Drake wants me alive, and you don't have the balls to go against him, do you?"

"Fuck you, Kat," he spat, the gun still raised.

"Don't call me that," Katrina hissed, her eyes narrowing in hatred for him and the name.

"So it's true." Pollard nodded toward the coyotes. "You can control them. That's how you got away from us. That's why all those fucking birds attacked us. I told Drake that, but he didn't believe me. He's going to shit, and if you think he wanted you back before, oh man, he's going to come after you himself."

Katrina didn't say a word. No way would she give them any information. If they were too stupid to figure it out, so be it. Steve had reappeared behind the other two men, his eyes on her. She gave him a warning look; she needed to find out where Drake was.

"Where's Drake's new clubhouse?" Katrina asked calmly.

"I can take you to him." Pollard gave her an empty smile.

"How nice of you, but I think I'll just show up on my own,"

Katrina replied with fake politeness, her smile just as empty.

"Still a smartass, I see." Pollard started to lower the gun, but one of the coyotes took a step, making him raise it again. "So what happens to you if I shoot one of those ugly bastards?"

"Nothing." Katrina took another step to shield the dog. "It's what will happen to you."

"Oh, and what's that?" Pollard cocked his head with an arrogant twist.

"I will kill you," Katrina replied, taking a step forward. "Go ahead, Pollard, or are you scared of what Drake will do to you?"

"Don't tempt me, Kat." Pollard sneered, the gun rising straight toward her forehead. "It's almost worth seeing your brains splatter for what Drake did to me when you got away."

"Oh, sorry." She tilted her head. "Did I get you in trouble?"

The gun clicked. "I told you not to tempt me."

A flash of brightness passed close to Katrina's head, and she felt a wave of heat. Her eyes widened as a ball of fire smashed into Pollard's hand, catching his sleeve on fire. The gun dropped to the floor. Strong arms wrapped around her, pulling her back as Blaze stormed past her, heading straight for Pollard.

Chapter 5

Blaze was disappointed to hear from Adam, who was reading Steve, that the place was deserted except for three members of the gang. He itched to get his hands on someone and dammit, the odds of that happening were slim since he wasn't the only one with those feelings. The rest of the Warriors were strung tight, wanting to get their hands on someone also.

"We got a problem," Adam said with a frown.

"What?" Sloan growled as the Warriors all made eye contact with each other.

"Steve just punched a dude in the face while still invisible." Adam chuckled then stopped immediately when Sloan growled. "It's okay. He's just fucking with him. It's actually working. Wait a minute. What the hell?"

"What?" Sloan demanded as Damon's phone went off.

"Somebody else is there." Adam put his hand to his temple before his eyes widened. "Holy shit!" His eyes shot to Blaze.

"That was Nicole." Damon also glanced at Blaze. "Katrina disappeared. When Nicole checked the cameras, she saw that Katrina broke into the garage and took one of the bikes.

She doesn't know where she went."

"I do." Adam jumped on his bike. "She's there. At the Iron Drakes."

Blaze was already heading out. He somehow knew without hearing Adam's words. He knew where Katrina had gone. Within minutes, he pulled through the open gate, spotting the bike Katrina had ridden, actually impressed that such a small woman could handle a bike like that.

"Hey, what the hell!" Sid stopped next to the bike. "That's my fucking bike she stole."

"Where?" Blaze asked the one-word question, ignoring Sid's outburst, his eyes scanning the area before landing on Adam.

"The house, over there." Adam pointed as they all spread out while Sloan gave orders as he ran alongside Blaze.

He didn't even look at the steps as he jumped them, landing on the porch. All he focused on was Katrina surrounded by coyotes and the motherfucker who pointed a gun at her. With no thought other than getting rid of the threat directed at her, he pulled his power and slung a ball of fire from his hand toward the bastard. Pulling Katrina behind him, he rushed toward the son of a bitch who dared threaten her.

Blaze felt a rage he had never felt before consuming his body as his large hand wrapped around the man's neck. Picking him up, Blaze punched him repeatedly in the face before slamming him on the floor. The bastard's arm was still on fire, his terrified eyes wide open as he frantically slammed his hand on the floor, trying to put out the fire. Undeterred, Blaze stepped on his wrist, hand still around his throat, letting his arm continue to burn.

"Blaze!" Sloan's voice broke through his heightened killing instinct. He wanted this bastard dead once he'd suffered. "We need him alive."

"Fuck that!" Blaze squeezed his throat tighter as his blazing eyes glared down into the man's soul. "He's going to hell tonight."

"Goddammit, Blaze." Sloan tried to push Blaze away from the man, but Blaze refused to be moved. "I order you to let him go. Now!"

Blaze cursed as he squeezed even tighter before finally releasing him. The man wheezed and gasped then rolled to his side, throwing up. Sloan actually pushed Blaze out of the way and off the man's wrist before he used his own foot to stomp out the fire, ignoring the man's screams of pain before he passed out.

Trying to calm his rage, Blaze turned to find Katrina gone. Son of a bitch! His eyes scanned until he found her bent over the unconscious girl on the couch. Her head lifted, meeting his gaze. "She needs help."

Looking down at the girl, Blaze frowned. "Slade," he called, nodding toward the girl.

Slade walked away from the two men who had been sitting at the table, but were now in custody and in handcuffs. He immediately rushed to the girl, lifting her eyelids. "What's she on, do you know?" he growled at the men. They refused to answer.

"Heroin." Katrina didn't hesitate as she picked up the girl's arm, showing the track marks.

Blaze watched as Katrina gave the girl one last glance before slowly backing away. She headed toward the coyotes, who then sat inches from her, their eyes never leaving her. It was really a sight to see. She stared at them for a few moments, then as one, they stood and calmly trotted out of the house into the darkness. She stared after them for a second before her eyes found his and then once again, they lowered to the floor.

Blaze walked up to her and used his knuckles to raise her face to his. "Breaking into the Warriors' garage, stealing a Warrior's bike, and facing down members of a motorcycle gang." Blaze didn't smile as he said those words, his voice even as he stared into her golden eyes. "I'm not falling for the shy girl routine."

When she didn't respond but continued to stare up at him, he felt a connection to her that made him drop his hand away from her smooth skin.

"I hope you're ready for the shitstorm heading your way." He frowned as he leaned closer to her, his mouth close to her ear. "And if you ever pull a stunt like this again, you will regret it dearly."

"What in the hell were you thinking?" Sloan had walked over, glaring down at Katrina.

Blaze reluctantly backed away but gave her a told-you-so look. As angry as he was at her, he wasn't happy to hear that same anger in Sloan's tone. Actually, it fucking pissed him off to the point he had to warn himself to keep his mouth closed and his thoughts to himself.

Katrina didn't answer right away as Damon, Duncan, and Jared led the three men out the door. "I didn't tell you everything and felt I needed to be here."

"So you decided to break into the garage and steal a motorcycle?" Sloan growled, his eyes narrowing.

"Yeah, about that," Sid, who was standing back, piped in. "If there is one scratch on my bike—"

"I can ride a bike better than I can drive a car," Katrina cut in. "Your bike is fine."

"You shouldn't be here." Sloan ignored Sid.

"You're right, I shouldn't." She shivered at the thought of what could have happened if Drake, her father, had been there. "But since I am, I can show you the layout and see if anything was left behind that could clue us in to where they might have gone."

Sloan and Blaze both glared at her without saying a word.

Jax walked in, looking annoyed; his frown grew seeing her. "Guess you being here explains the coyotes."

Katrina remained silent.

"Hey, she was trying to get that asshole to say where they went." Steve stepped in, and when everyone turned their glare to him, it was certain he should have kept his mouth shut.

"What in the fuck do you think you were doing?" Sloan rounded on Steve.

"Protecting a female," Steve replied without hesitation. "And I'd do it again."

"Do you have a read on them?" Blaze asked Adam, nodding toward the door the three men were taken out of.

"Yeah, and they have no idea where Drake and the club are," Adam replied, then frowned when Sloan and Blaze looked at him with disbelief. "Seriously, they don't know."

"And they wouldn't," Katrina responded, backing up Adam. "Drake isn't stupid, and when he feels a threat, he will pick up and move. No one knows until the move is being carried out. He always leaves two or three prospects behind if they have left something of value."

"Or waiting for something of value to come back." Blaze eyed her with a growl. He knew she would ignore him, but he had a feeling that her father wasn't going to just let her go so easily. If she weren't the daughter of the MC president that may have been a different story, but she was the property of the club, and MCs took their property seriously.

Chapter 6

Katrina acted like she didn't even hear Blaze because he was absolutely right. Drake wouldn't stop tracking her down, and the only thing that would stop that hunt was his death. Glancing over her shoulder, she saw Jenny sitting up with Slade talking to her.

"Looks like everything has been cleaned out," Jax was telling Sloan.

She needed to find out how long ago Drake evacuated the property; that would tell her what was left, if anything. She moved toward Jenny, who sat looking confused and still under the power of the drug. Yet, their eyes met and Jenny's gaze cleared.

"You're back!" Jenny cried out with a happy squeal, but then quickly looked around. "But you can't be here. You need to leave before he gets here." Jenny tried to stand, her frightened eyes searching around as she attempted to get to Katrina. Slade stopped her, but Jenny fought him.

"No!" Jenny screamed. "Let me go. She has to get out of here. This is what he wanted."

"It's okay, Jenny." Katrina grabbed her gently, edging her back down to the couch. The last thing Katrina wanted to do was sit on the couch, but she swallowed back her disgust and held Jenny as she cried. "Drake isn't here."

"You should have stayed gone." Jenny sniffed, her head resting on Katrina's shoulder. "It's gotten worse since you left. You're all he talked about, and then I heard them talking. He thinks you can control animals."

Katrina's eyes met Slade's then Blaze's. "Jenny, how long have they been gone?"

"Isn't that crazy? Nobody can control animals." Jenny continued her sniffling rant. "But Pollard swore to it, and I think Drake started to believe it because I heard them making plans on how they would use you."

"Jenny." Katrina didn't really want to hear any more; she didn't *need* to hear any more. She knew exactly what would happen if she fell under Drake's power again. Leaning back, she grasped Jenny's shoulders so she could look at her. "How long have they been gone?"

"Not even a week," Jenny replied, then bit her lip as tears flowed. "I think. I kind of lose time."

Katrina gave her a sad smile with a nod. "I know." Using the edge of the blanket, she wiped the tears from Jenny's face.

It seemed as if the drug fog Jenny had been under had started to clear. She looked down at herself as if finally realizing she was naked underneath the blanket, then shifted uncomfortably. Her angry eyes rose to meet Katrina's.

"Pollard raped me while I was out, didn't he?"

"I'm sorry." Katrina didn't know what else to say. Jenny was a beautiful girl, inside and out, but the drugs and lifestyle were taking their toll. She looked as if life had chewed her up and spat her out more than once.

"The bastard!" Jenny's chin trembled, but her head tilted back and her shoulders straightened. "I want out. I want out like you. Can you help me? Please, Katrina."

Katrina didn't know what to say. She could hardly help herself, but she knew she couldn't say no. "Yes, I'll help you."

Sloan had been standing close by, listening, his face set in stone. "Slade, find a rehab center that can take her ASAP."

Jenny looked up at Sloan, fresh tears flowing as she stood and walked toward him with the blanket wrapped around her. She looked so small and slight standing in front of the massive Warrior, but that didn't stop her from wrapping an arm around him, holding him tightly as she cried her gratefulness.

"Thank you," Katrina mouthed silently to Sloan.

Slade took Jenny back to the couch and started asking her questions while he was on the phone. Jill had taken Katrina's place and was consoling her. Katrina stood, knowing that Jenny was being taken care of, and glanced toward the steps then back to Sloan and Blaze, who were staring at her.

"If she's right, they've only been gone for less than a week, so there's no way they took everything." Katrina turned and headed toward the stairs. With each step she climbed, the memories slammed into her like a bad movie. She actually stopped in the middle to collect herself.

She felt Blaze as he paused on the step below her. His presence gave her peace of mind, making her feel safe.

"Katrina?" was all Blaze said, because it was obvious she wasn't okay.

"Sorry, just needed a second." She looked up the rest of the stairs, sighed a deep sigh, and continued. Going to the end of the long hallway, passing closed doors along the way, she stopped at the last door. As she reached out, a large hand stopped her from gripping the doorknob.

"Whose room is this?" Blaze gently moved her behind him, where Sloan, Sid, Jax, Adam, and Steve stood in a line.

"Samuel Drake's," she replied, then noticed she was being pulled behind the long line of Warriors.

"Would he set traps?" Jax turned his head slightly to look at her.

Katrina noticed Blaze had stopped and was looking at her, not opening the door. "No, but then again, I wouldn't put it past him."

"Proceed with caution." Sloan had turned back toward Blaze.

"Cover her," Blaze ordered, still not opening the door.

She was surprised when Jax took her in his arms and turned his back toward the door with her cocooned by his body. She heard the door open, heard orders being shouted, and then she was let go.

The Warrior line moved as they all made their way into the room. Katrina was the last to enter. Her eyes quickly scanned the room with disgust. Nothing of her mother's remained, but she was glad about that. Samuel Drake had never deserved someone like her mother.

The Warriors searched the room but came up short, which she knew they would. She made her way toward the closet and peeked inside. The closet had been cleaned out except for clothes hanging pressed against one end.

Stepping inside, she began removing the clothes, tossing them to the other side of the closet.

"What are you doing?" Blaze peered in, watching her, then quickly ducked back out when she threw more clothes toward him. "Katrina?" He growled her name.

Katrina ignored him, staring at the false wall, and knew

without a doubt, Drake didn't empty out everything. Feeling around, she frowned, realizing it was nailed shut. With a grin, she leaned back, lifted her leg, and with total satisfaction, she kicked against the wall, sending the false wall smashing into another wall.

"Take that, you bastard," she cursed as she peeked inside and chuckled. Turning, she then made her way toward Blaze and out of the closet. With a sweep of her hand, she motioned toward the hole. "And that is why I came."

Blaze looked at her for a second before squeezing himself inside. His curse had her smiling and the other Warriors staring. Once he came out, his surprised gaze landed on her, and then he gave her a nod of respect.

"What the fuck is it?" Sloan looked between them both.

"Guns, money, and God knows what else," Blaze said, then frowned. "But I don't think any of us can fit back there."

"I can, and it will be my pleasure." Katrina walked past them and disappeared into the closet.

"Son of a bitch." Sloan's curse trailed behind her; he actually sounded happy.

"And this isn't the only place. The garage closest to the house also has a secret room. Since no one was guarding it, I doubt anything was left there, but it might be worth checking." Katrina knew that what she was doing at that very moment was a death warrant. Samuel Drake would kill her for sure if he got his hands on her, yet, for some reason, that wasn't bothering her as much as she would have thought. She was much too excited to finally get revenge on the bastard.

"Why would he leave all that here?" Steve asked, nodding toward where Katrina stood.

No one answered as they all looked toward Katrina. And she knew exactly why he would leave anything behind.

"Because Samuel Drake is that arrogant, and he thinks no one would ever steal from him." Katrina looked over her shoulder into the closet, then back to the Warriors. "He thought wrong."

******

Blaze couldn't help but admire her strength. At first, she hadn't wanted to come anywhere near this place, and neither had he; he still didn't want her there. Yet, without her, they never would have known about the major stash of guns, money, and drugs hidden behind the walls.

For over two hours they worked as she tirelessly handed things out of the hole in the closet. He stayed close, grabbing them and handing them off to Steve as Jax and Adam took pictures and Sid logged everything. Damon, Jared, and Duncan had returned after locking the three assholes up. Damon stood watch while Jared and Duncan went to find the hidden room in the garage. Katrina gave them exact details on how to find it, but she had been right. It was empty.

Finally, Katrina stepped out from the wall. "That's it." She sneezed as wisps of dust flew out of her hair. Waving her hand in front of her face, she scrunched her nose. "It's so dusty in there."

Reaching up, Blaze clasped a handful of her hair. Its softness amazed him. As curly as it was, he would have thought it would be coarse, but what the fuck did he know about women's hair. He rubbed it between his fingers for a second longer before letting go. Their eyes met, his intense, hers surprised.

"Cobweb." His voice was rough, scraping his throat as the word escaped.

"Oh." She lifted her hands and ruffled her hair. "Thank you. Hope there are no spiders in this mess. I've actually thought about shaving it off." She sighed, pulling a sticky, stringy cobweb from her hair.

"No!" His tone was a little more demanding than he'd intended it to be, and thank fuck Sid found that moment to peek into the closet.

"Come on, guys." Sid huffed. "I don't want to be here all fucking night. Let's get a move on."

Katrina peeked around Blaze with a smile. "It's done."

"Well fuck, why didn't you say so?" Sid ducked back out of the closet and then reappeared. "Well, come on and help carry this shit to the van and stop staring at each other, or do you want me to close the door to give you some privacy so you can—"

"Sid, get the fuck out of here," Blaze warned as he backed up, then pushed Sid out of the way.

Sid chuckled, but moved. At Sid's words, Blaze had felt something he had never felt before: embarrassment. What the fuck was he doing, touching her, staring at her, alone with her in a fucking closet? As soon as he made sure she was safe, he needed to leave, move on. He did nothing better than moving on. Staying in one place was not in his blood, never had been and never would be; even a beautiful redhead couldn't change that.

Chapter 7

Katrina stayed out of the way as the Warriors continued to carry the stash out to the van.

"I still can't believe they left all this here." Steve picked up a large amount of cash, fanning himself with it before taking a big whiff as he looked at it longingly.

"They do this every time they feel the police may raid," Katrina replied, gaining the interest of every Warrior in the room. "If they have to move fast without any notice, they have confidence no one will find their hidden safe rooms. And death will come for any member who reveals where they are."

The room was deadly quiet as they all stared at her. None flinched at her words, knowing them to be true.

"They will come back like they always do when the heat is off them." Katrina shrugged as if what she had just said about death didn't bother her, and honestly, it didn't. It had been her way of life. "This is their main location."

"And you don't know where they are now?" Sloan asked, his eyes narrowed slightly.

"If I did, you'd know," Katrina replied, understanding his distrust, but not liking it. "They're all probably spread out, but they never run to the same place. Except when things calm down, they all end up back here."

Finally, the attention was off her as they collected the rest of the stuff. She followed them down the hall, the last in line, but stopped in front of one of the closed doors. Watching Blaze disappear down the steps, Katrina looked back at the door and bit her lip with indecision.

Knowing she would regret not doing it, she opened the door to her past one more time. The familiar smell of her old world hit her hard. The Baby Soft perfume she had used every day must have seeped into the interior of the room because the smell surrounded her. It smelled familiar, but it didn't bring her comfort, only anxiety.

The first object she spotted was her guitar. Her fingers itched to pick it up and play, something she had missed. When she'd run, she'd taken nothing with her. There were only two things in her room she would have taken: her guitar and the picture of her and her mother. She glanced toward her small bedside table and saw that it was missing. Not a big shocker, since things she cared about always seemed to end up missing. She was actually surprised her guitar was still there.

Slowly, she moved further into the room, her eyes seeing nothing but the guitar. Reaching out, she picked it up and brought it to her. Closing her eyes, she began to play. God, how she'd missed it. Jax had let her use his a few times while she watched Daniel for Pam and Duncan, but his had felt foreign in her hands. Her guitar felt like an old friend who had comforted her on many lonely nights.

As she quietly strummed, she looked around. The dust was thick and cobwebs hung in the corners, but other than that everything seemed the same. Her whole life had been a vicious cycle of drama that came with the MC, but once she'd closed her door, she'd always been able to escape for a short time, lost in her music.

As she stood strumming the song she'd played for Daniel, she sang along. Losing herself for just a second seemed natural to her, especially considering where she was. How many times had she done this? Hundreds? Thousands? No, most probably she had done this a million times before to escape the hell that resided outside her room.

With a sigh, she stopped, realizing that this was part of her past and she needed it to stay a part of her past, even the object that had been her best friend. Before she could lay the guitar back on the bed, a voice from her past filled the room.

"Don't stop, baby girl." Her father's voice surrounded her, turning the tiny moment of reminiscing into horror. "I've missed hearing you sing."

She didn't move, just stayed completely still, afraid to turn around to find him behind her, yet she had to know. With every ounce of courage she had, she laid the guitar on the bed then slowly turned. She was alone. Her father wasn't with her.

"I've been waiting for you, baby girl." His voice echoed in the room. "I knew you couldn't stay away."

His false endearment made her want to vomit as her eyes searched, finding a small box on her beat-up dresser. There were two lights on it; one was red. She knew that box. It was a Petcube. With a frown, she stepped closer. Her father was seriously demented. She didn't even know what to say. Although she was relieved beyond words, obviously, that he wasn't in the room, to know he had set this up to catch her coming back blew her away.

"It's time to come home." Her father's tone became more demanding. "Enough is enough."

"Come home?" She repeated the words that snapped her out of her stupor. "You had me beaten, you murdered my mother, and you're forcing me to marry a piece of shit that I hate."

"She didn't mean that, Breaker." Her father's whispered words sounded through the speaker on the Petcube.

"The hell I didn't. I meant every word." It was amazing how brave she felt. Maybe it was because her father wasn't in front of her, maybe it was her training with the Warriors, or maybe it was because she knew Blaze was close.

The red light on the Petcube began to move. She realized it was a laser. She watched it hit her shoe and move up her leg, up her body, then she squinted as it blinded her momentarily.

"You will come home, Kat." Her father's voice was no longer friendly. She was no longer his baby girl. This was Samuel Drake ordering her to do as he said, but she was no longer Kat. She would never be Kat again, and it was time he realized it.

"Never," she responded, looking directly at the Petcube and feeling freedom from just speaking that one word.

******

As soon as Blaze hit the stairs to find Katrina, the most beautiful sound he had ever heard greeted him. He knew she was singing quietly, but his keen hearing picked up her angelic voice instantly. He stopped on the stairs, listening, stunned. She was absolutely amazing. Disappointment hit him as her voice quieted, followed by rage when he heard a male voice. He knew for a fact everyone else was downstairs.

With ease, he jumped the rest of the steps and hit the floor running. Making himself slow to be prepared and in control, he stopped at the door to scope the situation. What he saw turned his blood to fire; his eyes blazed as he rushed into the room. A red target laser was centered on Katrina's forehead. With blinding speed, he pulled her into his arms, shielding her body before looking for the threat. He found none.

"It's the Petcube." Katrina's voice was muffled by his chest as he held her close. "On the dresser."

Blaze looked and saw the black box. Before he could say anything, a voice came from that area.

"Who's your hero, baby girl?" a man's voice asked pleasantly, yet held a hard edge. "Mind your manners and introduce him to your father."

Blaze felt her stiffen in his arms. "You're safe," he whispered before turning around, keeping her behind him. He noticed the other Warriors had entered but stayed out of the view of the small box.

"Who are you?" The voice had turned from pleasant to nasty in a split second.

Blaze gave the small box a glare and a sarcastic grin. "Never expected the president of the Iron Drakes to hide behind a pet toy."

"Oh, snap!" Steve's whisper reached his ears, but Blaze didn't react other than to raise his eyebrow.

"Listen, motherfucker." The voice turned deadly, but it didn't affect Blaze. He had faced down many mean bastards in his lifetime, and this man was no different. He would lose, he would probably die, but he most definitely would never lay a hand on Katrina.

"No, you listen, motherfucker." Blaze cut him off, leaning toward the box. "I will find you and when I do, I, along with the rest of the VC Warriors, will take you down."

"You have no idea who you're dealing with!" Samuel's voice shouted throughout the room. "No fucking clue who I know and what I'm capable of."

"Ditto, bitch," Blaze growled. "And you tell Breaker if he comes anywhere near her, he's a dead man."

Blaze was past the point of caring if he was baiting the bastards. He wanted them and wanted them bad. He could hear a man faintly in the background and knew it must be the bastard Breaker.

"Hey, Breaker, why don't you stop hiding behind that piece of shit and come on over, hmmm." Blaze couldn't stop. He was the best at pissing people off to the point of wanting to kill him. He just hoped the asshole took the bait. When no one said anything, Blaze grinned without humor. "Pussy."

"Kat, you are mine." Another man's voice came through the box. "Don't you ever forget that. I *will* find you."

Blaze felt her fingers clutch at his shirt, felt her shiver, and his rage knew no bounds. "The only thing you will find is me, fucker." Blaze glared at the box then raised his hand before looking at Sloan. When Sloan nodded, a ball of fire appeared, hovering in his hand. "You want to take anything from here, Katrina?" he whispered over his shoulder.

"No," she answered after a brief hesitation. "Nothing."

"Go with them." Blaze nodded toward Sloan. "I'll be right

there."

"Kat, don't you dare leave," Drake ordered. "I'm not finished with you."

Katrina stopped, and Blaze allowed her to take power by going in front of the box this one time because he knew for the moment she was safe. "I'm finished with you, and this is the last time I will ever answer to the name Kat."

Pride washed over Blaze as he witnessed her straightening her shoulders as she exited the room. Once she was gone, he turned his attention back to the black box, the fireball still dancing in his hand.

"Since you're too much of a pussy to face me, it's time for this to be over." A wicked gleam ravaged his face. "Be seeing you… real soon."

"What are you doing with—"

With a flick of his wrist, Blaze sent the fireball toward the box and watched as it exploded. Soon the fire took control. He calmly walked out of the room, and continued to set fire to the house as he exited. Once outside, he glanced at Sloan, who gave him another definite nod. With ease, he set every building on the property alight and gloried in the heat. The Iron Drakes would never be using this property again.

He turned to see Katrina looking a little lost as she stared at what used to be her home. He moved closer to her. "Are you sorry?" he asked, watching the flames reflected in her eyes. He found it wildly erotic and wanted nothing more than to take her in his arms and make her his.

She finally looked away from the fire to look up at him. "No." Her voice was firm and confident; he could tell she wasn't lying.

Sirens in the distance had them heading for their bikes. He chuckled as Katrina jumped on Sid's bike like it was nothing. "You sure you can handle that?" Blaze climbed on his, giving her a sideways stare.

"If you only knew," she replied, a smile breaking across her face. Once the engine started, she took one last look at the buildings then took off, leaving him with a half grin on his face.

He pulled out after her with a new purpose in his life. That one instant of someone trying to claim her had changed his whole perspective. No harm would come to her in any way as long as he lived, and even then, he would make a deal with the devil to make sure she was protected. Breaker was wrong. Katrina was his and no one fucked with what was his, ever.

Chapter 8

Katrina followed the Warriors into the garage she had broken into and carefully parked. The van continued to a different, smaller garage. With reluctance, she climbed off the bike. Everyone had exited quickly, except for Blaze and Sloan.

"Soon as we get everything out of the van locked up, stop by my office and then you guys are done for the night. First thing in the morning we'll start interrogations," Sloan called after them. Then his eyes fell on the alarm by the door before landing on her. "You owe me a new alarm."

"Yes, sir." Katrina nodded, averting her eyes from the smashed alarm.

"Go on." Sloan nodded toward the door, dismissing her.

She didn't really know exactly where to go. Was she supposed to help unload the van or was she to go to her room? Feeling she needed to help, she headed toward the small garage, where she heard the Warriors talking.

"Do you think Katrina ever had that happen to her?" Steve said as she stopped just outside the door.

"What?" Sid asked, moving an armful of guns from the van.

"What the bastard was doing to, what was her name?

Jenny?" Steve said, a look of anger and disgust on his face as he handed out more guns.

"I don't think Katrina is a drug head," Sid answered, then shrugged. "But who knows. Growing up around that shit all her life, she'd have to be a strong person to turn out different."

Okay, that hurt. It hurt badly. She straightened her shoulders and was about to step inside to defend herself, but just as quick, her shoulders slumped, and she turned to walk away. Let them believe whatever they wanted. What did it matter anyway? Sid was right. Was she that different from those in the MC?

"I am different," she mumbled, then repeated it as if convincing herself. "I am different." She had only taken two steps before her eyes, which were looking at the ground, spotted black boots. Slowly, her gaze traveled up a firm pair of thighs in faded jeans, slowing at the juncture of those tight thighs before shooting up to Blaze's narrowed golden eyes.

"Is there something you need to say?" Blaze asked, glancing over her head before looking back down at her.

Mortified that he had witnessed her humiliation, she shook her head. "No, what does it matter anyway?" she replied, tilting her head slightly, not wanting to sound like she was fishing for pity, because she wasn't. "They're going to believe what they want, no matter what I say. I either prove them wrong or will prove them right. Time will tell."

"Then I guess I'll have to say it." He cocked his eyebrow at her before moving around her.

"What?" Katrina asked with a frown, then realized exactly what he intended to do. "No! Please don't say anything." She grabbed his arm, knowing he stopped because he wanted to and not because of her trying to stop his huge body.

"You are not like them, Katrina." Blaze glared down at her.

"And how would you know that?" Katrina dropped her hand from his forearm. "You know nothing about me."

"I know." Blaze's tone held no doubt.

"Please… don't." Katrina once again reached out, but her hand stopped before touching him as she realized what she was doing.

"You or me," Blaze stated, ignoring her plea. "This thinking will be stopped tonight either by you or me."

"Why?" Katrina asked, really wanting to know why he was so concerned.

"Why what?" His eyes shifted slightly, and she had no doubt he knew exactly what she meant.

"Why do you care what anyone thinks of me?" She had seriously thought about not asking that question, but her curiosity won out. She really wanted to know the answer.

He hesitated, but his gaze didn't look away this time. "Because I do."

Realizing that was all she was going to get, she sighed. She didn't want to cause problems, so it was probably best she did this instead of Blaze, since they were his friends. Finally pulling her eyes away from him, she looked into the large opening of the garage.

"I am different," she announced inside the open doorway, her eyes lifting from the ground to land on Sid and then the rest of the Warriors, who had stopped what they were doing to look at her.

Sid sighed. "Listen—"

Katrina cut him off. If she didn't say what she needed to say now, she wouldn't say it at all.

"I'm not a druggie. Every day it was in my face, and I was even encouraged, but I never gave in. I was a straight A student in school and never missed a day. It was my escape from the chaos of the club. My mom fought to make sure no matter what was going on in the MC, I was allowed to go to school." Katrina's eyes roamed the group. She felt Blaze behind her, which in some small manner gave her the strength to keep talking. "I've always been judged because of who my father is. I understand it, but I refuse to tolerate it. It's not fair to me."

"I didn't really mean the drugs." Steve looked sheepish. "I meant, you know... what that asshole was doing to that girl while she was passed out."

Katrina cocked her eyebrow as she looked around at the rest of the Warriors who wore different stages of angry expressions while waiting for her to answer.

"No," she finally said, embarrassed that they would think that. "And I did everything I could to make sure it didn't happen to any of the other girls when I was there, and so did my mom. But most of those girls knew exactly what they were walking into when they came into the club. We helped the ones who wanted and needed help when we could."

Mistrust lingered in the air. They didn't trust her and she expected that. Seriously, what was new? As soon as anyone discovered she was part of the Iron Drakes, she was automatically labeled. When they found out she was the president's daughter, it was worse. Then again, how could she blame them? Didn't she just break into their garage and steal a bike?

She walked toward Steve, who had jumped down from the back of the van, and gave him a hug.

"Thank you for what you did for Jenny." She pulled away and stepped back before looking at all of them. "I know you don't trust me and I understand, but if I'm given the chance, I will prove where my loyalty lies and that is with the VC."

"We're not a trusting group," Jared remarked, then added, "Nothing against you personally."

Katrina nodded her understanding. "I get it, and I'm not going to lie. I have the MC in my blood, literally. As you've seen, I can pick a lock within seconds, I can disarm most alarms, I can ride any motorcycle you put in front of me no matter its size, I can lie without blinking an eye, I play a mean game of poker"—she held up a wallet with a tiny smile—"and I can pick anyone's pocket."

Steve stared at the wallet in amazement until he realized it was his. He quickly patted himself down then snatched the wallet out of her hand. "Holy shit, I didn't even know." Steve stuck it back in his pocket. "You're good. Real good."

After giving a bitter laugh, Katrina shrugged. "I had no choice but to be good, being the daughter of Samuel Drake." Katrina's frown deepened. "Failure was not an option."

No one spoke for a second, as if letting everything she'd said sink in. "Yeah, well I definitely want you to teach me how to pick a lock." Adam winked at her as he passed her. "That's pretty badass."

Katrina wanted to hug him so badly but held back. She couldn't help the grateful smile that crossed her face as she nodded at him.

"I seriously doubt it was seconds, and later tonight, we'll see just how good at poker you are." Sid gave her a sideways look as if sizing her up. "Be there with plenty of money."

The small amount of excitement she felt at the fraction of acceptance Sid tossed her way was dashed in seconds. "I don't have any money."

Sid gave her a smile then looked over her head. "Blaze will ante up for you."

Katrina glanced over her shoulder at Blaze, who just stood with arms crossed watching the back-and-forth. "I'll pay you back double."

"Oh!" Sid laughed along with the other Warriors. "That confident, are we?"

Actually she was, but didn't say it. Instead she turned serious. "We do have one thing in common." When no one said anything but all glanced her way, she looked them each in the eye. "Taking down the Iron Drakes."

******

To say he was pretty impressed by Katrina would be an understatement. In fact, Blaze was in awe of her, and that was honestly a first for him. He'd never been in awe of any-fucking-thing in his life. But the feelings from watching her stand up for herself among the Warriors was nothing short of awe. Jesus, he was a fucking idiot. One minute his total focus was to stay away from her, and the next he was following her around like a goddamn dog.

He had to physically make himself stay rooted when, after helping to empty the rest of the van, she walked away saying something about meeting up with them for the poker game after a shower. Just the thought of her body naked with water and soap made him groan.

"Shower got ya, huh?" Sid said as he shut the van doors. "Yeah, been there, done that. Actually, still there and doing that. Just the word shower from Lana's lips has me moaning and—"

"You know, Sid." Jared glanced from Blaze to Sid. "I think you better shut the fuck up before you find out how Blaze got his name."

"Shit." Sid snorted, shaking his head. "Just speaking the truth. No reason to get hot under the collar."

"Dude." Steve gave Blaze a sideways glance. "I've seen the shit he can do. Believe me, you don't want to piss him off."

Blaze knew Sid liked to push buttons and Jared loved to goad everybody, especially Sid. He really didn't give two fucks what they thought, but one disrespectful word about Katrina and they would definitely get a taste of exactly what he could do.

The Warriors made their way inside the compound, but

before they could go their separate ways, Sloan's voice blasted out from his office, "Get in here."

Blaze followed, and the first thing he saw was Katrina's image frozen on the computer screen on Sloan's desk.

"This girl knows what the fuck she is doing," Sloan said as they gathered around. He backed the tape up, then hit Play. "I'm fucking impressed, and I don't impress easily."

"Ain't that the damn truth." Steve snorted under his breath, then shook his head when Sid looked back at him with a grin, begging Sid not to say anything.

The cameras tracked Katrina until she reached the garage. For a split second, she looked up at the camera, and it was evident there was remorse in her eyes. She quickly knelt and went to work. In seconds, she had unlocked the door and was inside. The internal camera picked her up, and with another look of remorse, she smashed the alarm with her fist.

Sloan stopped the camera, turning to look at the Warriors. "Again, I'll fucking say I'm impressed." Sloan looked toward Blaze. "I see this as an asset as long as she is on our side. I want everyone to know how to pick a lock just as fast as her."

"Why the fuck do we have to learn that?" Damon scowled. "My foot does the same fucking thing, but faster."

"He has a point." Jared shrugged. "Never needed it before."

"Yeah, well I want it now," Sloan replied. "This is a good way to get in without anyone even knowing we were there. So shut the fuck up and learn it."

Blaze didn't say anything as one by one, the Warriors left with their order from Sloan. His eyes were glued to the computer screen where Sloan had paused the video. After Katrina had smashed the alarm system, her eyes had automatically gone to the camera she had known was there. Her beautiful eyes told him everything he needed to know about this woman. She was not a criminal, but a lost woman who had no choice but to learn that way of life.

"You need something?" Sloan asked, breaking him out of his thoughts.

With one last look at Katrina, Blaze lied, "No." He headed out of the office knowing exactly what he needed, and what he needed only the woman frozen on Sloan's computer screen could provide.

Chapter 9

Katrina stepped out of the shower feeling refreshed and clean. Walking back into that house had made her feel dirty, even though she had grown up inside those walls. The drinking, drugs, and sex had gone on no matter who was there or at what age. She had been the only kid to grow up at the MC, other than her brother. Her mom had tried her best to shield them both from everything, but being a curious little girl, not much had gotten past Katrina. She'd learned life at a very early age. Sometimes she was amazed by her own strength of staying on the straight and narrow. It would have been much easier to succumb to the life she was born into.

Wiping the mirror free of condensation, Katrina stared at her foggy reflection. She looked the same, but she knew she was different or at least she felt different. The freedom of being away from the MC was new and exciting. It was also a little scary, as if the free feeling would be snatched away from her at any moment, and if her father or his club found her, she had no doubt that was exactly what would happen. Pulling her lips back, she stared at her fangs and then back into her golden eyes. She was a vampire who communicated with animals. Actually, the vampire part was still more unreal to her than being able to understand animals. She had always had a special connection with them.

Running her fingers through her hair, she allowed the mirror to fog up again. After Becky and Sloan became a couple she had moved back into the compound. She had felt like a third wheel whenever Sloan was there, not to mention he made her nervous. Noise from her small room had her smiling and wondering what Sager was getting into. Without thought, she opened the door and walked out of the bathroom naked.

"Sager, what are you…?"

Sager lay on the bed, curled up, his eyes on the door. Katrina looked that way to find Blaze standing inside her room, his eyes, black as night, roaming her body. Her first thought was to cover herself, but her limbs wouldn't cooperate. The look he gave her was foreign, and she liked it, a lot, and so did her body; it was responding in ways that shocked her. Breaker had never been easy with her; in fact, he'd always hurt her. It had never been pleasant. So if Blaze could make her body feel this good without a touch, she couldn't even begin to imagine how he could make her feel in his arms.

"Out!" Blaze ordered Sager as he, without taking his eyes off her, stepped in front of the door so anyone passing couldn't see inside.

When Sager hesitated, Katrina sent him a silent message, adding not to blow this for her. As if knowing exactly what he was doing, Sager slowly stood, stretched, then jumped off the bed and creeped out the door.

Blaze closed the door and locked it. Not once did his eyes leave her. She wanted to say something, but her mouth was dry, and she had no idea what she could say. Okay, she was starting to feel a little uncomfortable and a lot turned on. Maybe she should grab a towel. As she turned to act on her thought, he stopped her.

"No."

His voice was low, deep, and firm. It was a command that made her body shiver in an excited frenzy of nerves. His eyes once again raked over her body, and she knew without looking that her nipples were hard and pointing directly at him, as if waiting for his touch.

Finally he moved, taking a step, then stopped. Her frustrated moan escaped, snapping his head in a tilt.

"You want me?"

His question confused her. Wasn't it obvious? She stood before him completely naked; she wasn't screaming or running to cover up. She was exposed to his mercy, yet he asked if she wanted him.

"Isn't it obvious?" Her voice finally showed up and spoke what was in her heart. She had never told a man she wanted him. Breaker—and why in the hell did she keep thinking of him?—was the only man to see her naked, the only man to touch her sexually. And if thinking of that bastard ruined this for her, she would kill him herself.

His eyes went straight to her breasts as a sexy half grin

curved his lips before he sniffed the air. With a growl, he closed the space between them, but instead of grabbing her in his arms, one large hand buried itself in her hair, moving the curly, wet mess between his fingers. He brought it up and inhaled.

Katrina allowed her hand to move to his chest. Even clothed she could feel his hardness and wanted nothing more than to be against him, skin to skin. She wanted to touch skin so badly she could taste it. Slowly, she glided her fingers up his chest to his neck, her thumb rubbing softly against his skin. With only a second of hesitation, she clasped the back of his neck and pulled him down close enough that she could place her lips against where her thumb had been. Yeah, wanting him didn't even come close to explaining what she was feeling.

******

Blaze had knocked repeatedly on Katrina's door and begun to worry when she didn't answer. He knew she was in there because he had heard the shower. Checking the doorknob, he had walked in at the same time she had opened the door to the bathroom and stepped out. If he had doubts about his feelings for her before, seeing her standing before him, vulnerable with nothing hiding her from his view, made any doubts he had vanish.

He stood still, waiting to see what she would do, but she had simply stared at him. And it wasn't fear he recognized in her eyes. It was a need that matched his own. Stepping aside, he called for Sager to leave, but blocked the door so no one could see the beautiful sight only for his eyes. Once the dog, which took its fucking time, left the room, he shut the door and locked it. He watched her reaction to that closely, but she didn't even flinch. Her eyes remained on his.

Once again, he just stood. He needed to make sure. His eyes raked down her body, stopping on her generous breasts tipped with pale pink nipples that begged for his touch. His mouth watered. His dick, which was already hard, hardened even more to the point of being painful. He could smell her desire with just a whiff of air.

"You want me?" It was a statement, but he posed it like a question just to hear her answer.

Her words almost drove him over the edge of any self-control he had left. "Isn't it obvious?"

He rushed her, but didn't want to frighten her, so he did what he had wanted to do since seeing her for the first time. He reached out and clasped a handful of her hair, rubbing the thick strands between his fingers. In his life, he had seen many things, but nothing as beautiful as the young woman standing naked before him.

Her hand against his chest felt right as it ran up to his neck. Her touch against his skin was liberating, as if having the power to break past his barriers and setting him free from his past. Not many touched him; he had allowed few to do so. The women he'd had in the past were usually taken from behind, and he'd done the touching, always. When she cupped the back of his neck, urging him closer, he allowed it and was fucking happy he did because her lips against his neck was mind-blowing. He couldn't even imagine what it would feel like when he was buried deep inside her. Jesus, it just might be the very thing that killed him, sending him over the edge to never return.

With his hand still buried in her hair, he gently tugged her head back, their lips so close her breath caressed him, and took what now belonged to him. No man would ever know the feel of her hair, the feel of her lips, or witness the beauty of her pale body. Fuck his good intentions of staying away from her. She was his. Mind, body, and soul. He claimed her as his own.

Knowing he should take it slowly, he pretty much fucked that up when their lips met. He crushed her mouth against his, his tongue parting her lips. She met his kiss with an urgency that matched his. His free hand landed on her ribs and slid down around to her bare ass. For someone with such a small stature, she had an ass that would bring any man to his knees, especially an ass man like himself. She had hidden a lot of herself in her oversized clothing, but he had known that she had a body underneath all that cloth.

His mouth left hers as he cupped her ass and with one arm, brought her up his body. His lips and mouth played against her skin as she rose higher, until her tits were face level to him. She had wrapped her legs around him and he wished he had removed his shirt so her bare pussy could rest against his skin. Her hands clasped loosely on his shoulders, pushing her tits together, and he could no longer resist. Taking one nipple in his mouth, he reached down with his other hand, which had been in her hair, to adjust himself. When that didn't work, he undid his jeans to free himself before he did some damage. His hand wrapped around his cock to give himself more relief as his mouth continued to taste her.

After a few moments of him pleasuring himself, Katrina's small hand touched his cock, almost sending him over the edge. His balls tightened painfully, but he fought with everything he had to regain control.

"Goddamn," he growled, taking her hand in his, showing her exactly how to take control, but she didn't need help. She pulled away from him, and he let her slide down his body. While she carefully unzipped his pants the rest of the way, he pulled his shirt off. He started to look down, but before he did, he felt wet lips take his length, and his focus went straight to hell.

Seeing Katrina's red head bobbing up and down along his cock was almost more than he could take. He had to stiffen his legs, which had begun to shake. One hand went directly to the wall in front of him to hold himself up. Holy fuck, she was going to kill him. His free hand automatically went to the top of her head as she continued. He couldn't find it in himself to stop her. What fucking man would? Not only was she taking his whole length, but she used her tongue in ways that he didn't think possible. Knowing he had to stop her before he totally fucked up the mood by exploding, he clenched his jaw and slowly pulled her off, all the while wondering if he was a fucking idiot.

"Was I doing it wrong?" Katrina glanced up at him, her eyes wide with desire.

"Jesus, where in the fuck did you learn to do that?" Blaze pulled her up off her knees. "And you definitely weren't doing it wrong."

"Really? I have no gag reflex so I figured I'd be pretty good." She looked proud. "I always wanted to do it, but—"

"What? You've never…?" Blaze couldn't have heard her right. Well, he heard about the no gag reflex, and what fucking man on the face of the earth didn't want to hear that? So, okay, how in the hell did he go about asking if she had sucked another man's dick without embarrassing her and then demanding who the motherfucker was so he could cut the bastard's dick off?

"No, but I've seen…." Katrina stopped, looking embarrassed.

"Never hold anything from me. I will not judge you, Katrina." Blaze tilted her chin up.

"I've watched girls do it before, but I never had anyone I wanted to do it with," Katrina said shyly. "Until you."

Blaze's growl was possessive. "And I'll be the only son of a bitch you do it to."

With a grin, she started to go back to her knees with excitement, but he stopped her.

Blaze groaned and chuckled at the same time. Fuck, she was insatiable. How fucking lucky was he? But it was his time to make her feel. "It's my turn now, beautiful." With that, he picked her up, kicked his boots and jeans off, and headed toward the bed, his eyes roaming all over her body the whole time. "Definitely my turn."

Chapter 10

He laid her on the bed, and neither of them wasted time. They knew exactly what they wanted and had no problem going for it. Katrina was in such a state of bliss she didn't realize how close he was to touching her between her thighs until his hand was already there. When he touched her core, she stiffened, and he followed suit, stopping.

"Katrina?" Blaze raised himself on his elbows above her.

"I'm sorry." Katrina bit her lip, looking up at him under lowered lashes. She should have been paying more attention, but this man had a mouth and hands that turned her mind to complete mush. She should have been ready for the pain, but his touch there had surprised her. "I'm fine."

"Has someone hurt you?" His voice was no longer soft. The desire in his eyes cleared as he stared down at her. "Do not lie to me."

Okay, this was not a conversation she wanted to have with this man, ever, and sure as hell not at this moment. "No." When his frown deepened, she sighed. "I know it hurts, but you have a way of making me forget about that."

Blaze growled with a scowl. "Hurt?"

"And well, it wasn't really pleasant like I thought it would be, but it was for him," Katrina replied, hoping she hadn't messed up by telling him this.

With a snort, Blaze angled up, resting on his side. "Oh, I'm sure the motherfucker enjoyed it," Blaze cursed, then continued, "Who? Was it that Breaker asshole?"

Katrina pushed away and sat up. She was disappointed when he let her, but unfortunately, the mood had shifted. She grabbed a pillow to cover herself up, but he snatched it and threw it on the floor.

"I had no idea I would ever be leaving the MC, so I gave in to him." Katrina shrugged, wishing with everything she had that she was pure for Blaze. As stupid as that sounded, she really wanted that for not only herself, but for him. "If I had known I'd meet you, it never would have happened. After the first time with Breaker, I tried to avoid him completely. I even did my best to set up other women to be available who wanted to be with him. Most of the time that worked, but not always." There, she'd put it out there. It was time to see how he responded.

"Did he hurt you?" Blaze asked again, his eyes had softened slightly at her words.

"I'm not naïve, Blaze." She avoided the question. "I've known what goes on since I was a young girl, too young to know, but I did. All I had to do was walk out of my room and see someone screwing on the steps, in a corner, on that nasty couch or the pool table. When I got older, I guess I wanted to experience something, and well, I got tired of Breaker pushing and pushing, so I gave in. I didn't see a life for me outside the MC. I was weak. I regret it, I hated it, and honestly, I don't even know why I want to do it so badly with you because as I said, it wasn't pleasant for me."

Blaze remained on his side, propped up on his arm and naked on her bed staring at her. He was quiet for so long she was afraid to even know what he was thinking.

"It always hurts the first time, Katrina." Blaze finally spoke.

"Really?" Katrina frowned because that definitely hadn't been her experience. Maybe there was something wrong with her.

"Any man worth a shit will make sure that after the initial pain, the woman will soon forget about the discomfort. Obviously this dumb fuck didn't do that," Blaze said with a growl.

"No, he just grunted while he—" Katrina started, but Blaze hissed.

"Enough." He pulled her into his arms. "If you don't want me finding the bastard to kill him right now, then don't say another word."

"I wish it had been you," Katrina said as she touched the side of his cheek. "I wish you had been my first."

Blaze lowered his head and kissed her lightly. "I will be your first because you will forget everything, and I mean every-fucking-thing about that bastard."

"I never had feelings for him," Katrina felt she needed to add. "I just felt at the time I had no choice. My father's word was law, and he was who my father had chosen for me."

"So, you won't cry when I take him out?" Blaze asked, and she knew he was teasing, but she wasn't. "Because that is what will happen."

"No." Katrina shivered with fear. "Because once he knows about this with you, he will kill me. I'm property of the Iron Drakes. Me running hasn't changed that, and with my father giving me to Breaker, I'm now his property. If you want to walk away now, Blaze, I'll understand. I should have told you all of this before it went this far."

Katrina was surprised when Blaze laid her back on the bed. He kissed his way down her body, across her stomach, and down to her core. His warm breath lingered over her, making her shiver with desire and need so strong she wanted to scream. His eyes told her more than his words ever could. He was not going anywhere.

****

As Blaze tasted Katrina's wetness while making love to her with his mouth, her words hammered in his brain. Walk away? Never! He stroked her with his tongue with a feverish need to cherish, to show her he was going nowhere. Knowing she was close, he rose, kissing and licking the inside of her thighs. Carefully he touched her. She was so wet with need that he wanted to ram inside her, but he needed to be sure she was completely ready. She would feel no pain from him; he would cut his own throat before he caused her harm.

His fingers touched her as one by one, he slipped them inside. She was tight, but with three fingers he pumped inside her, priming her.

She clutched his shoulders, trying to bring herself toward him. "Please, Blaze." She panted, pumping her hips up to meet his thrusting fingers. "I can't...."

A satisfied male grin broke over his face as he moved further up between her legs. He used her wetness on his hand to coat his cock.

"I love watching you do that." Katrina sighed between pants as she observed him moving his palm up and down his length.

Blaze groaned at her unembarrassed confession. With a few more yanks just for her, he pressed the head of his throbbing cock against her. Lifting one of her legs, he slowly pushed himself into her warmth and commanded himself to take it slow, because all he wanted to do was ram inside and fuck her hard. That would come later. Right now he was going to take it slow until she was ready. He used his power to heat his body and knew she was feeling it inside her when her eyes opened wide.

"Oh. My. God." She panted heavily, her head slowly going back and forth on the pillow. "That feels amazing."

Confident that she had adjusted to his size perfectly, he moved faster, watching her closely for any signs of pain, but he saw only pleasure, which was the only thing he ever wanted to bring her. Suddenly her heavy eyes opened, meeting his.

"You don't have to hold back, Blaze." Her voice was hoarse with desire. "I'm ready for whatever you have."

"I don't want to—" Blaze started, but she stopped him.

"If you want me to beg, I will." She gave him a lopsided smile. "I need more, please."

With a moan, Blaze picked up his pace, and she was absolutely right. She was more than ready for what he had to give her, because she gave as good as she got.

He honestly didn't know who took who over the edge or if it was a joint effort. He didn't really care. He lay on her with his weight mostly on his arms as they both breathed heavily without saying a word.

"Thank you," Katrina whispered with a sigh.

Blaze thought for a moment before lifting his head enough to look over at her. "What in the hell are you thanking me for?" He cocked his eyebrow at her.

She shrugged, her eyes shifting away, embarrassed. "For this." She smiled shyly when she looked back at him.

Reaching over, he gently pulled her closer. "You're welcome." He kissed her lips softly. "But it is I who should be doing the thanking. Those lips of yours are magic."

"I can't believe I told you I had no gag reflex." Katrina groaned, covering her face. "I did say that, didn't I? It's hard to think when you're looking at me with those eyes."

"Yes, you definitely said that." Blaze grinned, which he didn't do much, and it felt foreign on his face, but this woman had a way of getting through every wall and barrier he had spent decades building.

"Well, it's true." Katrina laughed while Blaze groaned. He watched her face become serious as she stared at him. "Blaze, I promise I don't expect anything just because of... this."

He was surprised and curious as to where this was coming from. She went from laughing to letting him off the hook, so to speak. "Why the fuck do you say that?"

Katrina played with a strand of hair, her eyes not meeting his. "I know who you are and I know what I am. I don't want to embarrass you or anything."

"Stop." Blaze shook his head. "First of all, what you are? I'll tell you what you are. You are a beautiful, smart woman who walked away from a life being you and not someone people assumed you would be. You're a good person, Katrina. Never forget that. And why don't we just take what is going on between us one day at a time?" he lied, knowing that she was his.

"Okay." Her eyes shifted to his as she nodded.

Blaze's eyes narrowed. "I don't play nicely with others. I'm not saying you're my property, you're more than that as a person. But I will say that no man will touch you. You understand?"

"Yes," Katrina replied, her eyes also narrowing slightly as her nose scrunched. "I don't play nicely either."

Blaze once again laughed. "Understood." He touched the side of her face before pulling away and grabbing his jeans. He pulled out money and handed it to her. When she looked offended, he quickly explained. "Poker money. That's why I came here."

"Oh." Katrina took the money with a chuckle. "I thought I was going to have to slap you."

"Wouldn't be the first time I've been smacked by a pissed-off woman." Blaze began to dress.

"Really?" Katrina did the same. "So, Blaze, exactly how many women have you had."

Giving her an "I will not be discussing that with you" look, Blaze grinned. "So you really think you can double my money?"

Katrina smiled widely. "Most definitely." She stood proudly. "Like taking candy from a baby."

He couldn't resist. He pulled her into his arms for one last kiss before they left. He knew Sid and the rest were probably wondering where in the hell they were, but he didn't give a fuck, and if he didn't pull away from her sweet body now, they would be waiting longer. Letting her go, he steadied her when she weaved.

"Have many women told you that you're a wonderful kisser?" Katrina asked slyly.

"Still not answering those questions, Katrina." Blaze chuckled as he opened the door and followed her out. He made damn sure he stayed behind her as he watched her gorgeous ass sway. Yeah, he was definitely an ass man.

Chapter 11

"It's about time." Shuffling cards, Sid eyed them. "Thought you might have come to your senses and decided not to show."

Katrina had been nervous, wondering if everyone was going to know exactly what she and Blaze had been doing, but Sid's words put her at ease. This she knew. This banter was comfortable to her, and she sighed in relief.

"Wishful thinking on your part?" She gave him a grin then headed for one of the empty chairs at the table. Jax occupied another of the chairs, and once she took her seat, only one was left.

Sid chuckled with a cock of his eyebrow but didn't respond. Jared headed over to sit in the only other empty chair.

"Hey!" Steve's voice shouted as Jared jumped up.

"What the fuck?" Jared glared down at the empty chair. "Steve, I swear I'm going to kill you. Get the fuck up."

Steve appeared before their eyes. "But I want to play and I don't have a good poker face. Plus, there are no rules saying an invisible player can't play."

"New rule." Sid frowned. "No invisible players allowed."

"Get the fuck up." Jared glared down at him until Steve stood with a huff.

"Jared, stop being so mean," Tessa scolded. "He just wants to play."

"Sitting on a man's lap pisses me the fuck off." Jared sat down, then looked toward Tessa. "Not a pleasant experience."

"Oh, I don't know." Tessa walked over and sat on Jared's lap hard, making him groan. "I think sitting on a man's lap is very pleasant."

Katrina watched Jared whisper something in Tessa's ear and felt a surge of jealousy, which was crazy. Or was it? Her eyes landed on Blaze, who had moved across the room to lean against the wall, talking to Adam. His eyes met hers, and she looked away. She wondered if she and Blaze would ever be that close.

"Yo, card shark!" Sid's voice broke through her thoughts.

"What?" Katrina replied, embarrassed to be caught staring at Blaze.

"Five card draw, starting ante is fifty." Sid continued to shuffle the cards as he stared at her.

"Fifty?" Katrina frowned, not even knowing how much money Blaze had given her. "As in cents?"

"Who did you play with, pussies?" Sid tilted his head, staring at her. His hands stopped shuffling. "Or five-year-olds?"

Okay, so it was going to be one of those games. Katrina pulled the money out of her pocket and gasped as she counted out ten hundred-dollar bills. Holy shit, Blaze had given her a thousand dollars of his money just to play poker. What if she blew it and lost it all? How in the hell would she pay him back?

"Change your mind, sharkie?" Sid teased with a serious undertone. "I mean, we usually ante a hundred, but you know, with you being…." Sid didn't finish the sentence, but grinned, watching her closely.

Katrina continued to look at the money, letting Sid's words sink in. The asshole. Knowing she could do this, she grabbed a hundred out of the stack and tossed it in the middle.

"A hundred it is." She was pleased to see Sid's shocked face before he quickly shifted back to playing it cool. Oh, yeah. She was going to be able to read him very well.

"Honey, as much as I would love to have you on my lap, shit just got serious." Jared gave Tessa a hard kiss then swatted her ass when she stood. Tossing his hundred in the middle, he grinned at each of them. "Get ready to lose your money, bitches."

Katrina cocked her eyebrow but didn't say a word. Sager had come to sit next to her, his big head resting in her lap.

"Okay, boys"—Sid winked at her—"and girl. Five card draw. May the best man win."

"How about the best woman?" Lana had come into the room, and kissed Sid on the cheek as he dealt the cards. "Kick their asses, Katrina."

Katrina gave her a smile of thanks as she picked up her cards and did a quick scan. Not bad, but not great. Looking up, she watched the reactions of everyone and realized they were good, real good. No sign of what they might hold at all. This was going to be harder than she'd thought. When she'd played before, which was hundreds of times, she played with drunk, drugged dumbasses, not sober, smart Warriors.

"I'll raise a hundred," Jared said, tossing in his money. Jax followed. It was her turn. She hesitated on purpose but finally tossed in her hundred. Sid did quickly as well.

When it was her turn, she discarded two cards and picked up the two Sid tossed her. Holy shit, she had four of a kind on her first hand. She knew her face was void of any emotion despite her insides quivering with excitement; she'd had a lot of practice hiding any feelings.

Jared glanced her way, his golden eyes studying her closely. A slow grin spread across his face. "I'll raise another hundred."

Katrina watched him just as closely. The only thing he could have that could beat her four of a kind was a straight flush or royal flush. There was no way he had that. Jax folded, so it was up to her.

She had to go for it. "I'll call your hundred and raise another hundred."

"Damn, look at all that money." Steve slobbered over Jared's shoulder.

"Steve, back the fuck up," Jared ordered with a growl.

"Chill," Steve said, but backed up quickly. "Where is all the hate coming from, bro?"

Katrina ignored Jared and Steve as she watched Sid. Her bet was in, and she waited patiently for Sid to decide. Without hesitation, he tossed in his money, and it was time for the truth.

"Okay, little girl, what you got?" Sid looked from her cards to her.

Katrina frowned and looked at Jared. "You first." She smiled sweetly.

"Three of a kind." Jared grinned then reached for the money. "No way do you losers have a better hand."

"This loser has four aces, so get your hands off my money."

Katrina tossed her cards down with a bigger grin. "Unless of course, Sid has a straight flush or royal flush." Her tone indicated she knew he didn't.

"Shit!" Sid threw his cards down, showing a straight.

Katrina laughed, raking the money toward her. "You guys up for another hand or have I proven my point?"

Sid tossed his cards at Jared. "Deal."

Giving a snort, Katrina sorted her money then glanced at Blaze, who winked at her with a nod. Even though it was just a stupid poker game, the pleased look on his face was better than any amount of money she could ever win.

Jared dealt as Damon walked into the room. "We just had the DA pull up with a shitload of cops."

As one, the Warriors stood, no longer just regular guys playing a game of cards. They were alert and warrior ready. Blaze walked past her toward the door.

"Stay here," he ordered before disappearing.

She nodded and watched as Lana and Tessa slowly made their way toward the door to look out. Katrina stood and followed. She watched as Damon allowed the police and DA to enter as Sloan came out of his office.

"And here you are again," Sloan said, his authority

overwhelming. "What do you want this time? Which Warrior do you want to arrest now?"

Evan Nico cleared his throat, obviously uncomfortable. "There's been an accusation that a Warrior has burned down a building, and we have evidence to—"

"Where's the evidence and who is accusing?" Sloan didn't let him finish.

Katrina frowned, looking closely at the man talking. Her eyes scanned the eight cops. Two were vampires. Her frown deepened, as did her concern. She looked back at the man in the nice tailored suit, his dark hair combed back from his face, and she gasped. She had seen him the day he had come to arrest Blaze, but she had not recognized him then. She knew him. Oh God, she knew him.

"You know I can't give that information away, Sloan." Evan tried to sound confident. "But know we have it recorded."

"And where is the recording?" Sloan countered back. "Because I'm not turning my Warrior over until I see it."

"Listen, I have the authority to—"

"I thought we had this conversation before." Sloan sighed. "You have no authority over me or any of my Warriors."

"If they break my laws, I do." Evan's anger flared, his voice lifting and face heating.

"Your laws?" Sloan's voice boomed.

"Yes, and he"—Evan pointed at Blaze—"is under arrest for arson. I also know you have three men in your custody. I want them returned to me immediately."

"Oh, my God," Katrina whispered.

"What is it?" Lana whispered, her eyes never leaving the men outside of Sloan's office.

Before things got out of hand, because every single male out there was getting antsy, the room ready to explode in violence, Katrina rushed out the door.

"I know you," Katrina said, drawing everyone's attention. "The day you came to arrest Blaze I didn't pay any attention, but I know you."

"I think you're mistaken." Evan Nico gave her a glance before dismissing her, but his confidence faltered, and everyone heard it.

"I'm not." Katrina frowned, then looked at two other men. "I also know you and you."

"Can you control this woman so we can finish our business?" Evan said, dismissing Katrina, but Katrina wasn't going to be ignored.

"I've seen you at the clubhouse," Katrina said, then nodded.

"You know my father."

"She's telling the truth." Adam sneered, his eyes never leaving Evan Nico. "He's had dealings with Samuel Drake."

"I have not had dealings with Samuel Drake." Evan's attitude changed in a flash. "I have been trying to take down their organization for a long time, and yes, I've been there and met with him, but only about his criminal activities."

"No." Katrina shook her head. "Unless snorting coke and screwing whoever was thrown your way is the way you do your business."

"I've never—" Evan started, but Katrina stopped him.

"Not you that I've seen, but you two, definitely." Katrina took a step. "You remember me, don't you?" she asked one of the cops, who was having a hard time keeping eye contact with her.

"No," the cop stated, his eyes shifting away from her toward the Warriors.

"Let me refresh your memory." Katrina took a step closer and noticed that Blaze had moved closer to her. "You mistook me for one of my father's 'girls.' Cornered me, and if it wasn't for the knife I always carry, you would have raped me."

"I've never seen you before in my life, lady," the man spat

with narrowed eyes.

"Then how'd you get that scar on the back of your neck?" Katrina countered.

It was obvious to everyone in the room that Katrina had not been able to see the back of the man's neck, but Steve walked behind him and whistled. "Somebody is about to get his ass kicked." Steve glanced at Blaze. "Big old scar and looks pretty much like a knife wound to me."

"And the reason you know about the fire at the clubhouse is my father has the recording on his phone through the Petcube," Katrina added, anger building inside her. When he didn't say anything but just glared, she figured to continue since no one was stopping her. "You knew me that day you came here, didn't you? Is that how my father knew where I was?" Katrina really wasn't asking. She had wondered how her father knew her whereabouts when his gang beat her that day. Now she knew.

"Truth," Adam added with a smirk when Evan glared back at him. "Actually, truth that he knew who you were, but he isn't the one that told your father where you were."

"It had to have been him," Katrina argued, pointing directly at Evan.

"I don't think you understand what exactly is going on here," Evan Nico finally said, shedding his good DA routine for the dirtbag he really was. "You have no proof of what you're saying, and who in the hell is going to believe Samuel Drake's little whore of a daughter? She's nothing but trash."

No one except for Evan Nico and the cops were surprised when Blaze went to tear the bastard's throat out. It took every Warrior there to stop him.

Chapter 12

The fury that hit Blaze hearing the bastard call Katrina a whore sent him into a dark place that even scared him. It took every Warrior there to stop him from killing the son of a bitch. Guns were drawn by the cops, but they were soon disarmed when Jill took them by surprise with her power.

Knowing he had to calm down so the Warriors could protect the women, Blaze eased his fight. "The women," he shouted as he was let go.

"Get the fuck out of here and never come back." Sloan sneered at Evan, who was now surrounded by the police. "We are cutting ties with all law enforcement."

"You can't do that." Evan pointed over one of the cops' shoulder. "You don't have that power."

"Oh, but I do," Sloan responded, his eyes black as night. "It is in our bylaws that once we know the human law has become corrupt, we cut ties and do things our way."

"Thank you!" Sid said, cracking his neck back and forth. "Because honestly, human ways were getting real fucking boring. Can we start killing them now?"

"I say yes." Jared grinned, revealing his long, sharp fangs.

"Hold on, now." Adam's hands rose. "Not all of them know what the fuck is going on so killing them all would be murder and well, we don't do that... do we?"

Katrina watched the fear cross their faces, even Evan Nico's, at Adam's words. The one who had cornered her in the clubhouse glared at her, but there was fear in his eyes.

"You are going by what this bitch says, the daughter of the Iron Drakes?" Evan shook his head. "She's a fucking liar. She's playing you for her father, and you're too blind to see it."

"Do I even have to respond on that?" Adam rolled his eyes, his body, along with others, shielding the women behind him.

"I don't know what you can do, freak," Evan growled toward Adam, "but your facts are wrong. You have no idea what you're bringing down on yourselves."

"If my father has you on his payroll, which I believe is true, then I know exactly what is coming, and I plan on stopping it," Katrina said, her eyes darkening. "And it's about time he, as well as his cronies, meaning you, are stopped."

Blaze was on edge, waiting for shit to fly, but damn, he was fucking proud of her for speaking her truth. He knew then and there she was a damn strong woman. Fuck it, his woman. She was *his* fucking woman.

"And you can tell him I said so," she added before turning around to walk out of the entry and back into the room she had come from.

Blaze grabbed Evan before he could take a step toward the retreating Katrina. "Motherfucker, it will take nothing for me to snap your head off."

"And here I thought Damon was the only one who did that." Jared looked thoughtful. "Wonder if Blaze could do it as clean as Damon."

Sid pulled out a twenty from his pocket. "I bet he can't. No way. Damon is an expert at decapitation." Sid snapped his twenty.

"Twenty?" Jared snorted, shaking his head. "That's all you got?"

"Until I get my poker money back, yeah." Sid frowned. "You taking this bet?"

"Never turned down a sure thing before." Jared pulled out his own twenty then glanced at Blaze. "Don't let me down, bro. Needs to be a clean decapitation."

Fear crossed Evan's face as he began to struggle. "Let me go."

Sid chuckled then looked at one of the cops next to him and elbowed him in the ribs. "You want in on this?" Sid grinned then sighed. "Damn, okay, but I'm telling you, Damon is a sure bet."

"Okay, Blaze." Jared gave the nod. "Rip that sucker off, but nice and neat."

"Jesus." One of the cops gagged then spun away.

"Dude, he hasn't even done it yet." Jared gave him a disgusted glare. "Grow some balls. Be a man, for shit's sake. This is good shit and a good way to make some extra money, as long as you bet on my guy there."

"Let him go, Blaze." Sloan finally stopped the Sid and Jared Show.

Blaze held the bastard for a minute longer before leaning in his face. "You even look at her and no one will be able to save you." He let him go with a shove before sneering at the rest of the men who had come with the bastard. "That goes for every single one of you fuckers. You go near her, I will hunt you down and I will not stop until I find you."

"This better be the last time I throw you out of my house, Nico." Sloan took a step toward Evan Nico. "We will be doing things our way until the corruption stops, and it will be stopped, no matter what it takes. You want a fucking war with us? Your mistake, because you sure as hell will get one. I'm done. Now get the fuck out while you can leave of your own free will."

"This isn't over." Evan pointed toward Sloan. "You can't do this."

"I've heard that before from you, and yes, I just did it." Sloan dismissed him, looking over at the other men. "I know a few of you, so you best determine which way you're going to fly because shit is about to get ugly, and you're going to be on the front lines."

"Are you threatening law enforcement?" Evan asked with fake shock.

"No, I'm warning them," Sloan added, then nodded toward the door. "Make sure they get off the property."

Blaze walked away because he didn't trust himself not to kill somebody. They didn't need his help at that moment, and he wanted to check on Katrina. Walking into the room, he found her instantly standing next to where she had been sitting at the table. Tessa and Lana saw him and quickly left her side.

"You okay?" Blaze gazed down at her bent head.

She nodded, but her words contradicted it. "No, not really," she whispered.

"I won't let anyone hurt you," Blaze vowed, his hand stilling her shaking one.

Katrina slowly pulled her hand away and picked up the

money she had won. "It's not me I'm worried about. My father won't stop until he has what he wants." Katrina glanced out the door then finally up at him. "And he obviously has more connections than even I realized."

"I'm not taking the money, Katrina," he said when she tried to place it in his hand.

She wouldn't even look at him, just wadded the money up and fled the room. His eyes darkened. Even he felt her pain that ran deep, and it angered him more than anything ever had. She deserved much more than life had given her, and he was determined to make sure her life from here on out was easier, even if it meant taking her father down.

******

Katrina was happy when Blaze didn't follow her. She really needed a minute. Once out the door, she noticed that everyone was gone, other than Sloan, who stood staring out the door. He turned when he heard her.

"I'm sorry," Katrina said, her eyes leaving the door to look at him. "I really didn't realize who he was the first time or I would have said something."

Sloan nodded, then frowned. "I know you're not like your father, Katrina."

Lifting her chin, she bobbed her head, trying to keep her tears in check; she knew if she spoke, he would hear the tears in her voice. His words meant the world to her. She respected Sloan Murphy and cared what he thought about her.

With a hard swallow, she cleared her throat. "Thank you," she finally managed to say before turning to leave. She had to get out fast before she lost it.

Finally making it to her room, she rushed in and shut the door. Sager had gone with Pam earlier so Daniel could play with him, and she was glad. She needed a minute with no one seeing her weakness, not even her dog. Noticing she still carried the money, she cursed and tossed it on her dresser. Crawling up on her bed, she lay on her stomach and gave in to the feelings rushing through her body.

Once the tears started, they wouldn't stop. Sobs racked her body as she buried her face into the pillow. How many times in her life had she done this very same thing and all because of one reason, but not the reason most girls her age did it? Not because her favorite pair of jeans didn't fit anymore or because the cute guy in school didn't like her. No, it was deeper than that. She hated her father, feared her father, her family... watched her mother murdered and hated herself because she couldn't do anything to stop it. Now she was here and putting people in danger because one thing she knew and knew well was her father and how he operated. He would run through anyone to get what he wanted, and he wanted her back, but not because he loved his daughter. No. It was to make a point to everyone that nobody fucked over the Iron Drakes. And more than that, no one fucked over

Samuel Drake, especially his blood.

Her mind focused on Daniel, and fear shook her body. If anything happened to that little boy because of her, it would devastate her. How could she stay, knowing she was putting them all in danger? Her father would wait. It may not be until years down the road that he got his revenge. He was uncommonly patient and could wait to make his strike.

She felt the bed shift and without looking, knew Blaze lay beside her, but she kept her face in the pillow. His arms wrapped around her as he pulled her to him, crushing her face into his chest.

"Why?" Blaze whispered in her hair.

Katrina hated to appear weak; it wasn't in her to show weakness in front of others. Blaze was different though. It felt natural to be able to turn to him for comfort, and that scared her. If her father knew, he would do everything in his power to remove Blaze from her life, just like he had done with her mother.

She shook her head with a sniff. "Just having a moment." Her voice, muffled from his chest, cracked as more tears fell.

When Blaze didn't say anything else but simply held her, she was relieved beyond words. She didn't know how he did it, but his body heated, offering her comfort, and he held her tight, his hand rubbing slow circles on her lower back.

"I wish I was someone else." She realized she'd said that thought out loud when he stiffened.

He pulled away from her, lifting her face to his. "I hope you did not just say what I think you said."

"I didn't mean to say that out loud," she muttered, then sat up away from him. "But that's all anyone will see me as. MC trash."

"Not everyone." Blaze sat up next to her. "And I promise to rid the world of those who think it."

Katrina's face scrunched up in a heartfelt cry, a true ugly cry. "Why?" Katrina couldn't even look at him. "Why me, when I know for a fact you could have any woman? Why me?"

Blaze was quiet for a long moment until she turned to look at him with her ravaged face. "Because…." He paused uncomfortably.

Katrina held up her hand. "You know, never mind. I shouldn't have asked that." She was a little hurt when she saw the relief on his face.

"Well, thank fuck for that." Steve's voice sounded in the room.

Katrina jumped with a gasp when Steve appeared, looking sheepish.

"I really didn't want to hear the big badass Blaze getting all flowery with his words and shit." Steve backed toward the door when Blaze growled.

"What the fuck do you think you're doing in here?" Blaze bellowed.

"Whoa! Whoa!" Steve held out his hands, looking legit scared to death. "Hold on, it's not what it looks like."

"It better not be!" Blaze rose slowly, his hands fisting at his sides.

"No, listen." Steve reached behind him, trying to find the door. "I swear I was just coming to check on her and was going to leave right away, and then you came in, shutting the door. So then I was stuck because if I had opened the door, then you would have known I was in here, and I really don't want to die."

"I know now and am debating on whether you live at this very moment." Blaze growled, taking a step.

"WHOA!" Steve frantically tried to open the door without turning around. "Blaze, man, I swear I wasn't here to make a move or spy on her. If any clothes started leaving her body, my ass would have been outta here. I swear it! I mean, I know she had a thing for me.... No, I mean... I just felt it was my duty to... you know."

"No, I don't fucking know." Blaze took another step.

"Jesus, why the fuck won't this door open?" Steve finally turned around, yanking on the knob, then squealed when Blaze slammed a hand beside his head.

"If I ever find you in this room again, nothing will save you," Blaze warned as he pushed Steve out of the way and opened the door with ease.

"Hey, how the hell did you do—" Steve's voice was cut off as Blaze slammed the door in Steve's face.

Katrina felt a tremble in her chin, and it wasn't a cry tremble, but a grin threatening to spread across her face. She looked from the door to see Blaze, who didn't look angry anymore. He openly stared at her.

"Ah, hey, Blaze... we cool, man?" Steve's voice carried through the door.

Blaze gave her a wink before swinging his arm back and slamming his fist against the wood. Steve's yelp was the only thing they heard before footsteps took off quickly down the hallway.

"He probably won't ever come in my room again," Katrina said, looking from the door to Blaze, a small grin on her face.

A different kind of grin lit Blaze's. "Good."

Chapter 13

Katrina sat with Jill, waiting for training to begin. She was anxious to get started, knowing that the others were further ahead than she was since her setback.

"Has Slade said anything about Jenny?" Katrina asked, hoping that the girl got help and stayed clean.

Jill glanced toward where Sloan stood with Jax and Blaze. "He's pretty tight-lipped about the doctor-patient stuff." Jill smiled proudly. "But I do know he took her to rehab, and I heard him talking to them today, so she's still there."

"Good." Katrina nodded, really meaning it. She wished she could have done more than leave Jenny there when she'd left, but she'd had no choice.

"Hey, you good?" Jill leaned back, relaxing on her elbows.

Katrina shrugged. "A little nervous since everyone is further along than I am."

"These guys have nothing on you." Jill snorted, glancing around at the men stretching, punching bags, and grunting. "We may not have dicks, but we kick ass."

Katrina shrugged, looking around at all the groups of guys talking. It was definitely intimidating being the only female in the new group.

"Anyone here able to control animals?" Jill cocked her eyebrow at her.

"No," Katrina acknowledged with a shake of her head.

"Exactly. See that big muscle head over there?" Jill gestured with a chin lift.

Katrina looked and saw one of the trainees who usually had something negative and sexist to say to her. "Yeah."

"With the flip of my wrist, I could send him sailing through the wall." Jill's grin was a little evil. "All that strutting around he's doing and those muscles mean nothing."

"Do it," Katrina urged with a laugh. "Please do it. He's an asshole."

Before Jill could respond, the muscle head glanced their way to see them smiling at him. He flexed his biceps a few times, grinning back at Jill, then her.

Katrina didn't smile back. Actually, she frowned as he made his way toward them, strutting just like Jill had said.

"Hello, ladies." He stood over them, flexing his muscles hard enough that his face scrunched, making it look like he had to poop.

"Hey." Jill sat up even more, then tilted her head. "What's wrong with your face?"

Steve walked up at that moment, looking at the guy. "Yeah, dude." Steve's eyes narrowed. "Looks like you need to take a shit or something."

Katrina tried to smother her laugh, but failed miserably. She didn't feel bad either. This guy, Rob, was always saying something about her and it was great seeing him uncomfortable, just like he had made her feel.

Steve looked down at her, dismissing the guy. "Hey, is Blaze still pissed at me?"

"I don't think so," Katrina replied, not really knowing the answer.

"What the hell did you do now?" Jill snorted with an exaggerated eye roll.

"Nothing."

Jill laughed, because Steve's tone clearly indicated he'd done something. "What did he do, Katrina?"

Katrina ignored Steve's warning look. "He showed up in my room invisible and didn't make himself known while Blaze was there."

With eyes and mouth open wide, Jill gasped a laugh. "Dude,

you're going to get yourself killed."

"So, you're letting the trainer in your room?" Rob looked at her, surprised, as he knelt down like he was part of the group. Everyone stared, but no one said a word. He then decided to make the biggest mistake of his life.

"Well, how about I come to your room later. I like tough girls." He turned his attention to Jill as he reached out to touch her face. Before his fingers could make contact, he was lifted off the ground.

"Oh, shit!" Steve stood quickly, shaking his head. He looked around at the audience now watching their fellow trainee being held in the air by one pissed-off vampire Warrior. "Well, for those of you who didn't know before, you do now. Jill belongs to Slade."

Everyone nodded their understanding with wide eyes, but no one said a word.

"So, my advice to you all is to steer clear unless you want the Slade Train to land on your face." Steve gave his head a sad shake as he looked at Rob, who was gasping.

"Why were you about to touch my mate?" Slade hissed in Rob's face.

When Rob didn't answer, Steve stepped closer. "Ah, Doc, I don't think he can talk with your humongous hand wrapped around his throat." Steve pointed at said hand.

Slade's head snapped toward Steve, who backed away quickly.

"Just sayin'," Steve replied, then flipped his hand a couple of times. "Continue."

"If I even see you look at my mate, I will kill you," Slade warned, his voice deep and hard as his attention turned back toward the man hanging from his hand.

"He's a doctor, so he knows how to…." When Slade glared at him again, Steve nodded quickly. "Shutting the fuck up. Got it."

Katrina watched with a fascination that was probably a little crazy, but when she glanced toward Jill, she swore she saw sexual hunger in her golden eyes as she watched her man protect her. Katrina wondered how that would actually feel and secretly hoped that one day Blaze might protect her like that—and wasn't that just sad and a little needy.

"Slade, I think he got the point." Blaze clapped him on the shoulder.

"I'd say shitting his pants is a pretty good indication he got the point." Steve snorted, then when both Slade and Blaze glared at him, he walked away, disappearing in the crowd of trainees.

Once Slade put the man back on his feet with a few warnings of dying an ugly, painful death, Blaze turned toward the group. "You are here to train and nothing more. Any female who walks onto these mats is to be respected, not treated like a piece of fucking meat for your enjoyment. This is the only warning you will get."

The trainees nodded with a loud, "Yes, sir!"

"And as you found out by this dumb fuck's mistake, the women may be mated to one of the Warriors, and believe me, that is something that will definitely get you killed," Blaze added.

"Amen!" Steve's voice carried, but he couldn't be seen. Blaze just shook his head.

Katrina had to turn away because she was smiling. Steve could do that to her, make her laugh when she shouldn't be laughing, dammit. She didn't want the trainees to think she was laughing at them.

"You find me funny?" Blaze said from behind her.

Turning, Katrina looked up and found nothing funny as he stared down at her. "No." She licked her dry lips. "But Steve...."

"Is an idiot," Blaze finished her sentence.

"I was going to say funny," Katrina countered with a small smile.

A small grin tipped the corner of his full lips. Then it was gone. "Get going on your laps."

Katrina noticed that everyone else had started running. Her eyes caught Jill, who wagged her eyebrows. Without saying a word, Katrina fell in step with her.

"Blaze is a fine specimen," Jill leaned over, whispering.

"That he is." Steve ran past them with a goofy grin. "He makes me all fluttery inside." Steve fanned himself as he passed.

"I'll be sure to let him know your true feelings," Jill called out after him.

"Shit!" Steve cursed, smacking himself on the side of the head.

Embarrassment heated Katrina's body, but she laughed then stumbled when her eyes met Blaze's dead-on. Yes, Jill and Steve were right. He was definitely one hell of a fine specimen.

******

"How's she doing?" Slade asked, moving next to Blaze.

"You're the doc, you tell me," Blaze responded, watching as the trainees worked on weapon disarming.

"Wish I could, but she hasn't come back to see me."

"Was she supposed to?" This time Blaze looked over at him.

Slade nodded. "She had Steve tell me she couldn't make it."

"For what?" Blaze asked, concerned. He'd thought she was doing fine; maybe he was wrong.

"Since she wasn't healing the way she should have been, I need to find out if there are other things that may be going on with her, like is she still having menstrual periods or—"

"Hey!" Blaze threw his hands up, stepping away from the information he wasn't comfortable getting. "Got it!"

Slade actually grinned.

Damn, what the fuck? He didn't need to know this shit about Katrina, but found himself asking. "So, what if she is, you know."

"What, having her menstr—" Slade asked, the grin still in place.

"Yeah, that, fucker." Blaze growled, not liking Slade giving him shit. This womanly function stuff was not something he was comfortable with.

Slade turned serious. "Well, it means she's not a true full blood."

Both Blaze and Slade were quiet, watching the trainees, Blaze paying more attention to Katrina.

Slade finally broke the silence. "I'm doing everything I can to find out what's going on with these man-made concoctions people are making to turn humans, but I'll be honest, and I fucking hate to admit that it's almost impossible. There are so many out there, and when we're lucky enough to find a vial of the shit, even the best—and I do have the best—who are working to decipher whatever we find are at a loss."

"So even though I changed her from her half-breed state…." Blaze really didn't even know what he was asking.

"If this is the case and she's still having human functions such as menstrual cycles, it means that whatever she has been given is somehow keeping her in a human state," Slade clarified, his tone dire. "We don't know the long-term effects of the man-made shit. Only time will tell."

"Can it kill her?" Blaze found himself asking, turning his head to watch Slade closely as he answered.

"I can't say, but I will tell you I'll do everything in my power to not let that happen." Slade nodded toward her. "Make sure she comes to see me. And if you see anything unusual with her that shouldn't be happening, such as not healing quickly, tiredness, and things that we as full bloods don't experience, let me know right away."

Blaze nodded. His stomach clenched as his eyes found her at the same time she glanced up. She gave him a small smile before getting back to work. Helplessness was not an emotion he was used to, and he didn't fucking like it. He never felt helplessness because he controlled his surroundings, his emotions, his life, but now this tiny woman had walked into his world, and he didn't know if he could keep her safe. Not only did that piss him off, but it scared him, another foreign emotion to him.

"We'll keep a close eye on her." Slade spoke as if sensing his thoughts. "She'll be fine."

Blaze headed toward the center of the mat. "She better fucking be."

Chapter 14

After showering, Katrina walked back out onto the mats. Her backpack was slung over her sore shoulder, so she switched. She had fallen pretty hard during a takedown, and her shoulder was killing her. Hearing Blaze's raised voice had her looking toward the door.

Jax, Caroline, and Blaze were in a heated conversation. She slowed, not wanting to walk up on them but really needing to pass them to leave.

"Hey, we're going out to get pizza." Steve stepped up beside her. "Slade's got something to do, so I asked Jill too. Want to come?"

Pizza was better than sitting alone in her room the rest of the night. She had hoped that maybe Blaze would ask her to do something, but she needed to stop that. Blaze never promised her anything, so it was best if she just went along with her boring life, and if it happened, it happened. Plus, she'd never had a normal life with friends so she welcomed the invite.

"Ah, hello." Steve snapped his fingers in front of her face. "Steve to Katrina. Come in, Katrina."

"Sure." Katrina nodded with a genuine smile. "Sounds good."

"Well, come on." Steve headed toward Blaze, Jax, and Caroline. "Let's make like ducks and get the flock out of here. Or something like that."

Katrina chuckled, shaking her head. Steve was always up; there was never a down moment with him, and he also said whatever came to his mind. It was nice because she never had to wonder about Steve. What you saw was what you got with him.

"Blaze, please do this." Caroline's voice was urgent.

Trying not to pry, Katrina hurried behind Steve, but wondered what was going on. Both Jax and Blaze looked pissed while Caroline looked upset.

"There's nothing good that can come out of this," Blaze growled, his voice low with a definite edge.

"You need to take care of your fucking business." Jax sneered at Blaze.

"You need to stay out of my fucking business," Blaze shot back, his voice growing louder as he leaned in toward Jax.

"She is my goddamn business and is suffering because of you."

Both men were almost nose to nose. Caroline shoved her way between them. "This is not settling anything and if anything, it's stressing me out more."

Katrina watched Jax relax slightly, but his glare was still deadly and directed straight at Blaze.

"Come on," Steve whispered, grabbing her elbow. Katrina let him lead her toward the door.

"Where the fuck are you going?" Blaze's voice stopped both Steve and Katrina in their tracks.

"Getting pizza," Steve squeaked.

"I'm talking to her." Blaze was staring straight at Katrina.

"Getting pizza," Katrina repeated Steve's reply without the squeak, but her voice was barely above a whisper. He was so damn intimidating.

"No, you're not." Blaze's eyes narrowed. "You're going to Slade's office, immediately."

"Why?" Katrina frowned.

"Because I said so," Blaze snapped with a frown of his own. "He said you've missed your follow-up. I told him you would be there after training."

Katrina felt like she was being chastised like a five-year-old. Embarrassment, as well as a little resentment, washed over her. With a short nod, she turned and walked out of the building.

"Ah, man. I'm sorry." Steve walked with her, staring over at her. "We'll bring you back some."

Katrina saw Jill standing next to a car and headed her way. "No need." Katrina opened the door, tossing her backpack in. "I'm going with you."

Steve slapped his hand over his face and gave a big sigh. "I see an ass kicking in my future."

"What's going on?" Jill asked Steve over the hood of the car.

"Well, Blaze forbid her to go get pizza and instead to get to Slade's office for the checkup she obviously purposely missed." Steve removed his hand, then sighed again and got in the car. "That's the appointment you had me cancel, wasn't it?"

Katrina didn't answer.

"Forbid?" Jill snorted, also getting in, and started the car. "Seems the Warriors like that word."

Again Katrina didn't say anything, but her eyes met Jill's in the rearview mirror and saw respect.

"You sick?" Jill asked, her eyes still fixed on Katrina.

"Nope," Katrina replied, her eyes not wavering.

"You getting pizza?" Jill asked, putting the car in gear.

Katrina nodded with a smile. "With extra cheese."

"That's my girl." Jill focused on pulling out of the parking space and then the parking lot. "Forbid, our ass. They need to wipe that word out of their vocabulary."

"Speaking of asses." Steve groaned. "Is there any way, any way at all, I won't be blamed for this."

Katrina didn't reply; instead, she watched Blaze walk out of the warehouse as they passed. He didn't even look their way as he headed to his bike. What had she expected, words of love from the Warrior? A sign of respect? Nope, just the same shit she'd run from. She had lived this life, being ordered around by men, disrespected. Yeah, not happening anymore. She wasn't a five-year-old, and she refused to be talked to as if she didn't matter.

"The blame is on me," Katrina assured Steve as soon as Blaze was out of sight.

"Not if I'm around." Steve snorted.

"If you want to drop me off, you can." Katrina hadn't considered that maybe Steve and Jill would get in trouble. She didn't want that; this was her decision. She told them as much.

Jill and Steve looked at each other before Steve turned to stare at her over the seat. "My middle name is Dangerous."

A loud snort from Jill filled the car.

"Hey, it is, or will be as soon as I change it legally, which I'm planning on doing," Steve said seriously. "And Jill just doesn't give a crap because no one is going to give her shit unless they want the Slade Train making a stop on their ass."

"I'm glad you came," Jill said, pulling into a parking lot. "One can only take so much of Steve."

"That's because there's so much awesome in this body." Steve hopped out of the car and shifted into a weightlifter pose.

Katrina laughed as she followed them inside. Once they found a table toward the back, she decided she wasn't going to worry about the consequences she would probably face for disobeying Blaze's orders. She was just probably one of the many women he had screwed in his life. Okay, where had that thought come from?

"She's been doing that a lot lately."

Hearing Steve, she realized the waitress was waiting to take her order. "Oh, just a small pizza with extra cheese," Katrina said, handing her the menu. "And a sweet tea, please."

"A small pizza?" Steve frowned at her. "Really?"

"Why? What did you guys get?" Katrina looked at Jill.

"He got a large and I got a medium." Jill grinned. "Honey, we don't gain weight anymore. I eat a lot of everything now."

Katrina smiled at the waitress, who waited. "I'm good with my order, thanks."

"Hey, do you know what's up with Jax and Blaze?" Steve asked, turning serious as soon as the waitress left to put in their order. "I thought they were going to come to blows before we left. Caroline was there too."

"I think someone in Blaze's past has been haunting Caroline." Jill thanked the waitress who brought their drinks. "And I don't think Blaze wants to hear about it."

"Caroline talks to dead people," Steve informed Katrina.

"I know," Katrina replied, more curious than ever. "Why wouldn't he want to take care of it if it's hurting Caroline?"

"You got me, but it must be some pretty bad shit." Steve cocked his eyebrow. "I mean, I can't really blame Blaze. Who the fuck wants to hear from dead people? Caroline and Lana are strong-ass women to be able to handle that stuff. I'd be pissing myself if some dead dude came waltzing up to me."

"I doubt they waltz." Jill rolled her eyes.

"And how would you know?" Steve narrowed his eyes at

her. "Have you seen a dead person?"

"Actually, yes." Jill cocked her eyebrow at him. "Aren't we technically dead?"

"Ah, good point." Steve thought for a moment. "But I mean dead, dead. Like in ghost floating around dead."

"Then no, I haven't."

He pointed in Jill's face. "Then you don't know if they waltz."

Soon their pizzas arrived, and talk turned to eating. Katrina couldn't stop thinking about Blaze. Why had he talked to her that way and why was he acting like that toward Jax and Caroline? She couldn't even imagine what Caroline went through with dead people coming to her and her sister, wanting to deliver messages to people, especially when those people didn't want to hear it. She had noticed the dark circles under Caroline's eyes and understood Jax's concern. Maybe Blaze wasn't who she thought he was. The thought made her heart hurt.

"Ah, shit!" Steve hissed, then looked at Katrina. "You're busted, babe."

Katrina looked up at Steve, then over her shoulder to see Damon walking toward them looking pissed.

Damon picked up a chair, turned it backward and straddled

it, then his eyes met hers. "Decided to disobey orders, did you?"

"I tried to tell her," Steve said with a shake of his head, then mouthed "sorry" to Katrina. "She should listen to her superiors."

Jill snorted. "Seriously, Steve."

Damon's eyes remained fixed on Katrina, but his eyebrow cocked at Steve's words.

"Guess Adam told you where we were." Jill took another bite of pizza.

"Seems someone was supposed to go to Slade's office straight from training but didn't show." Damon glanced around the small restaurant then back at Katrina. "Not a smart move. You have a price on your head, if you've forgotten."

"Kind of hard to forget," Katrina replied, knowing exactly what kind of a price she would pay if she were caught by the Iron Drakes.

"We got her," Jill said, tossing a big piece of crust on her plate. She then wiped her mouth. "Nobody would have—"

"Slade's on his way." Damon turned to look at Jill. "We figured that you all would know the danger, but obviously we were wrong. This isn't a game. This is serious."

Steve nodded as if agreeing with everything Damon said. "Very serious."

"It was your idea to get pizza, asshole, so stop acting like you're Mr. Innocent," Jill snapped at Steve. "Plus, we're in a public place. No way would anything happen. They aren't that stupid."

Katrina glanced at Damon, seeing he knew exactly what she knew.

"Tell them, Katrina." Damon tilted his head. "Tell them how serious this is."

Katrina cleared her throat as her past once again overwhelmed her. "He's right." Katrina hated this and wondered if she would ever be free from the MC. "I'm sorry. I didn't think, and I know better than anyone how they operate. Us being in a public place wouldn't matter."

Damon looked toward the door then stood. "Let's go." He threw down a fifty on the table.

Katrina stood to follow Steve and Jill, but stopped when she spotted Blaze, his eyes narrowed as he stared at her. He looked damn sexy when he glared like that. Seriously, her life was a mess, and all she could think about was how sexy Blaze looked when he freaking glared.

"If you're thinking about running, don't," Damon leaned down and whispered. "I'm pretty fast."

With those words, her feet began to move, and she finally looked away from Blaze only to see Slade glaring at Jill, but Jill was glaring back. Maybe that was what she needed to do. So taking Jill's lead, Katrina gave Blaze her meanest glare, which only earned her a smirk from that sexy mouth. God, she was pathetic.

Chapter 15

Blaze had left the warehouse to meet up with Katrina at Slade's office. Once there, to say he was shocked and pissed that she didn't show was an understatement. At first he feared she had been picked up by the Iron Drakes, but when Steve and Jill were not anywhere in the compound, he found Adam to confirm what he already knew. She had gone against his orders.

Now standing inside the pizza place staring at her, relief that she was safe was swift. A call had gone out and Damon had been the closest, but that hadn't stopped Blaze from breaking every speed law known to man to get there. He knew it was only a matter of time before the Drakes struck, and he didn't want Katrina left unguarded. Period.

Her miserable attempt at glaring at him actually had him grinning. She had spunk, which he respected, but she would learn to listen to him, especially now with the danger hanging over her beautiful head.

Slade was already giving Jill hell as they walked out the door. Katrina tried to ease past him with Damon following her, but Blaze pulled her out of the way to let Damon pass.

"Thanks, my man." Blaze nodded to Damon as he passed.

"We watch out for our own, so no problem." Damon gave

Katrina a pointed look before disappearing.

"You got something to say for yourself?" Blaze looked down at her as they stepped out the door.

Katrina pulled her arm out of his grasp. "Yes, I do." She met his gaze. "I'm not a five-year-old who needs to be ordered around."

"Obviously, you do." He let her walk away, his eyes going directly to her ass. "But definitely not a five-year-old." He cocked his eyebrow, watching her sway before catching up to her. When she opened the car door, he removed her hand and slammed it shut. Jill was already on Slade's bike after tossing Steve her keys.

"Take the car back," he told Steve as he led Katrina toward his bike.

"Always leaving alone from the party." Steve sighed dramatically as he disappeared inside the car.

"My bag." Katrina tried to go back to the car, but Blaze stopped her.

"Will be at the compound. You can get it later." Blaze pulled her with him, then stopped when he heard her gasp. He loosened his grip but didn't let her go. "What?"

"Nothing," she replied without looking at him.

"I know a gasp of pain when I hear it." Blaze's voice reflected his anger. "What's hurt?"

"Nothing."

"Katrina?" His voice hardened.

"Blaze?" Katrina's voice was sarcastic.

"Woman, you are going to drive me insane." Blaze sneered down at her.

"Yeah, well see you there."

Blaze cursed as he continued to his bike, but was easier with her. His eyes kept scanning the area; his senses were buzzing, alert for danger. He got on, then turned his head to look at her. "Do I need to physically put you on the bike?"

"No," she hissed, but still didn't slide on the bike.

When it looked like she was going to argue, he growled loudly. It seemed to do the trick because she hopped on behind him. He started the bike and waited for her to wrap her arms around him, but when she obviously refused to touch him, he reached behind him and did it for her.

"Hold on and don't fucking let go," he ordered. Rolling out of the parking lot, he headed in the opposite direction of the compound.

******

She wanted to be mad. She really, *really* wanted to be mad, but feeling her body against his as the motorcycle roared beneath them made it hard. She found herself pressed up against him as she watched the scenery pass by and wished with everything she had that her life was perfect and the man in front of her was hers.

The motorcycle slowed, and she squeezed her eyes shut, praying the ride wasn't over so soon, but it was. Finally, she lifted her head from his back and looked around, not knowing where they were. Reluctantly, she unwrapped her arms from around him and slid off the bike.

"Where are we?" she asked as he climbed off the bike.

"My place." Blaze put his hand on the small of her back and led her toward the front door.

Katrina was surprised as she took in the small house that had seen better days. The once white paint was peeling off, giving the house a haunted look. The shutters that weren't missing were hanging askew, and dead weeds had taken over the whole yard. With care, it could be a really cute house. Though she seriously doubted Blaze would appreciate living in a cute house.

"But I thought you lived at the compound." Katrina waited while he unlocked the door.

"I mostly do, but I have to get away from those assholes sometimes. When I saw this place, I bought it." Blaze opened the door, then stepped aside so she could enter.

Katrina walked in and sighed. It was an empty shell of a house. Only a kitchen table with two chairs that had seen better days filled the space. No curtains hung from the windows, only shades that were pulled down. No other furniture littered the room. There were no pictures, no life whatsoever.

"It serves my purpose." Blaze responded to her silence as if he knew exactly what she was thinking.

"It's nice, but empty." Katrina looked up at him with a frown.

"As I said, it serves my purpose." He shifted uncomfortably.

Okay, she was supposed to be mad at him, but all she wanted to do was take him in her arms to ease the loneliness she knew all too well. At least she felt that way for a short second until he went and ruined it.

"What possessed you to disobey me?" Blaze went from looking uncomfortable to stern, which in turn switched her emotions of feeling bad for the big vamp to seething at the arrogant ass.

"And what possessed you to think you could *forbid* me to do anything?" She shot back, then wished she hadn't emphasized the word because his eyes darkened menacingly.

"The word *forbid* never left my lips." Blaze took a step toward her.

Okay, if he was trying to intimidate her, it was working, but she was going to stand strong. "Pretty much the same thing in my book," she countered, proud her voice didn't break. "I promised myself when I ran from the Iron Drakes, I would never let anyone dictate my life, no matter what. It's a very hard habit to break, and one I could easily fall back into. Do you know how many times I got to go out with friends to get a pizza?"

Her words seemed to soften his features slightly. "No, but—"

"Never," Katrina interrupted him. "I could never have friends. It was *forbidden* outside of the club. I could have all the friends I wanted who were associated with the MC, but outside, it was not even a possibility. There wasn't one person inside the MC who I wanted to call a friend because every single one of them wanted something for that friendship, and most of the time the cost was too high, at least for me."

"Katrina—" Blaze tried to speak, but Katrina once again stopped him.

"I'm not telling you this to make you feel sorry for me. That was my life, my past, and I'm dealing with it." Katrina frowned at her words. "At least I'm trying to, probably not as successfully as I want."

Blaze cupped her chin, raising her face to his. All anger had left his hard features. "Telling you to do something for your own good is not forbidding you to enjoy something. You have missed your checkup appointments with Slade, and that will be corrected." He placed his thumb against her lip when she started to speak. "And as of right now, you will be accompanied by a Warrior when you leave the compound."

"I was with two Warriors," Katrina reminded him.

"Yes, Jill and Steve are Warriors, but not with the experience needed to deal with this alone." Blaze removed his hand but didn't move away.

Actually Katrina agreed with that. The Iron Drakes shouldn't be underestimated. She had momentarily forgotten that because she was so ready to be done with them. "You're right." Katrina sighed. "I should have listened to you."

"I'm what?" Blaze cocked his eyebrow, and a tiny slip of a grin tipped his lips. "I don't think I heard you correctly."

"You heard it, and I'm not repeating it." Katrina rolled her eyes, but also smiled. "I'll try to behave until this is over. But instead of acting like an overbearing ass being demanding, could you try asking? Being talked to like that was how I used to live. I want to forget."

She watched as Blaze thought long and hard about her request. "When it comes to your well-being and safety, I can't promise you anything, but I will try." When she remained silent, he continued. "But you will be seeing Slade sooner rather than later."

Katrina knew that was about as good as it was going to get with Blaze. A thought popped into her head. "What's your last name?"

That seemed to take him aback; his eyes darkened again. "Blaze."

"Blaze Blaze?" Katrina frowned. "Different, but catchy."

"Don't be a smartass." He growled as his eyes shifted away. "Blaze is all I go by."

She watched as he walked away, headed for the refrigerator, and pulled out a beer. When he offered her one, she shook her head. "Don't drink."

Blaze flipped the metal cap off with his thumb and took a long swallow. "You're different."

"Why, because I don't drink?"

"No. Can't quite put my finger on it, but I will." Blaze pointed at her with the hand that held the bottle.

"Well, fill me in when you find out." Katrina shrugged, then turned to walk deeper into the house. "I don't think I'm different from anyone else unless it's more boring."

"Boring would never be a word any sane man would use to describe you." Blaze's voice was so close to her ear, she shivered and leaned back.

As her back touched his chest, his strong arms wrapped around her waist. "I'm supposed to be mad at you," she whispered on a sigh.

Blaze raked her neck with his fangs. "Plenty of time later for that."

A scream of pleasure escaped her as his fangs broke through the skin of her neck and one hand cupped her through her jeans. All anger left her; only pleasure resided within her mind, body, and soul.

Chapter 16

Blaze knew he was fucked; he couldn't keep his hands off her. And when he wasn't with Katrina, he couldn't stop thinking about putting his hands on her. The attachment he had to her was stronger than anything he had ever felt, and now that he was tasting her blood for the first time, the connection slammed into him with surprising force. He knew she felt it as well. Her body responded to him as if they were one being. Pulling his fangs from her soft skin wasn't easy when all he wanted to do was continue feeding. God, she was sweet. Her blood tasted like the most expensive whiskey that had ever touched his lips, and as intoxicating.

"I'm going to take you, and it's not going to be gentle." Blaze hissed the warning softly in her ear. "Tell me now if that's not okay." He was already working her jeans down past her hips.

Katrina didn't answer, but she did help him lower her jeans, and then lay across the table bare-assed, looking at him over her shoulder, which was answer enough.

"Jesus!" Blaze wasted no time lowering his pants and taking his rock-hard cock in his hand. With his free hand, he touched her and probed to make sure she was ready for him. She was more than ready; her sweet juice ran onto his fingers.

Careful of her shoulder, he grasped her arm to give himself leverage as he slowly pushed his cock into her silky smoothness. Her body accepted him inside, clutching him to the point he cursed from the pleasure.

True to his word, he was not gentle. Careful, yes; easy, no, and she received him with a frenzy that matched his own. He cocooned her body with his as he lay his chest against her back and pounded into her. Her head rested on the table with her flaming red hair fanned out around her. Her eyes were closed. Her bottom lip caught in her teeth, and he had never seen anything more beautiful.

"You're beautiful." His voice spoke the vision he was seeing.

As her eyes opened slightly, her swollen lip was released by her teeth. "I want to touch you."

She could have asked him for anything, and in that moment, he would have sold his own soul, if he had one, to see she got it. Her modest request to touch him did just that, touched him like nothing else ever had. Slowly he pulled out of her, his need to take her fast and hard vanishing. He eased her up, removed her shirt, followed by her lacy bra. He frowned at the bruise on her shoulder, but didn't mention it; he would touch on that subject later. Before picking her up, he discarded his boots and jeans. Then with ease, he lifted her by the waist and with no problem, slid his cock into her warmth.

Her small hands caressed his shoulders, her fingernails biting into his skin, but he welcomed the pain. The pain was the only thing keeping him in the moment. His hands remained on her hips, keeping a slow, sensual pace.

She rode him with her head thrown back, so he let her pick the pace; he just steadied her with his strength. Blaze stood with his legs braced and gave her free rein, watching as she took control, something he never thought he'd enjoy, but he was fucking ready to explode witnessing her passion.

Katrina's head snapped up. Her eyes were black as night as they stared at him and then his neck. No words were spoken. Nothing needed to be said. He tilted his head so his neck was exposed to her. With a quickness that surprised him, she latched on. Her urgent but careful pulls had his dick hardening to the point of pain. As she drank, Blaze took back control and slammed her onto him over and over again until they were both spent.

When her fangs released him, she licked his wounds closed. Her head remained resting on his shoulder as she breathed steadily.

"Katrina?" He tried to see her, but her face was in the curve of his neck. Had she fallen asleep? But that was not possible. They didn't sleep; they didn't get tired. "Katrina?" he said, a little louder, with more force.

"I love you." The whispered words were just as clear as if she'd screamed them. She had said the words but still hadn't moved. The soft snore next to his ear told him what he'd thought: she had fallen asleep.

He stood with her in his arms, holding her close, and didn't know what the fuck to do. He honestly didn't know if the fear he felt, which was a first because fear wasn't a normal emotion for him, was because of her words or because she was sleeping, something a full-blood vampire never did.

Carefully he pulled his semihard cock out of her warmth and gently laid her on the table. She curled up, and he grabbed his leather jacket and covered her body as well as he could. After quickly pulling on his jeans, he grabbed his phone. Finding Slade's number, he called, pacing as he impatiently waited for him to pick up.

"Yeah." Slade answered on the third ring.

"She's sleeping," Blaze said, his eyes never leaving her. The silence on the other end said a lot.

"Where are you?" Slade finally said, his voice concerned.

"At my place, but I'll bring her to you." Blaze rubbed his eyes, actually feeling a little tired himself. What the fuck was she doing to him? "This isn't good, is it?"

"Let's just say it's different and not jump to conclusions," Slade responded. "I'll be waiting in my office."

Blaze hung up the phone and remained staring at her. With a

curse, he grabbed her clothes before reaching out. "Katrina." He shook her until she finally woke up.

"Was that a dream?" She sighed, then stretched, knocking his leather jacket off her and to the floor. She looked down at herself and smiled. "Guess not. Did I pass out?"

"You fell asleep." Blaze helped her sit up. "Are you okay?" He really tried to forget those three words she had spoken, but every time her lips moved, he was afraid she would speak them again. He honestly didn't know what he would say in return. The word love had never been in his vocabulary, ever, and he never expected it to be.

"Perfect." Katrina was watching him closely. "Did I do something wrong?"

"No," Blaze lied. Well actually, he didn't lie. She hadn't done anything wrong. What man in his right mind wouldn't want to hear those words from a woman like her? He just wasn't in his right mind, and he definitely wasn't the right man for Katrina. He knew that, but he couldn't fucking keep his hands or thoughts off her. "But you are going to see Slade."

"Now?"

"Yes, now," he replied. "Get dressed."

Katrina took her clothes he handed her. As the sleep seemed to clear from her eyes, she dressed. It wasn't until shock crossed her face that he knew she remembered the words she had spoken. The only thing he could do was turn away like the coward he was. *Fuck!*

******

Katrina once again found herself on the back of Blaze's motorcycle, but this ride was different. His body was stiff, almost foreign to her, and she knew why. She had once again spoken her thoughts aloud, a habit she'd had since she was a child that had earned her many slaps. She had told him she loved him and he'd rejected her words. He may not have said it, but his actions sure did. What did she expect?

Her fingers tightened on his jacket as he turned a corner, but she refused to put her arms around him, and he didn't force the issue. Rejection hurt, and she refused to knowingly put herself in that position. She blamed his stupid dick for her blunder. She knew she was being ridiculous, blaming his dick, but she was pissed at herself. When would she ever learn? Friendships and love came with a price, always. She had known she was in love with Blaze a while ago but had sworn to herself she would take the knowledge to the grave, whenever that would be. Unless he was to express the emotion first. Well, she blew that plan all to hell.

They arrived at the compound and Blaze stopped by the front door. "Go to Slade's office. I will be there in a second."

Katrina slipped off the bike without a word, but before she could take a step, he stopped her.

"I mean it, Katrina." Blaze eyed her. "Straight to Slade's office."

Nodding, Katrina pulled her arm from his grip as she walked away. Yes, thoughts of disobeying him again filtered through her mind, so maybe, just maybe, she'd end up bare-assed and facedown on a table. She was absolutely insane to even think that. She knew this wasn't a real relationship. She knew her saying she loved him was not a dream. The words had left her lips, and his actions since then told her everything she needed to know. She would not make that mistake again.

Before she knew it, and not even remembering walking down the hallways of the compound, she was at Slade's door. It stood wide open.

"Come in." Slade's voice echoed in the hallway.

Katrina cringed, wishing she were anywhere else than here. She hated doctors, always had, even doctors as gorgeous as Slade. Actually, that made it worse.

"Table." He pointed, then turned to grab a file.

She hopped on the table, then noticed Blaze had snuck up behind her and was leaning on the doorframe. Wasn't there such a thing as patient-doctor confidentiality? The look on Blaze's face told her to keep that thought to herself.

"How have you been feeling?" Slade asked, looking up from

the file.

"Fine."

"She has a large, painful bruise on her shoulder," Blaze answered. His eyes narrowed at her frown.

"Pull your shirt down from your shoulder." Slade set the file on the desk and headed her way. She did what he asked, making sure to remain still when he touched the sore spots. "When did this happen?"

"Tonight," she responded, pulling her shirt back over her shoulder. "During a takedown. Guess I landed on it wrong."

Slade frowned. He then turned to write something in the file. "Are you still having your menstrual cycles?"

Okay, this was uncomfortable. Her eyes slid to Blaze, who was staring at her waiting for her to answer. She glanced at the floor. "Yes."

"When you were human, were they normal and regular?" Slade waited for the answer, and when one wasn't forthcoming, he looked up from the file. "Katrina?"

"They were." She felt the warm blush of embarrassment rush her body.

"And now?"

"Not as regular."

"But normal or abnormal?"

"Is this really necessary?" Katrina wanted to die. The only person she had ever talked about her period with was her mother, not some drop-dead gorgeous doctor and definitely not with a man she'd just let screw her on a kitchen table.

"Yes," Slade replied, then glanced at Blaze. "Maybe you should wait—"

"Right here." Blaze's eyes narrowed as if daring anyone to tell him to leave. "She also fell asleep, as I said on the phone."

"Have you done that a lot since being turned into a full blood?" Slade leaned against his desk and crossed his arms just like Blaze.

"I mean, not a lot." Katrina shrugged. "I'm awake more than I sleep, but I do get tired."

"Do you get tired after a lot of activity?" Slade kept up his questions and then asked one she was in no way going to answer. "What were you doing tonight before you fell asleep?"

Katrina's eyes shot from the wall she had been staring at to avoid eye contact with anyone male, to Blaze, who was staring straight at her. What in the hell was she going to answer to that? Blaze looked away from her and gave Slade a cocked-eyebrow look that Slade obviously understood.

"Okay, I'm just going to do an exam on you, nothing major." Slade straightened. "Is that okay with you?"

"Do I have a choice?" Katrina gave it a shot.

"No," Blaze answered for Slade. "But I will give you some privacy."

Katrina watched as he closed the door with him on the other side and realized how lonely she suddenly felt. She wondered if Slade had a cure for a broken heart, because she had a bad feeling she was going to need one.

Chapter 17

Blaze stood outside the door waiting and thinking. He knew for sure she was aware that he'd heard her. Fuck, what a mess. Why in the hell couldn't things just be easy, no love involved? He cared for her, he did know that, but love? What the fuck was that anyway? Love, like, care—it was all the same goddamn thing, wasn't it?

"Oh, hey." Steve turned the corner and came to an abrupt halt.

Giving Steve a nod, Blaze kept his pose against the doorframe, arms crossed.

"You waiting to see Slade?" Steve glanced at the closed door.

"No."

"Oh, ah, is he in?"

"Yes."

"Hmmm, well, ah, is there someone in there?" Steve just didn't shut up.

"Yes."

"Oh, well. Okay." Steve leaned against the opposite wall. "I'll wait. I've had this itch... well, never mind. I'm sure you don't want to hear about it."

Blaze stared at Steve, knowing he was making the kid uncomfortable, but he didn't care. See, this was the real Blaze. He made people fucking uncomfortable. He wasn't made for love and all that stupid shit.

He kept his face blank as Steve fidgeted, then ended up with his arms crossed like Blaze before realizing what he'd done, so he dropped them to his sides with a curse under his breath.

"Hey, man, we good?" Steve finally asked, breaking the silence. "I seriously hate when someone is mad at me, and well, you look like you could, you know, kill me. Or is that just your resting face? Some people have happy resting faces, others have sad resting faces, but you have one of those rare 'I want to kill something' resting faces."

When Blaze continued to stare, Steve sighed then looked away. He really tried to not care for the guy, but Steve had a way about him that meant you just couldn't help liking the asshole. That didn't mean he couldn't make the kid sweat.

"Not that an 'I want to kill something' resting face is a bad thing." Steve continued to hang himself by talking. "Actually, it would help a lot when you don't want to talk to certain people and..."

Blaze cocked his eyebrow, trying to clue Steve in that that was exactly what he was doing with him.

"...and, well...." Steve seemed to get the message as the door to Slade's office opened. "Thank God."

"Make sure you see me in a week," Slade warned Katrina.

"She will," Blaze answered for her.

"You okay, Katrina?" Steve's brow furrowed in concern.

"I'm fine, thanks." Katrina looked uneasy at Steve's question.

Blaze glared at Steve with a low growl.

"You need to see me?" Slade broke in before Blaze could say anything.

"Ah, yeah." Steve rushed toward the door, staying as far away from Blaze as he could. "Seems I have another bad cause of diarrhea of the mouth and I got this itch...."

Blaze watched Katrina grin as Steve disappeared into Slade's office, but as soon as she looked up at him, her grin disappeared.

"She check out?" Blaze asked Slade, his eyes still on Katrina.

Before Slade could answer, Katrina spoke. "Yeah, she checked out." Katrina huffed. "I'm right here and can answer for myself. Plus, I don't see how it's any of your business, or does patient-doctor confidentiality not mean anything with the VC Warriors?"

Blaze was actually at a loss for words. Katrina rarely raised her voice and she definitely didn't give many people shit, but she'd given him and Slade a piece of her mind. He liked it, a lot.

"Fine," she said with a growl, then started to walk away. "Go ahead and tell him everything, not that I have a say in the matter."

Blaze watched her turn the corner before turning to Slade, who was grinning. "Going to have your hands full."

"Apparently so." Blaze smirked. "Seriously, is she okay?"

"As far as I can tell." Slade did turn serious. "I can't find anything wrong with her other than the human traits that are still present. We may never know the reason, but with those human traits, she can also age like a human, die like a human."

Blaze had already thought that. "You will do everything you can to—"

"I'm on it, Blaze," Slade assured him. "I'll do everything I can for her. I'm also going to Sloan with this. If she's like this, chances are so are the Iron Drakes who were changed with the same serum. They'll be easy to kill and they probably don't realize that yet, which is to our advantage."

All Blaze could do was nod because hearing that Katrina could be easily killed put things in perspective. In other words, shit just got real.

******

Saying these Warriors were overbearing was a total understatement. After today, she had no idea if she was going to be able to work with Tessa or not. She needed a job. Tessa had told her she could use extra help at the bar, which would be perfect. Pam and Duncan had offered her money for watching Daniel, yet she would never take anything from them for watching that cutie.

She was tired of being bored to tears when she didn't have training. Even working weekends would give her enough money to get what she needed, which wasn't much. The money Blaze gave her and that she won at poker was not hers, and she wouldn't spend a dime of it.

Speaking of Daniel…. "Trina!" Daniel shouted and ran toward her with Sager following at his heels. He either had a hard time getting the Ka sound in front of her name, or he just wanted to call her Trina, but she didn't care. This kid could call her anything he wanted.

"And what are you doing, young man?" Katrina made a big

showing of trying to pick him up. "Wow, what have you been eating? I can hardly pick you up."

"I eat like my daddy," he said proudly, puffing his little chest out. "Will you play with me?"

"Well, I don't know...." Katrina pretended to think long and hard.

"Please... please... plllleeeeaaassseee." Daniel clasped his hands in front of him.

Katrina saw Duncan watching them from up the hall and smiled before looking back down at Daniel. "I guess if I have to." Katrina sighed, then laughed when Daniel screamed in glee.

"Dad, she said she would."

"So she did." Duncan laughed. "You sure? I just have something to take care of. It shouldn't take me long at all."

"No problem," Katrina replied, letting the wiggling bundle of boy down. "Nothing I'd rather do."

"I'm gonna get my guitar." Daniel ran up the stairs, then ran back down. "Don't leave, Dad."

Katrina laughed, watching his antics as he once again headed up the stairs. He was a normal four- going on five-year-old, full of energy, he was very smart and knew things that for a young boy were amazing.

"How you doing, Katrina?" Duncan looked down at her, his eyes missing nothing.

"I'm okay," Katrina replied with a nod. Out of all the Warriors, Duncan was the one she was most comfortable with. She'd spent so much time with Daniel since she'd been there, that Pam and Duncan had really welcomed her into this tight group.

Duncan's stare stated he clearly didn't believe her. She was glad that Daniel was fast because he was coming down the stairs with his little guitar and Jax following him with his.

"Looks like you'll be needing this." Jax grinned at her as he handed her his guitar. "Little guy here knocked on my door saying you're giving him lessons today."

Taking the guitar, Katrina grinned. "Is that what we're doing?"

"Yep!" Daniel grinned back then headed into the game room. "Come on, Trina."

"Sorry," Duncan said to both of them with a laugh. "Once his mind is made up, there's no changing it, much like his mother."

Jax nodded but didn't smile. Katrina noticed, and she knew Duncan did also.

"How's Caroline?" Duncan asked the question Katrina wanted to.

Jax ran his hand through his hair in frustration. "Getting worse." He glanced quickly at Katrina, then away. "Something needs to be done before I go off on the fucker."

"I'll talk to him," Duncan replied with a sigh.

"Well somebody better, because I'm not going to watch her suffer much longer." Jax turned to head back upstairs. "If it comes down to choosing between him and her, the bastard dies."

Katrina's and Duncan's eyes met, but neither said a word.

"Trina, come on!" Daniel's voice carried out to them.

"Daniel, watch your manners." Duncan's tone wasn't harsh, yet Daniel understood he was pushing it.

"Sorry," Daniel called. "Trina, pleeease come on!"

A huge grin broke over Duncan's face as he rolled his eyes. Katrina slapped her hand over her mouth so Daniel didn't hear her laughter.

"I do what I can." Duncan chuckled with a shake of his head. "I'll be back soon. If you need me, just call. Pam may be back before me, but I'm not sure."

"No worries." Katrina held the guitar close. "We'll find some trouble to get into, I'm sure."

"That I have no doubt." Duncan left, still grinning.

"Come on, Trina." Daniel patted the floor with his hand. "See what I can do."

Katrina sat next to him on the floor. Sager lay between them, his eyes closed but ears alert. When he started to play, Katrina's brows lifted in amazement. He was a little clumsy with the chords, but holy crap, the kid soaked things up like a sponge. It wasn't perfect, but everything she'd taught him a week ago, he had down.

"Daniel, that is awesome," Katrina praised, truly stunned.

"I know." Daniel nodded at her with a seriousness that reminded her of a Warrior. Poor Pam; this little one was going to be a handful.

As they sat together, Katrina found herself relaxing, forgetting everything that was wrong in her life and enjoying the little boy's company. How refreshing it was to live through someone so young, if only for an hour.

"Play that song." Daniel watched her hands as she strummed.

"'That's What's Up'?" Katrina asked, and grinned when he nodded. "You remember the words?"

"Yep." Daniel put his guitar down. "But I don't want to play. You play and I'll sing with you."

When she had tried to find a song safe to teach him, "That's What's Up" by Lennon and Maisy had seemed perfect. It was a cute song that was easy to learn both the words and guitar. Daniel loved the song and learned it quickly, as he did everything.

"Are you sure you don't want to play?"

"I don't want to mess it up." Daniel frowned, touching the guitar.

She knew he wanted to play, but the little perfectionist didn't want to ruin it. He was far too stinkin' cute. "Daniel, we all mess up. I'll probably mess up, but that's part of learning something new."

"Really?" Daniel slowly picked his guitar back up. "So it's okay if I get it wrong?"

"Is it okay if I get it wrong?" Katrina asked him the same question.

"Sure." He grinned excitedly. "But I'll try not to, okay."

"Me too." Katrina laughed and then started the song with Daniel following. He messed up right away so Katrina made sure she did the same.

"See." Katrina stopped playing. "We both messed up, so let's start again."

Finally they got it together and began to sing and play. She was stunned by this boy. She knew he was special in terms of his abilities. For his age he was well advanced; seriously, what kid at almost five could play the guitar, remember words to a song, and play with ease? He was a complete joy.

As she always did while playing, Katrina got lost in the music, and once she was finished, she noticed that Daniel was no longer playing or singing, but had a huge grin on his face.

"You have a pretty voice," he said, then looked behind her. "Doesn't she?"

Confused, Katrina glanced over her shoulder to see they had an audience, and Blaze was among them. Embarrassed, Katrina turned back and leaned over toward Daniel. "Why didn't you tell me they were there?"

Daniel shrugged with the innocence of youth and stood. "Because the song wasn't done."

Katrina's eyes opened wide at his answer. Then she chuckled. He had a point. She stood with him, careful with Jax's guitar.

"Not only are you going to be waitressing, you'll be singing at the bar." Tessa clapped her hands. "That was amazing,

Katrina."

"I don't sing in front of people." Katrina's stomach revolted at the thought. Singing in front of people brought back too many bad memories.

"Bar?" Blaze broke into their conversation.

"Yeah, she's working with me at the bar on the weekends starting tomorrow night," Tessa said, excited, then walked out of Jared's arms toward Katrina, ignoring Blaze's growl.

Katrina wished she could ignore Blaze as easily as Tessa had, but from their conversation earlier, she knew this was going to be a battle she would probably lose. Yet she planned on fighting him on this. She wanted this job, needed it. With one last look, she saw Jared laughing after saying something to Blaze. All Blaze could do was glare at her, looking even angrier. It was becoming the norm.

Chapter 18

After Blaze had left Slade's office, he headed toward Sloan's. He had shit to do and needed to focus on his work. The faster he could make sure Katrina was safe, the faster he could sort out his feelings for her. He didn't know his ass from a hole in the ground at the moment, and it pissed him off.

Warriors had a protective instinct that went deep. How was he not sure that his feelings for the redheaded temptress weren't just that? Yeah, that was what he kept telling himself. Jesus, he was losing his mind because right now he heard her voice in his head.

The closer he got to the center of the compound, the clearer her voice became, and he realized it wasn't in his head, but coming from the game room. Jared, Tessa, and Adam stood looking in. Blaze knew exactly what they were looking at.

He stopped beside Adam and spotted Daniel and Katrina sitting on the floor, both singing and playing guitar. Noticing they were being watched, Daniel stopped playing and just listened to Katrina, who had her back turned toward them. Her voice washed over him and certain notes that she hit actually gave him chills. What kind of fucking pussy was he turning into?

As if her voice had put a spell on him, it took him a moment to realize she had stopped singing and was now looking directly at him.

When Tessa started discussing Katrina working for her, anger churned in his gut. She wouldn't be safe working in a fucking bar. He'd growled his disapproval but was ignored by both women.

"And you agreed to this?" Blaze glared at Jared, who held up his hands.

"Just found out about it, bro," Jared responded.

Tessa heard and turned. "What's the big deal?" She frowned, looking at them both. "She needs a job and I offered her one."

"Babe, we need to tighten up security some." Jared tiptoed around the issue.

"Pussy," Blaze sneered at him.

"Shut the fuck up, man," Jared shot back.

"The big deal is a very ruthless gang is after her and don't care who gets in the way," Blaze stated, being careful of what he said with Daniel still in the room. "And I believe that all of us are in danger and should be careful until the situation is taken care of. If your mate doesn't agree and lets you go to work, then he's an idiot."

Jared also looked toward Daniel, but Adam had taken him to the pool table, though Adam was still very much aware of the conversation.

"Listen, motherfucker, don't ever insinuate that I don't care for my mate." Jared had stepped up to Blaze, their faces inches apart. "She is never there alone during her work schedule, so fuck you."

"Hey." Tessa stepped between them. "My man takes care of me, so don't you worry about that, fire man."

Blaze had always liked Tessa; she said what she thought. He actually grinned at her. "Yes, ma'am."

"That's better. I like it when you Warriors play nice." Tessa patted them both on the arm. "So now about Katrina. She needs a job. A trainee's pay is nonexistent."

"Everything she needs is provided to her," Blaze argued, but should have known better.

"Oh, I've seen what the VC provides their trainees, which by the way are almost all men." Tessa snorted in disgust. "Male deodorant, jock strap, socks, men's underwear, and a one-size pair of sweatpants and T-shirt. Not to mention the smelly soap and shampoo in a tiny bottle. Seriously, look at her hair. You think that little bottle would last her any time?"

Blaze looked at Katrina, who stood staring at him with hope in her eyes. He'd never even considered what Tessa was saying and felt like shit for it. He knew they got a bag of supplies, but never realized what was in it because he never looked. Just tossed it their way to keep in their lockers. All trainees stayed off the property until becoming Warriors, and even then, some remained off property, but close enough that if called upon they could be there in seconds.

"You have money. I gave you money for the poker game, over a thousand plus what you won," Blaze reminded her. "Use that for whatever you need."

"That's not my money. I didn't earn it," Katrina replied with a shake of her head.

"Yes, you did earn it," he answered, before realizing by the look on her face she thought he meant something entirely different.

Before Blaze could respond, Jared spoke up. "Someone will be there during their work times. If not me, I always make sure someone will be. Nothing to worry about." Jared took Tessa's hand. "Plus, you got the trainees so damn busy, it will only be on the weekends. Chill, I got it."

Blaze still frowned, not feeling any better. Once Tessa and Jared left, he gazed down at Katrina. When she tried to walk past him, he stopped her. "I meant you earned that money playing poker, nothing else."

"Oh." Her face softened slightly.

"I know your past has been shit, Katrina." Blaze let his grip on her arm loosen. "But know I respect you and meant nothing else by my comment."

"Thank you." Katrina's eyes filled, but he watched her fight it and blink the blood tears away. "But that's your money, not mine."

"What difference does it make, Katrina?" Blaze growled, attempting to keep his frustration minimal.

"If you have to ask me that, then you don't know me at all." Katrina's voice sounded so sad he wanted to reach out and comfort her; instead, anger burned his chest.

"I know you better than most."

Her eyes widened at the whispered innuendo.

"And that's obviously going to change," she shot back, her eyes now narrowed.

He pulled her close, his head lowered so only she could hear his words. "Don't bet your sweet ass on that."

******

Katrina didn't know how to respond so kept her mouth shut. He confused her to the point she wanted to scream. Most of the time she was quick with her wit and could match words with anyone, but not with Blaze, never Blaze. It was unsettling.

"Come on, Daniel." Katrina turned away from Blaze for safer territory. "Let's get Jax's guitar back to him."

"Okay!" Daniel ran toward her, then did a one-eighty to grab his guitar. "Come on, Sager."

Sager stood and followed Daniel without hesitation. Katrina knew she had lost her dog. Actually, Sager had never really been hers. Katrina was happy that he and Daniel had found a special friendship, though.

"Hey, Blaze." Daniel stopped in front of the huge Warrior and looked up. He lifted his fist to Blaze, who bumped the little hand with his larger one.

"What's up, little man?" Blaze knelt in front of Daniel to be on his level.

"Just, you know, playing guitar and stuff," Daniel said, again sounding so like the Warriors, all cool and collected.

"You did a pretty good job," Blaze acknowledged with a grin.

"Yeah, I know," Daniel said in all seriousness. "Trina taught me."

"She's pretty good too." Blaze nodded, then started to stand, but Daniel stopped him.

"She's the best," Daniel said, his eyes swirling with color. He didn't have the eyes of a half-breed or a full blood. They were a deep blue that seemed to now swirl with light. "And if you don't face your past, you will lose her forever. Talk to Caroline before it's too late."

Everyone in the room, as well as Pam and Duncan who had just walked in, silently stared at Daniel in shock.

Just as quickly, Daniel turned back into a normal little boy as he spotted Pam and Duncan. "Mom!" Daniel ran around Blaze to jump in Pam's arms while Duncan grabbed the guitar before it hit the ground.

Katrina watched as Blaze slowly rose, his face a blank mask, but his eyes swirled with turmoil.

"Honey, why did you say that to Blaze?" Pam asked, her face giving nothing away.

Daniel shrugged his little bony shoulder. "I don't know," he replied, then looked over his shoulder at Blaze. "I just know stuff, and I like him, so I want to help."

Pam and Duncan looked over his head at each other. Daniel spotted the exchange. "I'm sorry."

"Don't be sorry. You did nothing wrong," Duncan told him.

Blaze finally moved and walked toward Daniel. "Your dad is right, Daniel." He once again did a fist bump with the small boy, with what seemed to be a forced smile. "You did nothing wrong. Nothing to be sorry for."

Wide-eyed, Katrina watched as Blaze walked away while Pam and Duncan headed up the stairs with Daniel. Adam walked up behind her. "Okay, that was fucking crazy." Adam stared after Pam and Duncan. "The kid is smarter than I'll ever be."

"Truth," Katrina said, then laughed at Adam's offended look. "Hey, you said it."

"Whatever." Adam grinned. "You need a ride to training?"

"Sure." Katrina nodded.

"Cool, I'm going to get a quick bite to eat with Angelina, and then I'll meet you here in about an hour," Adam said as he walked away.

Katrina didn't answer. She headed up the stairs and knocked on Jax's door. After a few minutes, Caroline opened. Katrina caught the gasp that wanted to escape her throat. Dark circles highlighted her red-rimmed eyes; she looked haggard and tired.

"Hey, I just wanted to bring Jax's guitar back." Katrina handed it to her.

"Thanks, I'll make sure he gets it." Caroline took the guitar and started to close the door, but Katrina stopped her.

"Can I come in?" Katrina asked, hoping to find out what was going on. The look on Caroline's face told her that wasn't going to happen.

"I can't tell you anything, Katrina." Caroline sighed. "I wish I could, but I can't. Any conversation about what is going on has to be with Blaze willingly. I'm sorry."

Katrina nodded as the door closed. She was more confused than ever. Blaze, with no last name, was becoming someone she didn't know at all, and what scared her was, did she really want to know him? If he could dismiss a woman suffering such as Caroline was, what kind of man did that make him?

Chapter 19

Beyond pissed, Samuel Drake stood staring at the burnt remains of what used to be the Iron Drakes main stronghold. He was enraged that anyone would dare do this to him, Samuel Drake.

"Don't see any of the shit we left." Reggie, one of the patched members, informed him. "I think it's all gone."

"You think? What fucking clued you in, dumbass? Could it be the ash and our burnt shit shattered to hell and back?" Samuel rounded on him and then backhanded him across the face. "I'm surrounded by fucking idiots."

"No, I mean, there's not even anything to suggest that it was here. Metal doesn't burn. We would have found some parts of the guns we had stashed." Reggie wiped the blood from his mouth.

Samuel looked away from what used to be the home of the most powerful motorcycle gang in the area to focus on Reggie. "Nothing?"

He shook his head. "Even if the police or fire department found anything, they wouldn't have found it all. There's nothing."

Looking around at the members, his nostrils flared before

his eyes went back to Reggie. "So what you are telling me is not only did those VC fucks burn my house down, they stole from me?" Samuel's eyes narrowed as he grabbed Reggie by the throat. "Is that what you're fucking telling me?"

"Yes," Reggie garbled, his eyes widening.

Samuel tossed Reggie to the side, his eyes searching out Breaker. "Is that your assumption also?"

"Yeah, Reggie's right. If it were here, we would've found some evidence of it." Breaker growled. "And only one person knew exactly where that stash was other than us. Kat must have shown them where to look."

Turning once again to stare at the destruction, his eyes caught something. Stepping over ash and blackened timber, he walked to a pole that was still standing. It was paper, untouched by fire and stuck to the pole with a knife. Samuel reached out and pulled it free, leaving the knife.

See you soon! was written on the paper signed by the Warriors.

Samuel Drake wadded the paper up and threw it as far as he could. His eyes were black as night with rage. "I want them dead. I want their mates dead. I want their families dead. I want their fucking pets dead, and I don't give a fuck if it's a goddamn goldfish. I want them all dead. I don't care how you do it as long as it's painful, but, and you better listen good, motherfuckers, I want that bastard who started this fire and Kat alive."

Samuel glared at each member, patched and unpatched, to make sure they understood his orders. "Is that understood?" Samuel shouted. "Because if you fuck up, it will be your life. Nobody steals from the Iron Drakes and nobody sets fire to my fucking house!"

Each member raised one arm with their fists pointed toward the sky. The yells coming from them would have scared anyone with any sense. The cries of rage and screams of revenge continued as fists pumped toward the sky.

In the midst of it all, Breaker walked to Samuel. "You promised her to me."

"You get her, she's yours." Samuel's eyes still flamed with rage. "As long as you make her suffer for what she did to us."

"I think you know me well enough not to have to worry about that." Breaker's grin held absolutely no humor, only expectation of what was to come.

Samuel did know that, and if he were a better man, he would be worried for his only daughter. She had broken the cardinal rule, just like her mother. *A snitch is a snitch and always ends up in a ditch.* That would be the easy way out, but unfortunately for Kat, Breaker wasn't known for his forgiving ways, and he had been on a hate bender since seeing her with that Warrior.

Samuel watched Breaker walk away, past the chanting members to his bike. It had begun. And soon the VC would regret ever hearing the name Iron Drakes.

******

Katrina felt unusually nervous. She started her job in about an hour and hadn't seen Blaze since yesterday in the game room. He didn't show up for training. Jax, Duncan, and Sloan had led the class. She had even gone to his room to return the money and maybe try to talk to him about Caroline, but he hadn't been there.

She definitely had shadows following her through last night and today though. Anytime she was out and about from her room, she was questioned about her leaving the compound and ordered repeatedly not to leave without someone with her.

Sitting on the edge of her bed, she glanced down at herself and hoped she looked okay. Tessa had told her to just dress normal, and well, this was about as normal as she could get with what she had.

Feeling confined, she stood and hurried out the door. She needed to get some fresh air before she went crazy. Heading away from the front of the compound, she walked out the back door near Slade's office. It was cold and a few snowflakes flittered about. She loved snow, always had. Christmas had always been her mother's favorite holiday and she had done her best to make it special for Katrina. Her brother, Craig, never wanted anything to do with them. She frowned. Just thinking her brother's name made her nauseous, angry and a little bit sad.

Not really paying attention, she walked along the building, catching snowflakes with her tongue and grinning like an idiot, trying to forget her past. It had been so long since she did something for the pure joy of it. Hearing a noise, she glanced over with her head held back and tongue sticking out to see Blaze staring at her from over the popped hood of Adam's car.

Slowly, she put her tongue back in her mouth and lowered her head before glancing away. Okay, that was embarrassing. She peeked his way once again and noticed how sexy he looked watching her over the open hood, his arm resting on it.

His face disappeared for a second, and then he was moving around the car and heading toward her. Grease streaked his arms. His large hands were also covered in grease, and damn, she had never been more turned on in her life. Holy hell, what was wrong with her? Maybe it was the black muscle shirt that stretched across his massive chest or the way his faded jeans hung low on his hips that had her wanting to take her clothes off and say screw it, screw me.

She shivered as he stopped in front of her.

"You need a coat. It's cold." Blaze's voice was low and deep.

She shivered again. "I'm okay." She looked up at him. "We're vampires, right? Cold doesn't bother us."

"Me no, you yes," Blaze responded before turning around quickly and going to the car. After reaching inside, he returned with his leather jacket and wrapped her in its warmth.

"Thank you." Katrina snuggled in the coat that was more like a leather dress on her.

He reached out to pinch a snowflake from her hair. "You're welcome."

"Hey, Blaze." Adam peeked over the hood. "Oh, hey, Katrina. Good luck tonight."

"Thanks." Katrina waved with a smile before looking up at Blaze. "Well, I'll let you go. I know you're busy."

Blaze frowned, then cursed under his breath, which she heard plainly. "Katrina, I'm never too busy for you."

Tears pressed hard against her eyes as the confusion once again clouded her mind. Not wanting him to see her tears fall, she quickly looked down. A red drop hit the ground, spreading red against the light white snow that had fallen earlier. It still shocked her that she cried blood.

"Hey." He bent to look at her face. "Look at me."

She couldn't bring herself to do it. Instead, she continued to stare at the ground that was starting to look like a crime scene.

"Katrina, look at me," he ordered. "I can't touch you with this grease on my hands."

Finally she found the courage to look up, wiping any trace of her tears away.

"Why are you crying?" Concern replaced the demand that had colored his voice just seconds before.

Katrina half laughed, half cried. "Because you confuse me."

The sadness she saw flash in his eyes for a brief second told her he was suffering from something in his past also, just like her, and maybe he couldn't help who he was, just like she couldn't help who she was.

"I'm sure I confuse you too." She gave him a sad smile, breaking the silence for him. Taking off his jacket, she handed it to him. "Thanks, Blaze. Maybe one day we can get our shit together."

He took the jacket, still staring at her before they both started to laugh.

"I think we are the ones with our shit together. It's everyone else who's fucked." Blaze gave her a grin. "Listen, Katrina—"

"No." Katrina shook her head. "Let's leave this on a good note, okay?"

Again, Blaze said nothing but watched her with those eyes that she knew could see right through her. Before she said to hell with it and jumped in his arms, she turned and walked away, letting the tears fall again. She refused to lift her hand to wipe them away until she was sure he couldn't see her. She was done being weak. This was her new beginning, with or without a happily ever after with her knight in shining armor—or in her case, a knight in a black leather jacket riding a Harley.

Chapter 20

Blaze watched Katrina until she walked back inside the compound. Glancing down, he stared at the blood from her tears spreading into the snow. No one had ever shed a tear for him, even when he was human. His life was rough then and it was rough now, but he had never expected tears from anyone, yet there was Katrina shedding not just tears, but blood over him.

Finally pulling his eyes from her blood, he turned and headed toward Adam. "Sorry," he mumbled, glancing under the hood at what Adam was doing.

"That's okay, man." Adam stood up straight and wiped his hands on a towel. "Let's give it a try."

Blaze stayed where he was as Adam went to start the car. It roared to life. Tweaking a few things, Blaze nodded as Adam came back around. "I think you got it."

"Hell yeah!" Adam grabbed tools and the towel before slamming the hood shut. "Thanks, I couldn't have done that without you. Where'd you learn to work on cars?"

"Don't really know," Blaze replied, not accustomed to giving any of his past away. "Just always liked fucking with them."

"Well, I'm glad 'cause I was stumped." Adam grinned, then looked behind him toward the compound. "She okay?"

"Yeah," Blaze answered, hoping that was all Adam was going to ask because more than hating talking about his past, he didn't like to talk about his relationship with Katrina. If he could even call it that. If fucking was a relationship, then he guessed they were in one.

"Good." Adam gave him a friendly nudge. "The girl has had it rough. You're a good man taking her under your wing."

Okay, that took him aback. What the fuck was Adam talking about? "Taking her under my wing?"

"Yeah." Adam walked around and shut off the car, then started it again and grinned when it immediately came to life. "I mean, you guys are a couple now and you're taking care of her."

"Whoa, what? We aren't a couple," Blaze said. *Are we?* "I mean, I watch out for her, but I'd watch out for any of my trainees if needed."

"Not like that, unless you're gay." Adam snorted, slamming the car door shut.

"Watch yourself, son," Blaze warned him with a narrowed stare.

"Come on, Blaze." Adam leaned against the car. "I may be a

little younger than you, but I'm not blind and neither is anyone else."

Blaze continued to glare, but that didn't faze Adam.

"Okay, so let's say I didn't have Angelina." Adam glanced around to make sure they were alone. "I'd be all over Katrina. Let me tell you, I could just picture her bent over with me slamming into that sweet ass. Getting hard just—"

Not even realizing it, Blaze had Adam slammed on the ground with his hand on his throat, knee on his chest and all he could see through the red haze that colored his vision was Adam's grin as he choked, which brought Blaze back to reality. He abruptly let Adam go. "Fuck!"

"Damn, you've got it bad." Adam jumped up, rubbing his throat. "Hey, man. I love my girl and have no feelings at all for Katrina. Just trying to prove to you that you do."

"You're an asshole," Blaze seethed, cracking his neck back and forth.

"True, but she needs you and I think you need her." Adam grabbed up all his stuff. "And, even though it freaked me the fuck out and I'm sure it did you also, little Daniel is right. You need to talk to Caroline."

"What makes you think any of this is your fucking business?" Blaze stopped Adam before he could say any more.

"It's not." Adam stood with his arms full, totally defenseless if Blaze decided to strike again. "But I know you're a better man than to let a woman suffer when you can do something about it. Fuck your past, Blaze. I know all the Warriors here other than me, Steve, and Jill know what's up with you, and honestly, I don't give two fucks as long as you got my back now, in the present."

Blaze didn't know whether he wanted to kill Adam or shake his hand. The kid had balls talking to him like that, and he respected the hell out of him. Then he thought of something and frowned.

"You reading me?" His voice turned deadly. If the fucking kid was reading him, Adam would die an ugly death. Fuck the handshake.

"Don't have to. Go talk to Caroline, Blaze," Adam said as he turned to leave. "We've all got a past, man. Deal with it and move the fuck on. You deserve that and so does Katrina."

"You're lucky I don't kick your ass, kid," Blaze called out after him.

"You're welcome." Adam chuckled as he disappeared inside. "Oh, and by the way"—his voice carried outside—"did you know yesterday was her birthday? Yeah, the big twenty-one. Thought you'd like to know and yes, before you ask, I did read *her*."

Blaze stood alone glancing up at the sky just like Katrina

had done earlier. If he wasn't careful, he'd be fucking sticking his damn tongue out catching snowflakes. "Jesus."

He grabbed his jacket and put it on. "Fuck!" he cursed when her scent wrapped around him, giving him an instant hard-on. Knowing he should take care of that before going to take care of other business, Blaze headed for his room, his cock hard as a rock from just her scent. Yeah, he knew exactly what he was giving her for her birthday.

******

Katrina was truly enjoying working at the Sand Trap. Everyone was nice. No one tried to grab her for a feel or cuss her out because she was too slow bringing their beer. She'd never worked in a bar before, but she'd served enough of the Iron Drakes and their friends that she was pretty much a pro. It had always been the women's "duty" in the club to take care of the men; she had been no different even as the president's daughter. Her mother made sure that nothing got too far out of hand, so she had been luckier than most of the girls.

Tessa was awesome and everyone loved her. Bobby took some getting used to, but he was okay. He obviously didn't like Jared and the feeling seemed mutual, but they got along for Tessa's sake, or so it seemed.

After wiping some tables, she walked over to where Jared was sitting and sat next to him. She hated to admit it, but her feet hurt.

"How you doing, little red?" Jared grinned at her over his phone.

"Good, other than my feet." She glanced over to see Tessa busy as ever and felt like a slacker. "Does she ever quit?"

Jared looked at Tessa with pride. "No, she doesn't, and that's why even though I beat her boss's ass, she's still working here, because he knows good help and would be an idiot to let her go. Plus, all the customers said they'd stop coming if he didn't rehire her."

"You beat up her boss?" Katrina laughed, shocked. "Why? What happened?"

"Let's just say he was disrespectful and made the mistake of putting his hands on what was mine." Jared actually glared at Bobby, who glanced their way, then looked elsewhere.

"I swear, you Warriors are a jealous lot." Katrina grinned with a shake of her head.

"Territorial," he corrected her. "And speaking of such, Blaze has been texting me nonstop."

"Oh, really?" Katrina's interest perked up.

"Yeah, really," he mocked with a grin. "Like you don't want to know what about."

Katrina stood. "I don't, not really."

Jared snorted then shrugged. "Okay."

"I mean, is it something important?" Katrina wiped his already clean table off, trying to look over at his phone.

Jared caught what she was doing and smashed the phone to his chest. "Maybe." Jared laughed. "If texting me fifty times to make sure everything is okay here and thinking I'm too much of a dumbass to figure out what he's really asking is important."

"Which is?" Katrina frowned, wishing she could grab his phone and run just so she could read the messages from Blaze. Yep, pathetic.

"Please, like you don't know." Jared's disbelieving chuckle stopped. "You really don't know."

Katrina just shook her head and was now wondering if she wanted to know.

With a sigh, Jared glanced down at his phone. "This is from Blaze: *Everything okay?* Me: *Yep.* Fifteen minutes later: *Any problems.* Me: *Nope.*" Jared scrolled through his phone. "That was more or less the first forty-eight texts. Blaze: *You guys still there?* Me: *Yep.* Then me again: *Dude, just ask.* Blaze: *What?*"

She couldn't help but grin when he did Blaze's voice. He actually sounded like him. Jared looked up to see her grinning.

"What?"

"Nothing." Katrina chuckled. "You just sound like him."

"Yeah, I do grumpy asshole real well," Jared said, looking back at his phone. "Me again: *Dude, just ask what you want to ask. Katrina is fine. She has five guys trying to give her a ride home, one actually got a dance, and she is leaving here with enough tips to retire on.*" Jared gave a snort with a sneaky grin.

"That's not true." Katrina wasn't grinning now.

"Yeah, I know." Jared snorted again. "Okay, this is Blaze: *You better be getting names of those motherfuckers. I swear if I walk through that door and find some bastard with his hands on her, I'll kill him. Get her the fuck out of there before I come there and tear the fucking place apart.*"

Katrina's head snapped back surprised. "He said that?"

Jared held the phone out to her so she could see the text, then pulled the phone back. "I didn't respond for a few minutes because I was busy laughing my ass off so he texted: *Hey!* Blaze again: *You hear me?* And again Blaze: *If you don't fucking answer me, I'll kick your ass first before I fuck those stupid motherfuckers up.* And finally my response: *Psych!* Blaze's final response: *Fuck you!*"

Speechless, Katrina stared at his phone before focusing on Jared. "Please don't tell him you told me," she finally said.

"Honey, I'm already going to get hell for fucking with him. Not that I care." Jared put his phone down, giving her a smile. "But I've poked the fire man enough and actually don't want my ass cooked, literally. So this is between us."

"Thank you." Katrina nodded calmly, but inside, her body quivered in excited glee. Was he jealous that some man might be showing her attention? It sounded like it.

Bobby called out to her and she gave Jared one last happy grin before getting her order. She could only hope that Jared was right. She never knew with Blaze, but it seemed he felt more for her than he let on.

Chapter 21

Blaze stood outside of Jax and Caroline's door. His hand reached to knock, then dropped. Closing his eyes tight, he cursed then knocked quickly before he walked away. The door opened, and Blaze felt like the biggest dick. Caroline looked up at him, her eyes sunken and red from little sleep.

"I'm sorry." Blaze hissed, seeing her state. "Fuck!"

Caroline actually smiled at him. "Don't be sorry. Just please tell me you're here to get this over with."

Nodding, Blaze walked inside when she made room and then closed the door behind them. Jax entered the room. His eyes narrowed on him, but he didn't say a word.

"If you don't mind, I would like to call Lana to help me," Caroline said; her voice sounded weak to him. "It's dangerous for me right now to open myself up and I'm afraid—"

"Whatever you need to do." Blaze didn't let her finish. What in the hell had he been thinking to let her go through this? He had been a fucking coward. Jesus, he hated himself right now.

He watched Caroline walk out of the room with her phone. He looked toward Jax, whose focus was on Caroline. Jax's features softened until he looked back at him.

"She's the only reason this has gone on as long as it has," Jax said to him.

"I didn't realize how much it was affecting her because I was too worried about myself," Blaze admitted, hating himself. "I'm sorry, brother."

Jax stared at him for a long second before nodding. "Just make it right. That's all I ask. No matter what, finish this fucking thing so I can have my mate back strong and healthy." Jax walked to the refrigerator and grabbed two beers. "This shit with her and her sister is fucked-up, but we deal with it."

Blaze took the beer offered and knew if he were Jax, he wouldn't be as cool. He'd want to kill the son of a bitch who made his mate suffer. What the hell did that say about him?

Caroline came out actually looking better than she had before she'd left the room. "Lana and Sid are on their way now." She smiled up at him. "We can go ahead and start."

"No, we can wait," Blaze said, not wanting to put Caroline through any more than he already had. "Why didn't you let Jax kick my ass?" he finally asked.

"It wouldn't have made a bit of difference." Caroline laughed, before taking a seat. "It would have made him feel better, but the problem would have remained. Until you were ready, there was nothing anyone could do."

"Well again, I'm sorry." Blaze finished the beer feeling uncomfortable. He had never told a person he was sorry so much, but dammit, he was, and he felt like a bastard. He didn't mistreat women, he cherished them, and look what he had done to Caroline, who was a gentle soul who only tried to help people.

"Accepted, so no more apologies needed." Caroline glanced behind him before returning her gaze to him.

"Are they here?" Blaze asked, feeling odd even believing what was about to happen.

"Yes," Caroline replied, her eyes searching his.

"You said ten were following me when we were working on your roof." Blaze frowned, wondering who exactly the ten were.

"There were ten, but as time passed, some left. There are six, five males and one female," Caroline informed him. "The others were what we call tagalongs. It's normal for them to disappear after a while."

"Female?" Blaze said aloud, more confused than ever. He'd thought he knew who it might be, but now he wasn't sure and he didn't like it.

She nodded, then tilted her head as she looked at him. "Why

now, Blaze?"

He shrugged, not really wanting to answer that question but knowing he had to. He just needed to figure out how to say it.

"Daniel?" Caroline answered her own question; her eyes crinkled with a smile. "I heard about what he said to you."

"The kid kind of shook me up," Blaze admitted, then chuckled with a shake of his head.

"Little Daniel has insight that is pretty amazing," Caroline replied, then shivered. "But I also think a certain female has something to do with you wanting to get your past out of the way."

Blaze glanced at Jax, whose face was a blank mask as he stared at him. Before he could answer, Lana and Sid walked in.

"Oh, you're lucky," Lana scolded him, but gave him a gentle pat on the shoulder. "I was about to hunt you down and kick your ass."

"Lana, leave him alone," Caroline told her sister.

"Man, Caroline, you ruin all the fun." Sid also clapped Blaze on the back then gave Caroline a kiss on the cheek. "I wanted to watch her kick his ass."

"Yeah, well at least he's here now." Lana set down her bag and took off her coat. "Let's get this over with. You ready, sis?"

"More than ready." Caroline stood, looking stronger by the minute.

"Wait." Blaze frowned, looking at Jax and Sid.

"Sorry, man." Sid gave him a look. "We aren't going anywhere. You might as well ignore us, because we won't leave our mates."

Jax agreed with a nod. "We already know most of the story. No judgment here."

"You have three main spirits following you who are persistent," Caroline started. "The first day you showed, they appeared and haven't left. There is a total of six, but two who stand out the most, how should I say, are demanding I guess, in giving you a message."

"My advice to keep me and especially Caroline safe is to stay," Lana warned. "This needs to be finished so they can move on and in turn, Caroline gets her life back. Our hope is that this will also help you, but we can't promise that. Only you will know the answer to that."

"I know everything, but Lana doesn't," Caroline informed Blaze. "If any of the Warriors know, it's not from me. I don't even talk to Jax about anything they reveal to me, which drives him crazy, but this is your story to tell."

"We remember when it happened, Blaze," Sid broke in, backing up Caroline. "So we're pretty sure who's here and why."

Blaze only gave a short nod, ready to get this shit done and over with.

"I'll go first, Caroline," Lana said, then looked behind Blaze with a frown. "Bryon Madison just stepped forward."

Blaze felt like he'd been punched in the stomach. It was one of the many names he thought about every day. He couldn't say anything, couldn't move to even nod that he understood what Lana had just said.

"What do you want to tell him, Bryon?" Lana tilted her head, staring at nothing or at least nothing that anyone else but Caroline could see. "You can use me if you'd like?" Lana held out her hand then dropped it.

"Lana," Sid warned, his body becoming alert.

"Shush." She shushed him, which made Blaze's lip twitch toward a grin.

Blaze looked back to see Lana staring at him in horror, a horror he understood all too well. He reached out when she swayed.

"Oh my God." She grabbed his arms, pulling him to her and hugged him tightly. "I'm so sorry."

Sid was right there, worry for his mate pulsating off him, but his eyes looked into his with understanding. Lana let him go, her face streaked with tears as she looked up at Blaze.

He knew right then it was time. "Don't cry for me." Blaze looked first at Lana and then Caroline, suddenly wishing that Katrina was there because if he were honest, he was doing this for her. Not for him, not for Caroline, not for anyone else but Katrina. He actually glanced at his watch to see what time it was.

"I'm sorry. It just took me by surprise." Lana wiped the tears from her face. "Okay, I'm ready."

"Wait." Caroline was staring at Blaze. "You're right. Katrina needs to be here."

"How did you know?" Blaze asked, totally shocked that Caroline knew exactly what he had been thinking.

"Not me, them." Caroline nodded behind him. "They know you very well and agree. They want her here."

Sid was looking at his phone. "Jared said they're back. He's sending her up now," he said, before clipping Lana's chin up. "You okay."

"I'm fine," Lana said with a wobbly smile before looking

back at Blaze.

Blaze stared off, wondering if he was making a mistake. Would Katrina look at him differently once she knew? But he couldn't worry about that. This had to be done. His eyes went to Caroline, and he knew without a doubt no matter what, it would be done tonight. No longer would he be the cause of her suffering. He didn't understand how her gift worked, but he knew how persistent the ones from his past were.

Jax went to answer the knock on the door. Blaze waited until he heard her voice before glancing her way and once he did, peacefulness settled over him, and he swore he heard a familiar voice inside his head whisper, *She's the one.*

******

Katrina was heading to her room when Jared came running back toward her. "Hey, Sid wants you up in Jax's room pronto."

"Why?" Katrina asked, feeling uneasy. She knew when Jax was working a lot, they stayed there at the compound. Actually, that was the way with most of the Warriors who had homes with their mates. They didn't like to be away from them or leave them unprotected.

"Didn't ask." Jared turned to walk away. "Move your ass."

She followed him to the front of the compound where Tessa

was waiting.

"I'll see you tomorrow." Tessa waved at her. "Good job tonight. Everyone loved you."

"Thanks." Katrina waved back while taking the stairs quickly. She had really wanted a soak in a bath as her feet were killing her. She just hoped whatever Sid wanted didn't take too long.

Her feet throbbed and she tried not to think about it too much because she knew that wasn't normal. She was a vampire; she shouldn't be hurting anywhere, or at least not for a long period of time.

Finally at Jax's room, she lifted her hand to knock, but the door opened before she made contact with it.

"Jared said Sid needed to see me," Katrina said, then stepped inside when Jax moved out of the way. She saw Sid, Lana, and Caroline, but her eyes fixed on Blaze, who stood with his back to her. Finally, he turned to look at her over his shoulder, and the torment she saw on his face hit her hard.

"What's happened?" Katrina feared that maybe her father had done something and was honestly afraid to hear.

Turning completely around to look down at her, Blaze's voice was deep when he said, "I'm getting my shit straight."

Chapter 22

At first, Katrina didn't know what he was talking about, but then she remembered one of the last things she'd said to him the last time she had seen him. She had said that maybe someday they could get their shit together. Not really knowing what this meant, she tilted her head to stare up at him and then nodded.

She watched Blaze closely and could see his inner struggle and hated it for him. She understood inner struggles better than most, but she knew the best thing she could do for him was to be there, be present, and listen. How many times had she wanted that very same thing? Many, many times. Well, she was there to offer him any support he needed.

"I murdered my brothers," Blaze said, his eyes never leaving her. "My VC brothers."

Okay, that wasn't what she expected, and she wasn't sure if she should respond. She made sure her expression never changed. She just stood and waited, letting him go at his own pace. For a man, not to mention a Warrior, expressing any type of weakness was not done; it didn't happen, especially in front of women. When Blaze still didn't speak, his eyes hard as if reliving the past all over again, she decided that maybe she needed to pull him back since it seemed he was speaking to her.

"And there must have been a reason." Katrina tilted her head, waiting for him to answer. "Why don't you start from the beginning."

Her voice seemed to pull him to the present. "My team was set up, but we knew we were being tricked. Our plan was flawless, or so we thought." Anger entered his tone, "We go in, take out the enemy, and I set the fire."

She felt Jax and Sid move closer, but didn't let her eyes move to them. She kept them fixed on Blaze. "What happened?" she whispered, urging him to continue.

"They—" Sid started when it didn't look like Blaze was going to continue, but Blaze broke eye contact with her to glare at Sid.

"No!" Blaze growled, then looked back at Katrina. "My brothers went in while I stood outside waiting for the go-ahead."

Katrina chanced walking toward him. She reached out and clasped his hand, never losing eye contact.

"Bryon came out and gave me the go-ahead, but the rest of the guys weren't there." Blaze's hand tightened on hers, but she stood firm. He could break her fucking hand and she wouldn't move. "He said they were out and on the other side of the building making sure no civilians were in range of danger."

He stopped talking. His eyes hooded over as if he were once again lost in the past. She tried to squeeze his hand to bring him back, but it wasn't working. He abruptly let go of her hand and stepped away.

"Goddammit!" he roared, the torment of that night escaping him. "I should have fucking known. That wasn't our plan. Our plan was to meet where I stood, and then I set the fire. We didn't break protocol and I knew it, fucking knew it."

Sid and Jax had moved even closer to Caroline and Lana, their attention focused solely on Blaze.

"But I went against my instinct. I knew something wasn't right, but with my leader shouting at me to go before it was too late, I did, not realizing the bastard standing next to me wasn't Bryon Madison, but a fucking shifter like myself." Blaze's chuckle sounded demented and out of control. "Fuck! Why did I fucking listen when I knew it felt so wrong?"

Katrina went to grab his hand again, but he moved away with a shake of his head. She refused to let the rejection hurt because she understood his pain. Instead she made herself stand her ground to be there when he was ready to reach out for her.

"I should have known, but none of our intelligence even pointed toward a possible shifter." Blaze rubbed his hand down his face. "Once I realized what had happened, I ran inside. My team... *my* team lay with silver chains across them, burning, and there wasn't a fucking thing I could do about it. I could walk in the flames, but they couldn't, and it was too late for me to save even one of them."

"But, I don't understand," Caroline said when Blaze became silent again. "Wouldn't they have healed?"

Blaze shut his eyes for a second before looking her way. "They would have lived, but we all knew their bodies would never heal from that kind of heat. They would have spent the rest of their days trying to heal only to have their bodies fail. Their minds would have been fine, but their bodies wouldn't, and for a Warrior, that is worse than death." He shook his head. "I have the ability to control the temperature of my fire, and my orders from the top were to make sure every fucking thing in that building disintegrated, and that's exactly what I did."

"This wasn't your fault," Katrina said and instantly regretted it when he glared at her.

"The fuck it wasn't," he shouted, then seemed to fight for control. "I wasn't a rookie. I was a seasoned Warrior who made a big fucking mistake that cost the lives of five of the best men I've ever known. Jesus, I can't do this."

Katrina watched as he stomped toward the door and she knew without a doubt if he walked out, he would be long gone. What she was about to do would either strengthen whatever they had going on or end it, but it had to be done. She finally knew what Jax had been arguing with Blaze about. His men, the five, were here and speaking to Caroline.

"If you leave, they don't get their closure, and neither do you." Katrina's words stopped him dead in his tracks.

******

Blaze had to get the fuck out of the room before he exploded and lost control. This was a bad fucking idea. He was a dangerous man when his control snapped and he knew it, but Katrina's words froze his movement. His head jerked around, pinning her with his eyes that he knew were flaming red.

"Closure?" he sneered at her. Logically he knew she wasn't at fault, but he couldn't stop himself. "You want closure? You want to hear exactly what the man you let fuck you did to his brothers?"

"Blaze!" Jax growled a warning, taking a step toward him.

"Step back, Jax." Blaze didn't even look his way as he stepped up to Katrina to lean over her. "As they burned, their skin sizzling on their bones, their screams filling the air, I took a fucking sharp piece of metal, and I cut their fucking heads off. Every single one of them died at my hand."

Blaze was too far gone in his self-hatred to truly register that she didn't even flinch in disgust.

"How's that for fucking closure?" Blaze spat and then found himself flying across the room, hitting the wall hard. He jumped to his feet immediately to turn on who dared touch him and was shocked to see Lana glaring at him.

"You best watch your mouth when talking to a lady, Johnny," Lana said, but it wasn't her voice and definitely not her strength.

"Bryon?" Blaze shook his head, glancing around at everyone then back to Lana.

"Who else, you dumbass?" Lana stood in a man's stance—her legs spread apart, hands on her hips. "Sorry, ladies. I tried to teach him better than this and I'm going to go ahead and apologize now for my language, but it's the only thing he fucking understands."

"Bryon?" Blaze again said, squinting as he stared at Lana.

"He's not too smart either." Lana snorted then looked down. "You know, I should kill you for making me do this. I swore I would not take over this poor woman's body because well, it's just fucking weird."

"Tell me about it." Sid frowned, staring at Lana. "Hurry the fuck up so I can have my mate back, and I swear if you hurt her—"

"Calm down, badass. I'm not going to hurt the little lady, and I actually picked her because I know this poor girl has been through hell with us." Lana turned toward Caroline. "I apologize for what we've put you through, but thank you for finally getting Johnny to remove his head from his ass."

"Johnny?" Caroline glanced at Blaze.

"Oh, yeah." He chuckled. "Johnny Bateman, but the guys nicknamed him Blaze, and it stuck. I was the only one who called him by his real name."

Blaze couldn't believe what was happening and could only stand there like an idiot watching it all unfold.

"Well, aren't you going to introduce me to your girl, Johnny?" Lana walked to Katrina with a smile. "What a beauty. Katrina, isn't it?"

"Yes." Katrina smiled nervously then took Lana's hand.

"Nice to meet you, Katrina," Lana said, then glanced back at Blaze with a sneaky grin. "I know he has his assholish moments, but he's a pretty decent guy."

Katrina nodded, her eyes going toward Blaze.

"Okay, well let's get this over with. I'm totally uncomfortable, and this bra contraption is killing me. How in the hell do you women wear this shit?" Lana shifted and tugged with a curse.

"Why are you here?" Blaze was still in a stupor. He didn't

even know what the fuck to say, what to do, and was seriously wondering if none of this was really happening and instead he was having a major fucking meltdown.

"I'm here to thank you, you fucking idiot." Lana's voice became hard and stern. "And to kick your ass if need be. You need to put what happened in the goddamn past, and that's a fucking order."

"How in the hell can I put what happened in the past?" Blaze finally broke free from his shock. "I fucking murdered—"

"You did not murder anyone, other than the ones responsible for what they did to us." Lana cut him off.

"What they did? I'm the one who—"

"Will you shut the fuck up for a minute?" Lana roared in the man's voice.

"The fault of what happened is with the intelligence who was working with the bad guys. It's rare that someone gets one over on the Warriors, but it happens. We weren't careful enough and trusted the wrong people. Our plan was solid and would have worked if we weren't double-crossed. You did your job like you were supposed to do. I know the shifter changed into me. I know what happened. We all do." Lana took a breath before continuing, "We knew what our lives would have been like if you'd pulled us out of that building like you wanted to do, and we all agreed to die that day.

Unfortunately, you were the only one who could do the deed. You did not murder us. We asked... no, we begged you to kill us."

"I should have known," Blaze said, his voice hard.

"I was the leader, Johnny." Lana's voice softened slightly. "I am the one to blame. You did your brothers right, and we thank you. Not only did you give us a Warrior's death, you sought and exacted revenge to those involved on our behalf. That is why myself, Thomas, Eric, Jack, and Davis have been fucking sticking around. We led you here, you moron, so we could finally say thank you, and of course tell you to get your fucking head out of your ass."

"So that's why you quit the VC," Sid said with a nod. "I always wondered about that."

"He quit so he could go after the bastards," Lana said, looking over at Caroline. "Which he did quickly and proficiently, just like a VC Warrior would."

"I can't—" Blaze started, but Lana was immediately in his face.

"You fucking can and you will, goddammit," Lana yelled. "Because if you can't, then we can't move on, and I'm ready to move on, my brother."

Blaze jerked away, leaned his head back, and cursed.

"One last thing." Lana grabbed his shirt and pulled him toward her. "Thank you for taking care of my Barbara."

"She's with you?" Blaze asked, hoping it was so. Bryon's wife, who was human, had never blamed him for what had happened. But he had sworn to Bryon before he killed him that he would take care of Barbara, and he did just that until she died from cancer. Blaze had told her he could change her so she could live, but she refused, ready to be with her mate.

"Yes, she is. She also wanted me to give you a kiss, but I absolutely refuse to do that," Lana spat in disgust, then looked toward Katrina before whispering to Blaze, "She's exactly like my Barbara. You treat her right or I will haunt you forever."

Lana stepped back, straightened her shoulders then, with a fisted hand, hit her chest hard. "You are my brother, Johnny Bateman, our brother." Lana took the same hand and clasped Blaze's forearm. "I was never so proud as when you became a Warrior again. Do us proud and keep us alive in you."

Blaze nodded, his emotions spiraling out of control. There was more he needed to say, but the words wouldn't come.

Lana nodded and with one last look at Blaze, turned toward Caroline. "Thank you for everything, and please tell your sister thank you for the use of her body. We will not be bothering you anymore." Lana then walked toward Katrina and pulled her into an embrace. "Stick with him, he's a good man. Just give him time."

One minute Lana was standing strong and the next she was sinking to the floor. Sid, who wasn't far away, caught her before she hit the ground. "Get Slade!" he shouted, but Jax was already out the door.

"I'm fine. He just left abruptly and it took me by surprise." Lana slowly sat up and rubbed her chest. "Why in the hell do you guys hit your chests so damn hard?"

Sid frowned, pulling her into his arms. "You seriously need to stop doing this."

Lana stood with Sid's help, her eyes seeking out Blaze's. With unsteady steps, she walked toward him. Tears swam in her eyes as she reached up and pulled him down so she could kiss him on the cheek. Then she let go and stepped back. "That was from Barbara." Lana stared at him for a second longer, making him uncomfortable. "You are a good man, Blaze. I know what you did for her."

"No, I'm not," Blaze disagreed, then disappeared out the door. He was far from a good man.

Chapter 23

Watching Blaze walk out the door, Katrina battled with herself, not knowing if she should follow him or not. She decided to give him space, but not for long. She could only imagine what he was feeling, and her respect for the man gave her pause to following him. He needed time, and he was so worth the wait.

"You okay?" Jax had walked up without her realizing it.

"Yes." Katrina pulled her gaze from the door. "Is Lana going to be all right?"

"She's fine, but Sid may need a minute." Jax glanced back at the couple. "Scary watching your mate go through something like that. I hate when it happens to Caroline."

"Hey, where'd Blaze go?" Sid looked around as he came toward them.

"He left." Katrina frowned. "Why did you want me here?"

Jax and Sid shared a look. "It wasn't my idea," Sid replied. "Blaze wanted you here."

Out of everything that had happened, that information shocked her more than any of it. "He did?" she asked, making sure she understood him correctly.

"Don't give him much time, Katrina." Sid nodded toward the door. "He needs you now more than ever."

He was right. Blaze did need her. With a quick glance toward Lana to make sure she was really okay, Katrina headed toward the door then turned toward them. "Thank you."

She quickly headed toward Blaze's room and knocked on the door. She wasn't surprised he wasn't there, but she had to check. She knocked again and tried the handle just to be sure, then headed toward her room. She knew for a fact he wouldn't be there, but they were the only two places she could think of at the compound he would be.

Throwing open her door, she was disappointed that he wasn't there, but as she went to close her door, she looked at her bed and gasped. Letting go of the door, she stepped inside toward her bed and picked up the new acoustic guitar that lay across it.

"Oh my God." She didn't have to look to see who'd left it. She knew. She held it close as tears fell down her cheeks. Considering she'd never held it before, it felt familiar, and she knew why. Blaze had gotten it for her, and that in itself made it familiar.

Carefully setting the guitar down on her bed, she wiped her tears away. She was sick of crying, even though these tears were a mix of happiness and disbelief. She was ready to start her life, and dammit, it was going to be with the Warrior who had stolen her heart.

With a new purpose, she gave the guitar one last look before walking out of her room, closing the door firmly behind her. She headed down the hall knowing where she had to go, certain where he would be. Hearing voices from the kitchen, she stepped inside. All activity stopped as the occupants stared at her.

"I need a ride," she said, her voice loud and clear.

"Katrina, what happened?" Tessa stepped toward her.

"Nothing." Katrina frowned, then looked around. "I just need a ride right now, and I know I'm not supposed to go anywhere alone, but if no one steps up, I'm taking off."

Tessa gave her a proud smile, then handed her a napkin. "You have blood on your cheek."

With a sigh of thanks, Katrina wiped her face and looked around. "Please, I need a ride now."

"Jared will take you," Tessa volunteered.

Jared shoveled the rest of the food he was eating in his mouth, dumping his plate in the sink. "Okay, calm down, little red." Jared kissed Tessa on the cheek before heading out of the kitchen. "Where we going?"

Katrina went to follow him, but Tessa stopped her. "Get your man, Katrina." Tessa gave her a hug then pushed her toward the door.

Glancing back, she saw Jax, Sid, Lana, and Caroline all giving her encouraging smiles. Confidence blossomed in her chest until Sid spoke up.

"If he gives you any problems, I'll kick his ass." Sid threw her a wink.

While thinking of Sid's words, she exited the kitchen to see Jared waiting for her. What if Blaze didn't want her to find him? Shaking that thought from her mind, telling herself it didn't matter, she passed Jared out the door.

"Where we going?" Jared asked as they made their way to the bikes. Sliding on, he made room for her.

"Blaze's place." Katrina realized sitting on the bike with Jared was nothing like riding with Blaze, not even close.

"Blaze has a place?" Jared asked, surprised. "That sneaky bastard."

Katrina didn't smile as she gave him the address. Then she held on as Jared took off. She didn't have to tell Jared to speed up, because he was driving like a maniac—going up on the curb to pass cars, taking turns that would have thrown her off the bike if she hadn't been holding on. Within minutes, he was pulling up to Blaze's, and Katrina had never been so relieved in her life.

"Holy crap." She slid off the bike. "Who the hell taught you how to ride?"

"Pretty impressive, huh." Jared grinned, then killed the engine and stared at the house. "What a dump." He snorted, then shook his head.

"No, it's not," Katrina defended. "It's… nice."

Jared snorted again as he got off the bike. He then leaned against it and stared at Katrina, who stared right back. "Well, are you going to go see if he's here? I'm not leaving until I know for sure."

Katrina glanced back at the house. The courage that had filled her moments earlier had completely vanished. Not seeing his bike, she looked back at Jared. "His bike's not here. Let's go."

"Chicken?" Jared cocked his eyebrow at her.

"No, I just think maybe it's too soon." Katrina kicked a pebble by her foot, then looked back at the house. She wanted to go, but she wanted to… ah, dammit. She didn't know what she wanted.

"You care for him?" Jared asked, looking far too comfortable leaning against his bike with his arms crossed. She really wanted to give him a nudge and knock him over.

"You know I do." She frowned, inching closer to him so if

she got the chance, the nudge could happen.

"Then why run, little red?" His cocky grin had her lifting her foot.

"I'm not running." Frustrated, she stomped her raised foot.

"Good, then turn around and talk to the man." Jared turned and lifted his boot over the bike before looking over her shoulder. "You got her?"

Katrina's eyes widened like saucers, then narrowed dangerously at Jared. "You're an asshole," she whispered before his bike roared to life.

"I know." He winked at her, then gave Blaze, who apparently was standing behind her, a nod before taking off.

Katrina remained still, working on her earlier bravado. Then with a sigh, she turned and gave him a half smile and a wave. "Hi."

Shirtless and bootless, he leaned against the doorframe. The only thing that adorned his body were his jeans that hung low on his hips. His lips curved slightly as his eyes left hers to search the area. Pushing himself away from the door, he came down the steps toward her, grabbed her hand, and led her inside.

The house was dark, but her eyes adjusted quickly. Turning, she watched Blaze lean against the closed door, watching her intently. "Why are you here?"

"I didn't want you to be alone," she answered honestly.

"Katrina, I've been alone most of my life," he replied after a few seconds.

"So does that mean you want to be alone for the remainder of your life?" The words were out and she couldn't pull them back. She bit her lip, afraid of his answer.

He moved away from the door, heading deeper into the house and away from her. "Katrina, I don't know what I want at the moment." Blaze growled his frustration. "What happened tonight just brought back bad shit for me. This isn't really the time to—"

"You know, I get it," Katrina said, quickly cutting him off. "I just wanted to thank you for the guitar. It was really a nice thing to do, and well, I thought maybe you needed a friend or something."

Blaze stood in the middle of the room near the kitchen table. The item brought back very vivid memories. Her eyes then roamed his body, stopping at the tattoos that continued from his arm onto his back. They were beautiful markings that fit the man. When he didn't say anything, discomfort settled in her chest. It was as though she didn't belong there. The sensation hit her hard. If she didn't belong there, with the man who knew her in the most intimate way, where did she belong?

Bolstering her courage, Katrina said, "I think what you did was brave." Katrina would have her say and then she would leave. "It took courage."

Blaze gave a bitter laugh, but didn't turn around. "There was nothing brave in what I did, Katrina."

"Yeah, well most brave men would say the same," Katrina responded, wishing he would turn around so she could see his face.

"You think you understand me, but you don't." She got her wish as he turned around while he spoke. "I killed my team. They died by my hand. I choose to be alone in my life because I don't deserve the happiness that should have been theirs. Is that enough, Katrina?" His voice sharpened, agony chasing every syllable. "Is that what you came to hear? No? Do you want me to lie and tell you that after tonight my feelings are different about what I did? My conscience is clear and I'm free to move forward? Are those the words you're waiting for?"

Katrina stared at him, only seeing a man so full of pain she felt the hurt. "Actually, I didn't expect you to say anything. I just wanted to be here as your friend and to thank you for the guitar. No one should be alone. I know that better than anyone and yet I was. Our situations are different, but still the same. Whether you want to take advantage of that or not is your choice. Just know I'm here or... somewhere." Katrina felt better getting that out. Whether her words made sense to him or not, she didn't know, but she'd said them and that was that.

"Our situations are not even close to being the same." Blaze narrowed his eyes at her.

Katrina shrugged her shoulder but didn't break eye contact with him. "Think what you will, Blaze. Believe that you are the only one who has been put in an impossible situation to only fail at saving those close to you." Katrina backed toward the door. "But it's just a way for you to push anyone who cares for you away. You had a perfect opportunity tonight to have closure, yet you're too selfish to take it. It was handed to you and you're selfishly shoving it away. I would give anything to have that same chance."

"What in the fuck are you talking about?" Blaze shouted, his hands fisting at his sides.

"My mother, you fucking asshole." Katrina was done being nice and rational. Fuck him. She had tried to be there for him, but if he wanted a fight, she was willing to give him one. "I would have given anything to have her come to me, to have closure."

"You didn't kill your mother, Katrina." Blaze's voice calmed somewhat, but still held frustration.

"Didn't I?" Katrina looked up at him. "She died trying to save me. She died trying to give me a better life. She fucking died because of me. So fuck you and your attitude of 'no one has your situation' because if anyone understands, it's me, you big fucking dick."

Katrina turned and pulled the door open with enough strength to slam it against the wall and took off. Not caring where she was going, she jumped the row of bushes to the right of the house and headed across a field. She heard him calling her name, but she didn't stop. Actually, she sped up when she heard him pounding behind her.

Glancing around, she noticed all the trees so used her powers. Birds flew out heading straight toward Blaze, with special instructions to not hurt him, but to block his path to her. Hearing him curse, she chanced a glance back only to see him fighting his way through the wall of birds flying in front of him. With a smirk, she made sure other of her animal friends were on standby.

Chapter 24

"Son of a bitch." Blaze dodged and waved birds away. They were so fucking thick he could hardly see Katrina, but he did know she was gaining ground and he was losing it. With a roar, he fought his way through the mass. As he felt a sense of accomplishment, a fucking herd of deer jumped in front of him, making him fall and slide on his stomach.

He looked up from the ground to see Katrina disappear into a line of woods. "Dammit." He stood and took a running leap over the deer, then kicked up his speed, leaving the animals behind. He looked over his shoulder, satisfied that he was in the clear, until he looked back in front of him and stopped so suddenly his bare feet pulled up grass and dirt.

"You have got to be fucking kidding me," Blaze said out loud as he stared at seven skunks with their asses in the air and looking at him over their backs. "Katrina!" he yelled with his hands on his hips.

He listened closely and didn't hear any running. No way did she get far enough from him that he wouldn't hear her. Scanning the tree line, a thought came to him as he noticed the birds and deer had caught up to him. His head snapped to the side when he heard a chuckle. So she thought this was funny, did she?

"Show yourself or I'm going to start cooking me some

dinner." He formed a fireball in his hand and held it up. "You know you're not supposed to be alone and if it comes down to you or them, I'm choosing you. I know you're out there. Don't make me do it."

"You wouldn't do it," Katrina yelled from the woods.

Blaze's eyes narrowed toward the direction of her voice. "Don't try me!"

"You won't do it," Katrina repeated, then stepped into his view. "I'm fine, Blaze. I'll call Jared and be out of your way."

"Fuck Jared," Blaze shouted. "Now call them off."

A light mist of freezing rain began to fall. He could hear the breathing of the deer around him, feel the breeze of the birds' wings and was reminded that Katrina really was an amazing woman. He let the fire burn away and stood staring at the beautiful sight she made standing on the edge of the woods as if she belonged with the scenery.

"I'm sorry," he shouted as the freezing rain came down in earnest.

"So am I," Katrina shouted back.

"What in the hell are you sorry for?" Blaze frowned.

"For calling you a big fucking dick."

Blaze actually laughed, and now he couldn't stop laughing. He bent over, hands on his knees, and let emotion overtake him. Jesus, he was losing it and it felt fucking good. Wiping his eyes, he noticed the blood mixed with the wetness of the rain. Standing straight, he saw that she had moved closer, but still had the protection of the animals between them.

"Call them off," he said gently as his eyes took in her beauty. The cold and rain had crystallized in her curly long hair, giving her an angelic look. Damn, she was beautiful, and much more deserving of someone other than him.

"Do you promise to let me be your friend?" she questioned with a tilt of her head.

"Call them off." His tone became stern, but soft.

Katrina looked at the animals, and he knew she was relaying a message. The birds flew away as the deer, with their graceful gait, began to depart. The skunks, however, stood in the same exact position, looking at him.

"I don't think they got the message." Blaze nodded at the skunks.

"That's because you haven't promised me." Katrina cocked her eyebrow. "To let me be your friend."

Blaze sighed as feelings of not being worthy of her friendship, love, or whatever she felt for him, swarmed him. "Katrina, you are much more to me than a friend."

Stepping over the skunks, Katrina walked into his arms. Blaze held her so tight she squirmed. When he picked her up, she wrapped her legs around him as his lips met hers. He opened his eyes slightly, relieved to see the skunks waddling away. Yes, the woman in his arms was special, and he was going to make damn sure from this moment on he would treat her as he should.

******

Katrina had no idea and really didn't care how long they stood in the clearing kissing. One thing they hadn't done a lot of was kissing and holy crap, could this man kiss. She did, however, realize that she was no longer cold. He was heating his body for her, but honestly, his kiss alone would have warmed her enough.

He pulled away, his eyes searching hers. "You said you loved me in your sleep," Blaze blurted, his arms tightening around her. "Do you remember?"

"Yes." Katrina leaned her forehead into his. "I didn't mean to say it out loud, but I won't deny it."

"Do you still feel that way?" Blaze tilted his head and kissed the corner of her mouth.

"Yes, I do." Katrina licked his bottom lip, earning a moan from him. "And it's okay if you don't feel the same."

Blaze pulled away from her, his eyes darkening as they

roamed her face. "I don't really know what love is, Katrina. As stupid as that sounds, it's true."

The rain fell harder, but it didn't seem to faze either of them. "Of course you know what it is, Blaze. You have love for Bryon and your team. I also saw it when you talked about his wife, Barbara."

Seeing doubt in his eyes, she didn't want to push the issue, not wanting to drive him away. "Love is just a strong like, Blaze. Nothing more, nothing less." She touched his cheek. "It's just something that is."

He frowned when she shivered, then turned and headed out of the woods and across the field. "We need to get you warm."

She let go of the love issue, knowing it made him uncomfortable, and that was fine. She laid her head on his shoulder as he carried her back to the house. Once inside, he closed the door with his bare foot and took her into the bathroom. Without setting her down, he reached in and turned on the shower.

******

While the water heated, Blaze set her on her feet and removed her clothing, slowly kissing a path to each article of clothing. When he started to remove his jeans, she stopped him and knelt to do the same as he did for her. Except when his cock sprang free, she took him in her mouth, and he loved the sound of her groan. He didn't try to stop her this time. He let her continue, using steel control to keep from exploding in her mouth. He ran his hand through her hair and even helped her set a tempo. His legs began to shake with the pressure he was putting on them to keep control. Using his free hand against the wall as leverage to keep upright, he slung his head in fucking bliss.

Knowing he was close, he glanced down to see her staring up at him with her mouth around his cock.

"Jesus, you're going to kill me." He slowly pulled her off his swollen cock and lifted her to her feet. Then he took her mouth with his. He could taste himself, and how fucking sexy was that.

She pulled away from him and stared at him wide-eyed. "You just kissed me after I—"

"Sucked my cock." He finished for her with a sensual grin. "What's wrong with that?" He kissed her again, making sure his tongue tasted every inch of her mouth.

"Absolutely nothing." She moaned, grabbing his hand and pulling it toward her soaked pussy. "Total turn-on."

Blaze laughed, plunging two fingers inside her warmth. Katrina held on to his arm, riding his fingers.

"You are a fucking turn-on." He growled, pulling his fingers out of her before picking her up and placing her in the shower.

Grabbing the soap, he lathered his hands and began bathing her with as many suds as he could; as far as he was concerned, there was nothing sexier than seeing her tits lathered by his hands. He turned her around and did the same with that fine ass. Then he gave her a smack.

"Oh, God!" Katrina cried out, making Blaze give a satisfied smile. Knowing she liked a little spanking made his dick twitch.

"You like that?" He gave her another smack just under the cheek, then rubbed some of the pain away.

"Yes." Katrina reached up, cupped her own breast, and then pinched her nipple. "Please, Blaze." She tried to turn around, but he stopped her.

"Hold on, baby." He lifted her leg and put her foot on the edge of the tub. He worked up some lather and cupped her pussy. "If you liked having your ass smacked, you're going to love this."

He gave her a tap on the pussy. She moaned. He did it again, but harder and she screamed. Yeah, he'd found her level. He continued with a good pace until he felt her grow weak. Now it was time to get some relief himself. He edged her under the warm water to wash away the lather, then turned her toward him. His mouth smashed down on hers.

Damn, he wished he had a bed, but he didn't so he picked her up and sank her down on his cock. Needing leverage, he pushed her against the wall and fucked her hard. Her fingernails dug into him. Then her fingers tangled in his hair pulling his neck back. A moment later, her fangs sank into his neck. He groaned, knowing she loved to feed from him while his dick was deep inside her.

He held back his release as long as he could while pounding into her. Having felt her come more than once, with his head slammed back, he let go and released inside her. His body shook, his teeth clenched, and his dick pumped his seed into her.

Finally returning to his senses, he looked at her to find her smiling at him. "Friends?" she asked before she burst out laughing.

Blaze knew then and there what love was. That was exactly what he felt for the woman in his arms. It had to be, as there was no doubt he would give his life for her.

Chapter 25

Katrina sat on her bed, playing her new guitar. Strumming the strings with a smile, she was the happiest she had ever been in her life. She had stayed at Blaze's until just a little while earlier, when he had to come in to work for a meeting. She was due at the bar that night for her second shift, and then she had training tomorrow.

While humming a tune, she thought about the time she had spent with Blaze. After the shower, which she would never in her life forget, they had talked for hours about mostly good things, but also things from their pasts. They'd both wanted to get the past out of the way so they could move on.

She had drifted off in his arms as they'd sat on the floor, him leaning against the wall. When she'd woken, he'd been staring down at her. What a way to wake up! She chuckled at the thought, then sang softly as she waited for Blaze to take her to work.

Closing her eyes, getting lost in the song, she quietly played. She hit a wrong chord and laughed, shaking her head.

"You are beautiful."

Katrina jumped, then smiled, pleased by his words, but embarrassed. "You scared me." She put the guitar down. "That was a fast meeting."

"Yeah, it was." Blaze glanced at the guitar. "You like your birthday gift?"

"So much!" Katrina reached out and touched it, then frowned. "How did you know about my birthday?"

"Adam."

"How did Adam…? He read me, didn't he?" Katrina snorted when Blaze nodded. "He really needs to stop doing that."

"This time I'm glad he did because I wouldn't have known about your birthday." Blaze grinned, then became serious in a flash. "But he has been warned to stay out of your thoughts."

"Thank you." Katrina chuckled, then jumped up. "Oh, and before I forget."

She headed to the small dresser and opened a drawer, embarrassingly revealing how little she had. She pulled out a shirt and unfolded it. After grabbing the money hidden inside, she tried to hand it to him.

"I don't want that money back, Katrina." Blaze refused to take it.

"I'm not giving you a choice." Katrina wadded it up the best she could and went for his pocket, but he was too quick and moved out of the way.

"No." Blaze grinned when she persisted.

"Dammit, Blaze. Take the flipping money back." She caught her finger in one of his front pockets, but once again he evaded her.

Carefully, he grabbed her wrist, stilling her. "You can get in my pants anytime, but not to put money in them."

Katrina huffed and tried not to laugh. "Seriously, Blaze!"

"Hey!" Steve called out from the other side of the closed door. "Sloan wants to see you guys, pronto."

Blaze opened the door still grinning, which in turn made Steve grin.

"Hey, Blaze." Steve went in for a knuckle bump. "What's up, bro?"

Katrina nodded toward Steve who was trying to get Blaze to knuckle bump him, but Blaze didn't move. It didn't matter though, because as soon as Steve saw the money in her hand, his brows lifted.

"Holy shit!" Steve stepped closer. "What the fuck did you do at the bar to earn that kind of tips?"

"Oh, Steve," Katrina whispered as she watched Blaze's calm, cool mood change in the blink of an eye.

"What the fuck is that supposed to mean?" Blaze rounded on him.

Steve rolled his eyes and sighed. "Katrina, know that I really like you, but I'm not talking to you anymore because it's just too fucking dangerous for a dumbass like me." Steve turned and walked away. "Don't forget Sloan wants to see everybody in the game room pronto."

"Blaze, he didn't mean it." Katrina stepped in his line of vision. "He's Steve. He says stuff, but he's a really good guy. Actually, he's the main person who helped me when I first came here and wanted nothing in return. Please make nice with him."

"I don't make nice, Katrina." Blaze glanced down at her.

"Try for me, please." Katrina leaned into him while looking up into his eyes. "Please."

"For you, I will try." Blaze nodded, but stopped her hand from slipping the money into his pocket. "And you may be a good pickpocket, but you suck at trying to give it back."

"I'm not going to spend this." Katrina walked to her dresser and put the money back. "It will stay in there forever because I won't spend it. I mean it… for-ev-errrrr."

******

Blaze chuckled when she spread the word forever out. He

had been so blind during his self-hatred of his past, but hearing her words calling him out had opened his eyes. No one understood him more than she did. He cared for her more than anything or anybody he had ever cared for in his life.

"Hey," he said when she closed the dresser drawer.

"What?" Katrina looked up at him, her wide eyes always so expressive as if waiting for what he was going to say. No one, for a long time, had cared what he had to say.

"Why don't you use that money to fix up the house?" Blaze took the leap. He was a smart man and knew it was heading that way anyway so he may as well jump now.

"The house?" Katrina frowned, then her eyes opened wider. "Your house! Really? Oh my God. Yes, a million times, yes. I'll fix it just the way you want it. Wait, hold on."

Blaze watched her search around the small room until she found paper and a pen. She jumped up on the bed, sitting cross-legged with the pen ready.

"What colors do you like?" she asked, tapping the pen to her chin. "Not black though. I know you like black because that's all you wear. You know you'd look really good in blue, a dark blue."

"Whatever color you want. You pick." Blaze leaned against the wall, amazed. This once shy, quiet woman had bloomed before his eyes, and he'd been almost too dumb to have missed it by pushing her away. He saw the flash of excitement at his offer, but then she shook her head.

"No, I'm not picking the colors." Katrina rolled her eyes with a laugh. "You pick."

"No, you pick the colors to our house." Blaze watched her closely.

"Blaze, stop being difficult." Katrina sighed. "I'm not picking the colors of your house, just like I won't pick anything else, but I will see it done."

Blaze pushed off the wall and sat in front of her on the bed. "How about you understand what I'm saying and you pick the colors of *our* house."

"Ugh, I'm not... wait... what?" Katrina dropped the pen, which landed in her lap, but her eyes never left his. "Our..."

"...house," Blaze finished for her. "Unless of course you like this little room so much and—"

Blaze didn't get to finish. Katrina was in his arms and hugging him tightly. Her body shook as she held him. "Please don't be teasing me," she whispered. He heard the tears in her voice.

"Hey." He tried to pull her away so he could see her, but she clung to him like glue. "Hey!"

"No, I don't want to let go because I might be dreaming," Katrina said into his neck.

"Katrina, stop." Blaze laughed and finally pried her away a little so he could see her face. "Why would you say that?"

"Because good things don't happen to me," Katrina said, then wiped her eyes. "Holy cow, I've been blubbering a lot."

Her words broke him. Many times he had faced adversity, faced monsters ready to destroy him, yet only her words broke him. "Well, you better get used to good things happening to you." Blaze gently tipped her chin up. "Me and you are a team now. You hear me? Now answer my question. Can you fix our house up to be a home for us?"

Katrina's chin wobbled. She bit her lip as though trying to stop them from trembling. "Yes, I would love nothing more."

"Good, now we better get going before Sloan comes to find us." Blaze helped her off the bed. "And, Katrina, I would never tease you about something like that. Those days for you are over."

Katrina reached up and tugged him down, kissing him softly on the lips. "Thank you," she whispered with another kiss. "So much."

Blaze deepened the kiss as he wrapped his arms around her, pulling her close. "You might take those words back." He smirked into her hair. "I'm not the neatest person."

"I don't care." Her voice was mumbled against his chest. "Just don't leave the toilet seat up."

It took him a minute, but his head slammed back as his laughter filled the room. God, it felt good to laugh again. It felt good to feel again.

Chapter 26

Katrina felt like she was walking on air as they made their way to the game room, her hand held tightly in his. A nagging sensation nipped at her, but she pushed it away. She was going to be happy, dammit. She deserved it. She wasn't naïve enough to think her father wasn't going to strike, but for this moment, right now she was going to enjoy being a part of something good. That included having a friendship… a relationship with a man who cared enough for her that he asked for nothing in return. Or at least, nothing she wasn't willing to give.

The doors to the game room were closed. "Oh, no," Katrina whispered, glancing up at Blaze. "I'm sorry. I made us late."

Blaze shook his head with a sigh. "This might be ugly." He reached for the doorknob. "Sloan hates when someone is late."

"Wait." She grabbed his hand. "We have to have a reason. Think of something."

"Hmmm, how about you couldn't keep your hands off me?" Blaze answered seriously, then grinned when she punched him.

"Don't you dare." Katrina huffed before cocking her eyebrow at him. "And your hands were pretty darn busy, mister."

"No, I think it was you who was trying to stick *your* hand down my pants, if I remember correctly." Blaze went to open the door again, but Katrina stopped him again.

"I was trying to put money in your pants." Katrina hissed, then rolled her eyes when he laughed. "Seriously, what are we going to say?"

"That you couldn't keep your hands off me." Blaze quickly grabbed the knob and shoved open the door.

"HAPPY BIRTHDAY!"

Katrina screamed and jumped behind Blaze. She peeked around him to see everyone laughing, smiling, and obviously there for her. Tessa, with her beautiful smile, ran up and pulled her out from behind Blaze.

"Come on, birthday girl." She rushed her inside the room that was decorated with balloons, streamers, and even Sloan Murphy, who gave her a small nod.

Becky smiled at her before rushing up and giving Katrina a hug. "Happy birthday, Katrina."

"Thank you." Katrina returned her smile, still stumped that this was for her.

Daniel raced to her wearing a party hat and carrying one in

his hand. "Here, Trina."

Katrina knelt and allowed him to put the hat on her. "How do I look?"

"Pretty," he said shyly. A moment later, he blew a party favor in her face before running off.

By the time everyone came and wished her a happy birthday, Katrina was lost for words. She'd only had one birthday party in her life, and it had included a drunken brawl with bloody presents, as well as plenty of booze, drugs, and sex.

Nicole walked up to her and smiled. "You a little overwhelmed, hon?" When Katrina nodded, she gave her a glass. "Here, take a drink of this. It will help."

Gratefully, Katrina grabbed the glass, needing water to get rid of her dry mouth. She lifted the drink and the sickening smell of alcohol hit her. She quickly handed it back to Nicole. "I'm sorry, but I don't drink."

Taking the glass back, Nicole hugged her. "I'm sorry, I seem to keep forgetting that."

Daniel returned and clasped her hand, leading her to where the presents were. "Come on, Trina. Open mine first!" He looked at Duncan, then added, "Pleassse."

"Absolutely." Katrina laughed, her eyes meeting Blaze's; he stood with the Warriors. Staring at him as he watched her intently, she couldn't find the will to move or look away. A grin tipped his lips and he winked. Butterflies swarmed her stomach; she could have easily stood there all night gazing at him, but Daniel was having none of it.

"Come on, Trina." He shoved a gift at her. "Guess what it is!"

Pulling her gaze from Blaze, she looked at the gift in her hand, then held it to her ear. "It's an... elephant."

Daniel laughed loudly. "Noooooo."

"Are you sure?" Katrina held it up to her ear again and gave it a little shake. "Oh, wait. It's a... motorcycle."

"Ah man, you stink at this." Daniel giggled, then pointed at it. "Just open it. You'll never guess."

Opening it, Katrina savored every single minute of it. It was her first wrapped present she had ever received on her birthday that wasn't bloodstained.

******

Blaze couldn't take his eyes off Katrina as she sat among the women, letting Daniel help her open all her gifts. After reading the card from each gift, she stood to hug the givers.

"Just got word that the Drakes are on the move," Sloan casually said from beside him. "We know they're going to strike, just not sure when, so I've had eyes out watching. Got a hit today. They were seen downtown, maybe five or six."

Blaze frowned, taking another drink of his beer, his gaze fixed on Katrina as he listened to Sloan. "The strike is coming soon," Blaze replied, his eyes narrowing at the thought of them getting their hands on Katrina.

"I've told everyone to be vigilant. This is probably going to get ugly." Sloan frowned. "But we'll do whatever we can to make sure she's safe."

After giving the update, Sloan left, leaving Blaze to consider what could happen next. He knew what would happen to Katrina if the MC caught her, but he'd die before that happened.

Hearing her laughter, he watched as she stood and headed toward Steve. She wrapped her arms around him in a big hug. Steve, wearing a huge grin, hugged her back until he saw him watching. The change on Steve's face was comical as he shoved Katrina away.

Katrina frowned, before glancing his way. Blaze gave her a "what?" look, then grinned when she narrowed her eyes at him as she went to sit back down.

Shit, he guessed he needed to make nice. Finishing his beer, he tossed the bottle in the trash and headed toward Steve, who looked like he was ready to make a run for it.

Blaze stuck out his hand, making Steve jump back and stare at his hand in horror. "Thanks for everything you've done for Katrina since she's been here." Blaze held his hand out and waited.

"I swear I didn't want to hug her, but she just ah… huh?" Steve's eyes traveled from Blaze's large hand to his face, no doubt the words sinking in. When they did, Steve took Blaze's hand in a handshake. "Ah, man, I thought fire was going to shoot out of that big hand of yours."

Adam, who was standing next to Steve with Angelina, rolled his eyes.

A grin tipped Blaze's lips. "No fire, just a handshake."

Steve let go of his hand looking uncomfortable. He then peered at Katrina. "And don't thank me. Katrina is my peep. I'd lay down my life for her."

At that moment Blaze examined Steve in a new light. As fucking goofy as he was, he was a loyal Warrior and obviously a good friend to those around him. Blaze didn't know much about friendships, but he did know loyalty.

"I have no doubt about that," Blaze responded, and meant it. "You're a good man, Steve."

Blaze glanced toward Katrina, who was watching him as she helped clean up the wrapping paper. She mouthed "thank you" to him with a radiant smile. With a nod, he moved away from Steve and Adam, but heard Steve say, "Holy shit, I thought I was a goner."

A huge smile broke over Blaze's face. Even though he made nice with Steve, it was good to know he feared him and would think twice where Katrina was concerned. She was his and very soon, he would make that official.

"Did I do well?" He took the bag of trash from Katrina.

"You did well." She smiled up at him. "I knew you could play nice."

"Yeah, best not get used to it." Blaze gave her a fake frown. "I have a reputation to uphold." He leaned toward her to give her a kiss.

"Hate to interrupt, kids, but we have to go to work." Tessa grabbed the garbage bag to throw away more trash. "She riding with me and Jared or are you taking her?"

"I'm taking her. Then I have to take care of something, but I'll be back." Blaze glanced toward Jared, who was making his way over. "You got them until I get there?"

"Absolutely." Jared nodded without his normal snarky grin, and both Tessa and Katrina picked up on it.

"Okay, what's going on?" Tessa put her hand on her hip. "I know you well and I know that look in your eye."

Blaze and Jared shared a glance, then he gazed down at Katrina. "They're on the move."

The anger that rushed through his body at not only the fear in her eyes, but the acceptance that this was her life burned like raging fire.

"I won't let anything happen to you," he vowed.

"I know." Katrina gave him a smile, but the fear behind her beautiful golden eyes called to him. "Just be careful."

Chapter 27

Blaze had not only dropped her off, but along with Jared, he had walked through the bar eyeing everyone, getting a read on the customers, and checked around the property. Then he left with a warning to stay inside and in sight of Jared at all times. He definitely didn't get an argument from her. All too well she knew the threat was very real. For the first time in her life, she felt safe; it was a wonderful feeling.

She wasn't surprised that her father was taking his time. He was good at being patient before striking at the enemy. It was a perverse satisfaction he took in knowing that someone was waiting for his wrath. It was also what made him a force in the MC world. He was unpredictable, and that was what made him so dangerous.

Heading across the bar, she glanced at Jared, who had taken a spot in the corner, his back to the wall as his eyes scanned everywhere and everyone. They fell on her for just a second before moving past. This was a different Jared from the one she had come to know. This was the Warrior he really was. Usually Jared was joking, laughing, and playing pool with the customers, but not tonight. Tonight he had the air of "stay the fuck away from me," and people were paying attention.

"Hey, get that table over there in the corner for me." Tessa nodded, her hands full.

Katrina quickly went that way and noticed a large man in a cowboy hat, his head bent looking at his phone. Weird, she'd never seen him walk in.

"Hi." Katrina stepped up to the table and noticed the light above was out. "I'm Katrina, can I get you a drink?"

His head lifted slightly, but not enough to show his full face. "I'm good, ma'am." His western drawl was slow and deliberate, almost hypnotizing. "Thank you."

The door opened, drawing Katrina's attention. Adam and Steve walked in, tossing her a wave. She returned it, then looked back to her customer. He was now looking at her with deep golden eyes glowing from under his cowboy hat.

"Uh, can I fix that light for you?" She glanced at the light. "I don't mind."

If her heart weren't already taken, this man's smile would have ripped it right out her chest. "I like the dark," he replied, his smile still in place. "But thank you again, ma'am." Katrina had a pretty good people sensor, as she called it, and didn't feel threatened by this man at all. There was a time when she'd had to be suspicious of everyone, mainly because her father was a ruthless bastard. Regardless, even though she felt there was no threat, she would make sure Jared knew about him.

"Okay, I'll check on you in a bit, but if you need anything, just wave me down." She returned his smile, then added,

"And please, me and ma'am just don't go together. I'm Katrina."

The only response she received was a nod and that same melting smile before he pretty much dismissed her to look back at his phone. Katrina cocked her eyebrow then headed toward Jared, picking up empty beer bottles and glasses on her way. Holding the empties to her chest, she slid into a chair across from Jared.

"Hey, little red," Jared said without really looking at her. She had never seen Jared so focused before; it was pretty damn impressive.

"There's a guy over there, sitting at the table with the light out." Katrina did a sideways nod toward the table.

Jared glanced that way then back at her. "He's good" was all he said. Then he dismissed her just like the cowboy in the corner had.

Alarms went off at that moment. She knew from experience when something big was about to go down, and something big was definitely about to hit. "What's going on, Jared?"

"It's under control, Katrina." Jared frowned at her.

"Where's Blaze?" Fear tightened her throat. When Jared didn't answer, anger slammed into her chest. "Where is Blaze?"

"Shit!" Jared hissed, then leaned toward her. "We got a hit on where they are. They're going to get them. Now go back to fucking work so I can focus on what the fuck is going on."

"No." Katrina had a bad feeling. "It can't be that easy. Something isn't right."

That got Jared's attention. "What?"

"There's no way my father would be that careless," Katrina hissed. "Why didn't anyone say anything to me. I know them. I know how they operate."

"We know what we're doing. This is not our first rodeo." Jared glared at her, but there was also concern behind his glare.

"With the Iron Drakes it is." Katrina cursed as she nervously glanced around. "If anything happens to them...." She couldn't finish.

"Nothing is going to happen," Jared growled, then reached out and squeezed her hand. "We have—" The door opened, and his eyes darkened dangerously.

"Get to the back. Now," he said as he stood. Katrina started to turn to look, but he growled, "Now!"

Standing, Katrina then took two steps to do as Jared ordered, but stopped when she heard the name she despised, spoken by the man she despised even more.

"Hey, Kat!" Breaker's greeting didn't sound sincere, and everyone in the bar heard the venom in his tone. "You've been a bad girl." His tsking sent chills down her spine.

Katrina watched as Bobby sent people out the back door, but they only returned as more Iron Drakes forced them back inside. Slowly she turned around. Her eyes landed on Breaker and she wanted to throw up. Then she glanced to his left to see John staring at her, wearing a prospect vest.

"John?" She frowned as she put two and two together. The shock of seeing him momentarily left her speechless.

"Oh, yes. I almost forgot." Breaker put his arm loosely on John's shoulder. "John here is the reason we've known your every move, and on a personal note, which Warrior you've been fucking. They really need to check their potential Warriors out better."

"Why?" she asked John, who had been so nice to her during training and seemed earnest when helping her. Now she knew why; he was on her father's payroll.

"The pay is better." John shrugged. "And I needed the money. Nothing personal."

"Nothing personal?" Katrina tried to keep control, but all she wanted to do was smack the indifference off his face. "You have no idea what you've done, you bastard."

"Damn, where did that spunk come from? I'm really liking it." Breaker tilted his head, his eyes roaming her body with appreciation. "You know, Kat, you look so good I don't think I'm going to care that you're a Warrior slut."

Jared stepped in front of Katrina, his body rigid. Steve and Adam also stepped forward.

"You have two options, asshole." Jared cracked his neck back and forth.

"Two?" Steve glanced at Jared. "Death is only one."

"Yeah well, we have witnesses so I have to give them two," Jared countered, his voice hard.

"Ah, I get it." Breaker laughed. "You two are the funny guys of the group. Well isn't that special, but I'm already bored."

"I really don't think anyone in here will care if we just go with one option." Adam growled the words while cracking his knuckles. "Because this asshole needs to fucking die."

"Oh, I agree." Jared looked from Breaker to the other four assholes. "But I really think Blaze wants… him." Jared pointed straight at Breaker. "And I'm a loyal brother so I think we can keep him alive."

"Yep, bored. Now, here are my options." Breaker held up his phone. "This is a—"

"Phone." Jared rolled his eyes. "Now I'm fucking bored."

Knowing Breaker well, Katrina could tell Jared was getting under his skin, badly, and that wasn't good. While they bantered back and forth, she glanced around and counted nine Iron Drake members. Most she knew. One asshole even gave her a sarcastic finger wave. Breaker had a short fuse, and God only knew what he would do if Jared pushed him too far. Too many innocent people were in danger, and she couldn't have that happen, couldn't live with it.

"What do you want, Breaker?" She looked back at him, digging deep for Kat, the girl she had tried to bury and forget. It didn't look like that would ever be a reality.

"You, Kat." Breaker's eyes stayed on Jared for a second after his response before snapping to her. "That's what all the Iron Drakes want, you. You know the saying, a snitch is a snitch and always ends up in a ditch. Like mother, like daughter is another saying that comes to mind."

"Fuck you, Breaker," Katrina spat, her control shot to hell. She knew what he'd done to her mother, what they all did to her mother. She hated him, hated them all.

"Ah, damn girl!" Breaker adjusted his crotch. "You're getting me all hot with that attitude."

"Okay, fuck this." Jared went for Breaker, but Breaker stepped back, holding up the phone.

"You take one more step and I will blow this fucking place up," Breaker shouted, his thumb hovering over the phone. "Just one push and this place is going up in one hell of an explosion. Now we, and we meaning us vampires, will probably survive. But the humans, including your gorgeous mate, Tessa, will not." His eyes shot toward where the customers stood. Then he winked at Tessa.

Katrina knew this was not a bluff and prayed that Jared realized it too. But the threat against Tessa along with the wink set Jared off. Thankfully Adam stopped him.

"Good move, young Warrior," Breaker said to Adam. "Now on to option two. I walk out of here with Kat and everyone lives. It's really an easy decision if you think about it. One of ours, for all of yours."

No one said a word as Breaker stood with his phone out, his thumb still hovering. A strange sound whizzed through the air as a thin piece of leather wrapped around Breaker's wrist, snapping the phone out of it.

"Hope you have an option three, asshole." A familiar western drawl filled the room.

Breaker cursed, freeing himself from what looked like a whip, his eyes black with rage.

Everything happened in a blur. Adam and Steve scrambled for the phone while screams echoed as gunshots rang out through the small bar. Katrina spotted Jared heading for

Breaker, but a scream of pain stopped him. Terror filled Katrina as she slowly turned to see Tessa falling face-first onto the wooden floor. Bobby tried to stop her fall as he yelled for Jared.

"No!" Katrina followed Jared, but someone grabbed the back of her hair and started to drag her. Using her strength, she tried to untangle unseen hands from her hair. Her struggle stopped suddenly as a roar of pain and rage rattled the walls of the bar. Her eyes briefly saw Jared with his head back, his mouth open in rage as he held a lifeless Tessa in his arms.

"Dammit, Kat." Breakers fist tightened in her hair as he continued to pull her. "Stop fucking fighting me or I'm going to knock you out."

Katrina fought hard, but he was too strong. One minute she was being dragged, the next she was free, and hearing Blaze's voice, she knew he was the reason.

Chapter 28

You got a bad feeling about this?" Sloan kept watch as Damon, Duncan, and Jax escorted members of the Iron Drakes to the van.

"Definitely." Blaze's eyes scanned the area. "Where are the rest of the bastards?" He had searched each member closely looking for that fucker, Breaker, but he wasn't among them.

Samuel Drake, with his hands confined behind his back with silver cuffs, was led out by Slade. Their eyes met. A slow grin spread across Samuel's face before he turned his attention to Sloan.

"Good catch, Warriors." His grin turned into a smirk. "Didn't see you coming at all. You guys are good."

"Shut up!" Slade gave him a push.

Sloan didn't say a word and neither did Blaze as Slade all but threw Samuel into the van. Something wasn't right. He reached for his phone; Jared hadn't responded to his text. He sent another one.

"Who gave you the information about where they were?" Blaze asked, still checking his phone. His body was strung tight waiting for Jared's reply.

"A trusted informant, but I don't know who he got the information from." Sloan cursed, his angry eyes staring at the van then to the house. "Motherfuckers were waiting for us. No fight, just put their hands up and surrendered."

Blaze turned and headed for his bike. "We need to get to the bar, now!"

The laughter of the Iron Drakes from the back of the van had every Warrior rushing for their bikes.

"Goddammit!" Sloan started yelling orders.

Blaze didn't wait. He knew they were close to the bar, another bad sign. These fuckers had set a trap, a trap they'd walked right into. Shit!

Blaze pulled up to the bar with the rest of the team following him. When Jared hadn't checked in with him, he'd known something was wrong. He heard gunshots before even pulling into the parking lot. He dropped his bike without care as he flew to the door. "Fuck!"

As soon as he opened the door, he ran into someone and that someone was dragging Katrina by the hair. His arm reached out instinctively, rage fueling every movement. Grabbing the man by the shirt, Blaze spun him around, headbutting him in the face and knocking the bastard out instantly. Blaze reached around, trying to detangle the man's hand from her hair. The fucker was knocked out cold, so trying to get her free, holding the bastard off her, and scanning the scene was not easy, but he finally released Katrina.

"Are you okay?" Blaze still held the fucker just in case he came to, but he needed to know she was okay. "Dammit, Katrina, are you hurt?"

Katrina had made it to her knees. "No, but Tessa was shot."

"Shit! Slade!" Blaze yelled as he dragged the unconscious man and tossed him to Adam, who was restraining the Iron Drakes who hadn't taken off out the back when the rest of the Warriors appeared. "Make sure this fucker is secure."

Slade ran in, heading toward Tessa. Blaze helped Katrina to her feet, his eyes going to Jared, who held Tessa close, refusing to let her go. Reality hit Blaze hard; he could have lost Katrina. That thought scared him more than anything ever had.

He pulled her close, his gaze still searching for danger. The rest of the Warriors were making sure the Iron Drakes were restrained. One of theirs was down. Respect and worry were thick in the air, the atmosphere somber.

Katrina shook in Blaze's arms as she watched Slade work on Tessa, Jared finally letting her go for him to do so. Adam stood quietly, his face an unreadable mask as he stood over his sister. The customers had been taken outside and were being questioned.

"I need to help," Blaze whispered in her ear. "Stay right here and do not move."

Katrina only nodded, her eyes glued on Slade.

"I mean it, Katrina," Blaze warned, then kissed the top of her head. "Right here."

"I promise," Katrina said, still watching as her hands fidgeted.

Blaze turned and headed toward Steve and Sloan, who were talking to a man in a cowboy hat. He positioned himself so he could keep an eye on Katrina, who remained alone.

"Blaze, this is Ronan McDonald," Sloan introduced as Blaze shook the man's hand. "If not for him, this place would have been nothing but rubble."

"What?" Blaze frowned, taking his eyes off Katrina.

"Yeah, they had a bomb planted, and that sick fuck had it set with his phone. If it weren't for him and his whip, which was fucking awesome by the way, we would've been toast," Steve said, then pointed toward Breaker, who was just coming around.

Blaze glanced back at the guy Steve pointed to and took a real good look. "Motherfucker!" Blaze headed toward the man, realizing now it was that fucker, Breaker.

"Stop!" Sloan grabbed Blaze then got in his face. "Not here.

You'll get your chance, but not here."

Blaze jerked away, then nodded, fighting for control. "You're asking a lot, but fine. Just know I want that bastard."

"Done." Sloan nodded.

"We found the bomb." Damon walked up, his face a mask of rage. "It's been disengaged by Duncan. It would have leveled this place. These fuckers don't play."

"Yeah, well neither do we," Sloan growled. "Start clearing these fuckers out of here and put them in the van with the rest of them. I don't care if you have to break their fucking bones to fit them all in."

"Goddammit, where in the fuck is that ambulance?" Slade's voice rang out, drawing their attention.

"It's just pulling in," Jax called, then looked at Sloan. "And so are the local police."

"Fuck!" Sloan frowned, then looked toward Tessa. "Hold them off until they get Tessa out."

"Done." Jax nodded as he turned to walk back out, Damon, Duncan, Sid and Steve following.

Blaze wanted nothing more than to take Katrina out of here, but the good news he hadn't been able to share with her yet would have to wait. Her father was in their custody. She was safe. His eyes went to Jared, and his stomach dropped at what could have happened.

******

Katrina couldn't take her eyes off Tessa as Slade worked on her. She refused to look at Jared, afraid she would see hate in his eyes because if it weren't for her, Tessa would be her vibrant self, rushing around serving the customers who loved her.

She moved quickly out of the way as the paramedics rushed in. Jared would not let them put Tessa on the gurney; he did it himself then rushed out with them, holding Tessa's hand. Slade followed while shouting orders on the phone.

Her eyes followed them and then fell on Breaker. He was on his knees with his hands behind his back, smirking at her.

"You go against your family, and this is what happens. You'll always be a Drake," Breaker said, the smirk still in place. "Just think, Kat, if you had stayed where you were, none of this would have happened. This is your doing."

Everything in her body tingled as if she had just been struck by lightning. The rage and hatred she felt for him, for the MC, fueled her body, shooting her forward without thought. Lifting her leg, she kicked him in the face as hard as she could.

"You bastard!" Next, she kicked him in the stomach, but she was aiming for his balls. She went to do it again but was picked up and pulled away. "I fucking hate you! Do you hear me? I hate you!"

"Katrina." Blaze moved into her line of vision when she continued to struggle to get to Breaker. "Katrina!"

With effort, she calmed herself enough to focus on Blaze. "I want to go to the hospital." Her chin trembled, but she kept control. No way would that bastard see her break.

Sloan had walked over. "Go on." He gave Blaze a knowing look that wasn't lost on Katrina. "We got this here. Keep me informed on Tessa until we can get there."

Blaze nodded, took Katrina's hand, then headed toward the door, but stopped in front of Breaker, keeping the bastard out of Katrina's view. "I will see you real soon," he growled down at him, then looked at Sloan. "Motherfucker is mine."

"Done," Sloan replied again as he followed them out, sending Steve inside to help Ronan keep watch.

"Shit!" Blaze cursed, and Katrina frowned, seeing all the cops. One stood arguing with Duncan. Admittedly it was a one-sided argument, since Duncan stood rigid with his arms crossed, looking bored.

"Go on, we've got this." Sloan headed toward Duncan and the yelling cop.

Blaze quickly took her hand and led her to his bike. He let her go long enough to pick up his bike, then got on.

Before Katrina could slide on behind him, she looked toward the van.

"There she is," one of the Iron Drakes shouted. Jax glanced her way then pushed the man inside the back of the van.

"Kat!" her father's voice screamed out from the van. "This isn't the end. I almost got you, Kat!" Her father's laugh frightened her; it always had.

"Get on, Katrina," Blaze ordered, his eyes black as they stared at her.

"How many will you let die, Kat?" Her father's voice carried easily to her. "You know this ain't over."

Sloan had walked over and taken her arm. "Get on the bike."

Katrina glanced at the ambulance, then back to the van. He was right. This wasn't over. She let Sloan help her on the bike. Blaze didn't waste time getting out of the parking lot. Katrina held on tight, her gaze on the van, her father's words repeating over and over again in her mind.

It was a short ride to the hospital and Katrina was off the bike almost before Blaze stopped. "Dammit, Katrina." Blaze tried to steady her and the bike at the same time. "Be careful."

"Sorry, I just want to hurry." Katrina was wringing her hands together so hard that Blaze cringed and stopped her.

"This isn't your fault. You know that, don't you?" Blaze forced her to look at him. "Don't you?"

"Blaze, of course this is my fault. I brought this to your door and now Tessa is paying the price." Her voice cracked. "Didn't you hear him? It's not over. It's never over with the Iron Drakes."

"Listen to me. You are safe. No one is going to touch you or anyone else. Do you hear me? We've got your father, Katrina." Blaze searched her face before pulling her into his arms and whispered against her hair, "You're safe now. None of them will hurt you or anyone else again."

She wanted so badly to believe him, but she knew her father. He would find a way; he always did. She nodded against his chest, keeping her thoughts to herself, for now. Once she'd controlled herself, they hurried into the emergency department and quickly found Adam and Jared. Adam met them while Jared sat with his elbows on his knees and his head in his hands.

"She's in surgery. Slade's with her, but he called the best surgeon in," Adam informed them, trying to sound strong, yet every emotion was evident in his eyes. "The bullet is close to her heart, and they don't know if...."

Katrina reached out and wrapped her arms around him.

"She's going to be fine." She repeated Blaze's words he had just spoken to her. "Tessa is a fighter, Adam."

Adam squeezed her tight before letting go. "She is."

Katrina glanced over at Jared; he looked so alone she didn't know what to do. Something told her that he needed someone, but she was afraid to take that chance. Pushing her fear aside, she walked toward him, then knelt at his feet and touched his arm.

"I'm so sorry," she whispered, not knowing what else to say.

"Don't you fucking blame yourself." His quiet order was stern, his head still down, not looking at her. "Tessa cares for you like a sister. She wouldn't blame you, neither do I, and I will not tolerate you blaming yourself. You understand me?"

Katrina remained quiet. What could she say? The only thing she really understood was that her father was causing havoc in not only her life, but the lives of people she cared for.

With his head still in his hands, his eyes lifted and met hers. "I can't lose her," he whispered back. "I really can't lose her, Katrina."

"You won't." Katrina reached out and took him in her arms. "You are not going to lose her, Jared."

Katrina didn't know how long she held Jared and didn't care, but she heard quiet voices behind them and glanced around. Warriors filled the space, all comforting each other. Slowly, Jared let her go; the pain in his eyes was unbearable. Standing, he helped her to her feet.

Katrina bit her lip to stop the sob caught in her throat. Unable to utter a word, she nodded. He clasped her by the back of the head and kissed her on the forehead before walking away.

She felt Blaze's arms come around her and she sank into his strength, something she needed so badly.

As hours passed, the tension and worry peaked. Sloan finally arrived looking pissed, but kept to himself. Katrina sat in the chair with Blaze next to her holding her hand. With her eyes roaming the group, it struck her that she was part of this close-knit family and would be damned if anyone or anything tried to ruin that.

A moment later, Slade headed toward them, and the room became silent. He stopped halfway as Jared met him. They talked quietly and then Jared took off running down the hallway, and Slade came closer to them.

"She's alive," Slade announced, looking at Adam who was holding on to Angelina. "But we're not out of the woods. The bullet nicked her heart. If she survives the next forty-eight hours, she will still have an uphill battle and her life will never be the same. This isn't good. And honestly, me and the surgeon are both surprised she is still alive."

Katrina swallowed hard. It wasn't fucking fair. Her father had disrupted so many lives and once again a life would be altered because of his evilness. She glanced in the direction Jared had fled. Two lives would forever be changed.

"I'm sorry." Slade looked at Adam.

Adam only nodded, then cleared his throat. "Can we see her?"

"One at a time." Slade waved Adam toward him. "I'll take you. Jared's in there now. Everyone else might as well go home. There's nothing anyone can do at this point. If you pray, I'd say she could use some right now."

Shell-shocked, Katrina sat rigidly. She heard the soft, quiet cries from those around her, but all she could do was sit and stare. This wasn't supposed to happen. Blaze squeezed her hand, then pulled her out of her chair and held her.

"It's going to be okay," he whispered into her hair, but this time, she didn't believe him.

Chapter 29

Katrina punched the bag as hard as she could over and over again. Each punch released some of her pent-up rage. It had been a week since Tessa was shot and she still wasn't allowed to see her. All she was being told was she was recovering slowly, that was it. She had asked Slade every single day. His response was always the same. Man, if he wasn't so big, she would punch him in the gut. Jared was never around, which she understood, and Adam just didn't talk to anyone other than Angelina.

She hit the bag again, then kicked it wishing it was her father's face as well as the DA's. That fucking weasel, the DA she knew was working with her father, found a way to take control over the arrests of her father and his men. How could that even happen? The system was rigged and crooked, and always had been.

This time she used elbows, pounding the bag as hard as she could. She knew her father's arrest had been a setup to spread the Warriors out so they could take her. She knew the Drakes all too well. Her father had also ensured that he and his club would not be under the Warriors for long. She had no doubt he and the asshole DA had worked it out beforehand.

Her father had a far reach and until they realized that, they would never take down the Iron Drakes. She had been watching the court docs online and told Blaze she wanted to be there, but he refused, saying that he would be there to make sure justice was done. She even said she wanted to testify against them, but Sloan felt there was no need since they had a solid case. She knew better. She also knew that it would be a miracle if her father and the rest of the MC actually made it to their court date.

"Fuckers!" She unleashed on the bag like it was one of the three men she hated the most. Her father, Breaker, and the DA asshole, whatever his name was.

"Calm down, killer." Blaze wrapped his arms around her, receiving an elbow in the stomach. "Hey!"

"Stop. I'm working out." She wiggled out of his grasp and continued to hit the bag.

"Katrina!" Blaze stopped her and turned her to him. "What's wrong with you?"

"That's really a loaded question." Katrina swiped a strand of hair out of her face, but it sprung right back. "Ugh, I'm going to cut this mess one day."

"No, you are not," Blaze ordered with a growl, nudged her hand out of the way to move the strand himself. "Now tell me what's wrong."

"I'm just grumpy." Katrina huffed then tried to go back to the bag, but he stopped her again.

"That I know." He grinned but lost the grin really quick at her glare. "What I don't know is why."

"Okay, you really want to know?" Katrina tried to take the boxing gloves off, but couldn't, so she used her teeth to pull the straps.

"Here, let me." Blaze took them off for her. "Now tell me."

Dammit, why couldn't he be a dick right now so she wouldn't feel so bad about being a bitch? "I'm pissed."

"Yeah." Blaze nodded, cocking his eyebrow.

"No one listened to me about my father and his dealings with the DA, obviously," she started, and when Blaze started to open his mouth, she shook her head. "You want me to tell you? Because if so, you need to let me finish before you try to defend."

Blaze crossed his arms and leaned against the wall. "Please, continue."

Katrina narrowed her eyes at the hint of sarcasm in his voice. "I want to go to the hearing of my father and the rest of them."

"No." Blaze didn't even blink.

"Why?"

"Because."

"Without my testimony, they're going to get off. That is if they make it to their court date, which is doubtful," Katrina warned. "They always get off."

"Not this time," Blaze responded with maddening confidence.

"How can you be so sure of that, Blaze?" Katrina sighed, feeling defeated.

"Because we have others who have stepped forward to testify against them with enough evidence to put them away for a long time." Blaze reached out and removed the unruly strand from her face again. "Why do you want to put yourself in that position when you don't have to, Katrina?"

She knew the answer to that question but doubted he would understand. "Because I've stayed silent for so long."

"Once they hear what these people are going to say, there is no way any of them will get off." Blaze pulled her into his arms.

Katrina allowed it this time, pressing her cheek against his chest. She wasn't as sure as he was. She and her mother had thought the same thing so many times, only to have her father come back a free man.

"Is that all?" Blaze asked, his large hand rubbing circles on her back.

"No." She shook her head. "I want to see Tessa. All I get from Slade is 'she's recovering slowly.'" She mocked Slade's voice.

"And you don't believe him?" Blaze looked down at her, and she could tell he was trying not to grin.

"I mean, yes, but no." Katrina shrugged. "I just want to see her. I won't upset her or anything. Is there a reason she doesn't want to see me? Does she blame me for what happened to her?"

Blaze was silent for a minute. "Go shower while I make a phone call."

"Oh my God. Does she blame me?" An overwhelming sense of panic threatened to take Katrina to her knees. Blaze knew something and wasn't telling her. "Is she really okay?"

He tipped her face up to his and kissed her softly. He then pointed her toward the showers and gave her a gentle push. "Go shower."

"You're so demanding," Katrina mumbled as she did what he said.

"You didn't seem to mind it last night," he shot back.

Katrina rolled her eyes even knowing he was right. She

hadn't minded it at all last night.

******

As soon as Katrina walked out of the women's shower room, Blaze hung up the phone. "Get your stuff."

"Stop being so damn bossy." Katrina knew she was a pain in the ass, but she couldn't help it. When she worried, she was snippy with some bitchy thrown in. She blamed it on her red hair.

Blaze didn't rise to the bait and waited for her at the door. She didn't question him when she got on the bike to where they were going. It wouldn't matter anyway; she wasn't getting anything she wanted. Okay, not only was she being snippy and bitchy, she was wallowing in self-pity, feeling sorry for herself.

Suddenly her mood dawned on her. She was due for her period. She snorted and rolled her eyes. Of course her luck would be to finally have an out by being a vampire, and ta fucking da, the whole vampire thing didn't work for her. She still had her period. Or as Slade called it, her menstrual period. She snorted again. Yeah, she was pissy with the doctor.

"What are you snorting about," Blaze called over the roar of the engine.

"Nothing," she called back, then sighed. He wouldn't

understand anyway. Then she saw it and wanted it. "Hey, can you stop so I can get a chocolate milkshake?" Yep, her period was about to show with a vengeance.

Blaze didn't question it; he just pulled in and rode up to the speaker.

"Welcome to Pete's Burgers, can I take your order?" The guy's voice sounded as if he would rather be saying anything other than "Welcome to Pete's Burgers."

"Yeah, I'll take a large chocolate shake. Do you have extra chocolate by chance?" Katrina bit her lip, then her gaze met Blaze's in the mirror. "What?"

"Nothing." Blaze looked away.

"Ah, nope, just regular chocolate," the guy's voice answered. "Anything else?"

"No, that's it." Katrina was still looking at the menu. "No, wait. I'll take a large, no make that a jumbo order of fries."

The intercom crackled and was silent for a minute. "Ah, we don't have jumbo." The guy seemed real confused. "We can supersize it."

"Then supersize them fries, dude," Katrina replied into the intercom, then noticed Blaze's shoulders shaking. She smacked him on the shoulder. "Hush!"

The intercom was silent for a minute. "Pull around to the window."

Blaze slowly inched up, then stopped at the window. "That will be five-fifty." The guy at the window stuck his head out. "Nice bike, man."

"Thanks." Blaze stood, reaching into his back pocket pulling out his wallet and handed the kid money.

Katrina looked in the window to see all the girls staring out trying to see Blaze. Hell, she couldn't blame them. She glanced at his ass while he accepted the change and put his wallet back in his pocket before sitting and riding to the next window. He was a fine-looking man, no doubt about it.

"Hi." The girl at the window smiled at Blaze. "It will be just a minute."

Blaze gave the girl a nod as he adjusted his stance on the bike.

"I bet all the girls want to ride your bike."

"And what's that supposed to mean?" Blaze glanced at her in the mirror.

"Nothing, just an observation."

"Jealous are we?" he teased with a grin.

"No, not at all." She felt like smacking him, but refrained.

"Damn, baby," a man's voice called, followed by a whistle. "You can ride my—"

"Motherfucker, you best keep on driving." Blaze glared, showing fang at the guy in the truck who had been busy staring at Katrina rather than focused on who was in front of her.

"Holy shit! My bad, man." The guy peeled out, almost hitting a car backing out of a parking place.

"Jealous much?" Katrina snorted, then took her shake and bag of fries when the girl handed them out the window. "Thank you," she politely told the girl, who was still staring at Blaze.

Blaze growled, but took off carefully since she had her hands full. She didn't even question pulling up to the compound. They had been spending time at the house fixing it up here and there. Her mind had really been on other things, so not much had been done.

Once inside, she headed toward her room, but Blaze stopped her and led her in the opposite direction. They went through a door she had never seen before, and then he pushed an elevator button.

"I didn't know there was an elevator," Katrina said before sucking on her shake. Seeing him watch her, she pulled it out of her mouth and offered it to him. "You want some?"

His eyes darkened as a grin appeared.

"Of my shake." She rolled her eyes, but her insides quivered at his look. The elevator doors opened, and they stepped inside. Blaze pushed a button and the doors closed. "Seriously, elevator music?"

"Sid thought it would be a nice touch for when we take people to the cells downstairs." Blaze chuckled.

"So where are we going?" Katrina frowned. Too busy feeding her face, she had no idea what was going on.

The door opened into a long hallway and at the end was a door. Blaze held the doors open as Katrina walked out and they headed to the door at the end. Blaze knocked and they waited.

The door opened, and Katrina saw Jared, but her eyes then focused on who stood behind him.

"Oh my God!" Katrina set her food down and rushed past Jared. "You're okay."

"I'm fine." Tessa smiled, showing gleaming fangs. "Never been better."

Chapter 30

Blaze watched Tessa and Katrina talk excitedly. He knew Katrina had been worried about Tessa, guilt weighing her down. He hadn't known anything until he'd called Jared, asking if Katrina could see Tessa for only a few seconds. That was when Jared had told him he'd turned her.

"How's she doing?" Blaze asked, looking away from the women.

"Good, still having a little problem with control." Jared frowned, then shrugged. "It takes time, but she's doing really well. After the surgery, she wasn't coming out of it. Slade told me to make the decision because things weren't looking good. And even if she came out of the forty-eight-hour period okay, her life wouldn't be the same as before. He really couldn't promise anything. It was a no-brainer for me. I went to Sloan and he got it approved. Even if he hadn't, I would have changed her, but I wanted to try the right channels first, and we had time to do that."

"I'm glad for you both." Blaze slapped him on the shoulder.

"Wish I knew which motherfucker shot her." Jared's voice was fierce, his eyes darkening. "But bullets were flying everywhere."

Hearing that, Blaze frowned, thinking that Katrina could have also been shot and wondering what would have happened to her. He didn't even know if she was a full-blooded vampire because of the human traits she still possessed.

"What?" Jared broke into his thoughts.

"It's nothing." Blaze shook his head, then his brows dipped. "Can I ask you something?"

"Shoot." Jared leaned against the counter.

"With Tessa being human for most of the time you've known her, she had, you know…." Blaze looked at him as if he should know exactly what he was talking about.

"Ah, no, not really," Jared replied. "Had what?"

"Her girl thing." Blaze waved his hand like that said it all. "You know."

Jared stared at him for a minute. "Her period."

"Yeah," Blaze said a little too excitedly.

"What about it?" Jared was now looking at him like he was some fucking weirdo.

"What did she do? I mean, did she have a lot of pain, or how did you know she was, you know, doing that?" Blaze was falling all over his fucking words, but dammit, this wasn't normal talk for him.

"Jesus, man." Jared chuckled. "Had a hard time spitting that out, didn't ya?"

"Fuck you," Blaze hissed. "This isn't something I've ever talked about before."

Jared looked over at the milkshake. "Chocolate?" He nodded toward it.

"Yeah."

"She eating weird shit?"

"If dipping french fries in her chocolate milkshake is weird, then yeah."

"Moody, snappy, and crying a lot?"

"Definitely." Blaze frowned.

"Yep, she's on her period…. Hey, wait a fucking minute." Jared looked at Katrina and then to Blaze. "How the fuck is that possible? She's a vampire. We don't have periods."

Blaze cocked his eyebrow at him.

"Fuck, you know what I mean. Her, them, female vampires don't have periods."

"She does." Blaze frowned.

"Does Slade know?"

"Yeah, and he can't explain it. The only thing he can figure is what she was given to change her into a half-breed was tainted." Blaze glanced over when Katrina laughed. "She has human traits such as sleeping, her thing—"

"Period," Jared supplied.

"Yeah, that, and she doesn't heal like we do." Just talking about it made it all too real. "Even me changing her into a full blood and her feeding from me hasn't helped."

"Well, man, if anyone can figure it out, it's Slade. He is one fucking hell of a doctor." Jared opened his arms up for Tessa to step into them. "He'll figure it out."

"Figure what out?" Katrina finished off her shake, then tossed it in the trash. When Blaze and Jared shared a look, she frowned. "What?"

"As soon as Slade gives us the go-ahead and we can get out without having to worry that Tessa is going to eat a human, we need to go to dinner." Jared cut off what could be an uncomfortable conversation about women's monthlies.

"I'm not going to eat a human." Tessa smacked Jared.

"Damn, woman." Jared rubbed his chest. "Remember your strength."

Katrina laughed. Blaze loved to hear her do just that. She leaned against him, the movement natural. He didn't know what he would do if something happened to her. The thought both terrified and angered him.

******

After saying bye to Tessa and Jared, they walked to the elevator hand in hand. Once inside, she laughed again at the elevator music.

"Thank you," she said once the doors closed.

"For what?" Blaze pushed the button before looking down at her.

"For making sure I saw Tessa. Did you know?"

"No, not until I called while you were in the shower." Blaze once again held the door open so she could step out. "But don't say anything. They want to be the ones to tell everybody."

"I won't," Katrina replied, then frowned. "But I hope they told Adam. I didn't even think to ask."

"They did. Jared told me that he, Sloan, and Slade are the only ones who know." Blaze stopped, looking down at her. "You want to go to the house?"

"Sure," Katrina said, but then smelled something amazing.

"After we see what's cooking. Man, that smells good."

"But you just had a large shake and jumbo fries." Blaze laughed, following her toward the kitchen.

"I'm hungry." She smirked at him over her shoulder.

Katrina pushed open the door to find the kitchen packed. Everyone was there, even Sloan.

"What's going on?" Katrina asked Steve, who was standing next to the door with a bowl.

"Chili cook-off." Steve grinned, then pointed with his spoon. "Cowboy Ro there challenged Sid to an old-fashioned chili cook-off."

"It smells delish." Katrina took a big whiff.

"Okay, come and get it," Sid called out, his gaze then shifting to Ronan. "Let the best cook win."

Katrina enjoyed everyone's banter as she stood in line to get a taste of chili. She grabbed a small bowl and dipped from Ronan's pot. She glanced up at him and grinned. "You ever take that hat off?"

"A cowboy only takes his hat off for one thing." He winked at her.

"Watch it," Blaze warned with a glare.

"Sorry," Ronan replied, not sounding sorry at all.

She tasted the chili and moaned. "Holy crap that's good."

"No, it's not." Sid frowned at her and pointed to his pot. "This is the good stuff."

"Oh, I'm sure it is." She quickly got another bowl and dipped a little out and took a taste. "Oh wow, this is awesome. I mean absolutely awe inspiring. I've never—"

Sid glared at her over the pot. "When did you become such a smartass?"

"Since coming and hanging out with you guys," she shot back.

Thinking about that for a second, Sid nodded. "Sounds about right."

Once everyone had tasted the chilies, Sid tossed out paper and pens. "This is pot A, which stands for tastes like ass, and this is pot B"—he pointed to his pot—"which stands for the most beautiful chili you've ever tasted."

Once everyone voted, Sid handed the votes to Jill. "Would you please count the votes?" Sid leaned down toward her. "Count them twice so I don't have to call for a recount."

"I will," Jill replied, then began the count. It only took her a few minutes to finish. "The winner, after counting the votes twice by Sid's orders because he trusts no one, is… pot B!"

Everyone cheered as Sid beamed. He reached over and shook Ronan's hand. "This is still my kitchen, still my rules."

"Read it, learn it, and by God, do it!" everyone shouted at the same time.

"Fuck you, guys," Sid growled, his scowl turning into a grin. "Assholes."

Katrina went back for seconds and sat on Blaze's lap. Even though everyone was having a great time, there was a heaviness in the air. Slade was asked repeatedly about Tessa, his answer the usual, "she's recovering slowly." Every time Katrina heard him say it, she rolled her eyes; it still pissed her off even knowing that Tessa was okay.

"So is Ronan staying on here with you guys?" Katrina leaned back asking Blaze.

"Why? You like cowboys?" Blaze growled against her ear. "Careful with your answer. A man's life depends on it."

"No, I don't like cowboys." Katrina sighed. With a grin, she then said, "I obviously like overbearing Warriors who like to growl a lot."

"Then yes, he's staying on," Blaze said after a minute of thought.

"That's nice." Katrina stood up from his lap and looked over her shoulder at him. "Maybe he could show you how to use that whip."

Katrina laughed at the shocked look on his face as she walked away. How she loved baiting that man just to see that sexy "wait until I get you alone" look in his eyes.

Chapter 31

Katrina brushed paint on the wall, trying to decide if she liked the color or not. She'd thought Blaze was going to kill her at the hardware store, but she hadn't been able to make up her mind. Now seeing it on the wall, she was again second-guessing it. Glancing at Blaze, she figured he was in a foul mood and decided to just keep painting.

Before going to the hardware store, they had stopped for her appointment with Slade. He still didn't know why she had human traits and all he could tell them was to be careful. Well, that helped! She didn't blame Slade. Katrina knew it was whatever Bones had concocted. Jesus, she was lucky to be alive. She could live with the human trait stuff, well the periods sucked, but it was whatever. Blaze seemed to be taking it harder than she was.

Taking another peek at him, she watched as he rolled the paint on so hard it was defeating the purpose of painting because he was taking it right back off. After putting her paintbrush down, she stood and walked over to him.

"Why don't we take a break?" She took the roller from him and put it in the pan.

"You don't like this color either." Blaze didn't ask; it was a statement.

How in the hell did he read her so easily? "Well, ah… that's not the point, but I don't know if I do or not."

"Damn, woman." Blaze sighed, shaking his head.

"I know. I know." Katrina bit her lip and glanced at the wall. "I mean, I like it and then I don't. But it doesn't matter since you're just rolling it off with all that Warrior power."

Blaze looked at the wall and frowned, seeing she was right. Where he had painted, the old color showed through.

"What's wrong?" Katrina asked, taking his hand in hers. "And don't tell me nothing because ever since we left Slade's, you've been grouchy."

"I don't get grouchy," he grouched, then narrowed his eyes. "I get—"

"Grouchy." Katrina cocked her eyebrow.

"I don't like not having control," Blaze finally said.

"Shocker." She grinned, then swiftly wiped it from her face when he gave her a look. "Sorry."

"You should be a full blood, without any human traits. I think that something I did when I changed you—"

"Stop." Katrina wrapped her arms around him. "Nothing you did is the reason, and you know that. It's whatever I was given, and it is what it is. We will deal with it and I promise to not be such a bitch when it's my time of the month. Deal? Because we both know that's what this is all about," she teased, but her smile faded at the seriousness of his face.

Blaze was silent for a long time as he stared down at her. "I love you." He broke his silence with those three words Katrina had hoped to hear from him. "And I don't know what I would do if something happened to you."

"I love you, Blaze. So much. And I'm going to be fine because you won't let anything happen to me." She reached up and kissed him softly.

Blaze took her in his arms and returned her kiss possessively. The painting forgotten, they stood in their unfinished living room enjoying being in each other's arms. Nothing else mattered at that moment.

******

The phone ringing on the kitchen table was being ignored. Blaze heard it but knew whoever it was would leave a message or call back. He was busy. It stopped only to start again. Pulling his mouth away from hers was not easy when he wanted to continue tasting her.

"Dammit," Blaze cursed.

"Tell them to go away," Katrina whispered, trying to take his mouth again.

"I better get it." He kissed her quickly as the phone stopped, then started again. "Shit!"

"The life of a Warrior." She sighed dramatically.

Blaze laughed as he headed for the phone, but his eyes caught something outside. A strange feeling came over him as his eyes adjusted to the person in front of his house. Breaker sat on his motorcycle across the street. That couldn't fucking be. Blaze quickened his pace to get a hold of the motherfucker until he watched him raise his hand.

Stopping Blaze saw the phone, and then Breaker smiled with a wave. Blaze turned, and with a speed that was unseen by the human eye, he ran and grabbed Katrina who screamed in surprise. He had almost made it out the back of the house before the explosion hit. He used his body to shield Katrina the best he could.

Fire surrounded them, but the only thing that touched Blaze was the debris. They had hit the ground hard, the power of the explosion knocking them flat. He got to his feet with Katrina in his arms taking a second to glance at her. She was quiet with her eyes closed.

"Fuck!" He moved further away from the heat. His eyes searching behind him for any sign of the bastard, but he couldn't see through the fire.

Finding a safe place, he laid Katrina down to check for any wounds. "Katrina." A few burns littered her arms, but other than that, there was no obvious damage to her body. Once again, he scanned the area for danger. The sound of sirens was coming close. With the fire department down the road, he was sure they'd heard that fucking blast. His ears were ringing like a motherfucker. "Katrina! Goddammit! Please wake up."

He checked his pocket for his phone and then remembered he'd never picked it up. "Fuck!" He tried again to get her to wake up, but still, her eyes remained closed. The burns on her arms were blistering, and he didn't know what in the fuck to do. The rage and helplessness building inside him was too much. Leaning his head back, he roared his pain.

Feeling a hand on his arm, he snapped his head back down, his chest heaving, to see Katrina looking at him.

"I'm okay." She touched her head before her eyes focused on her arm. "I think."

"I'm going to get you to Slade." He started to pick her up but heard motorcycles roaring toward them. He stood, putting himself between any danger and Katrina. Those motherfuckers wanted to dance, he was ready. His relief was swift when he saw that it wasn't the Iron Drakes, but his brothers.

They rode straight past the burning house toward him and Katrina. Slade was off his bike first, running toward them and sliding down next to Katrina.

"Where are you hurt?" Slade looked at her arms and frowned, then glanced toward Duncan. "We're going to put her in your car and get her back to the compound. I have nothing with me for these burns."

Picking her up carefully, Blaze followed Duncan toward the car. "She also got knocked out. It must have been when we fell."

"Why the hell aren't you answering your fucking phone?" Sloan bitched, his eyes black with anger. "An informant called saying the Drakes were out, and we knew they were going to strike before we had a chance to come after them. When you didn't answer, we figured the worst and headed this way."

"I didn't have a fucking chance to answer my fucking phone. I saw that bastard Breaker sitting out in front of our goddamn house holding his fucking phone and knew if I didn't get her out of there, we wouldn't be having this conversation right now." Blaze glanced down to make sure he wasn't jarring Katrina too much as he moved closer to Duncan's car. "Why in the fuck is he out? And how in the hell did he know where I lived?"

"The DA cut them a deal." Sloan sneered. "Motherfucker cut them a deal, which I warned the mayor could possibly happen. And if I could guess, Nico, who I'm sure knows when and where every Warrior takes a shit, gave him your address."

"I told you," Katrina whispered against his chest, but they all heard her.

Blaze didn't say anything; his rage was too deep. The police as well as the fire trucks and paramedics were pulling in. He ignored the cops' questions as well as the paramedics offering help. He didn't even look at his smoldering house. No, he looked straight ahead, planning deaths, a lot of deaths.

Once inside the car, Blaze held her tightly against him. He knew she was in pain and it was killing him.

"Are you hurt?" Katrina asked, her eyes searching his.

Blaze took a minute to answer; he actually had to glance away from her and look out the window. There she was with burns, possibly a concussion, yet she was asking him if he was hurt. "I'm fine," he finally got control enough to say. "Let's worry about you."

Once at the compound, Blaze rushed inside with Katrina and followed Slade to his office. Jill was already there waiting, a worried frown on her face. Slade gave instructions on what he needed, and Jill got busy. Blaze hated it, but he laid her on the table.

He stood by her side as Slade and Jill cleaned her burns. Katrina tried to be brave, but it was too much. Tears ran down her cheeks, but she didn't cry out. She even looked at him repeatedly to assure him she was okay.

The longer her pain went on, the more the rage built inside him. His control was close to snapping. Once she was wrapped up, he sat next to her. "Better?"

"Yes." Katrina nodded. "I'm just really tired."

His concerned gaze shot to Slade, who immediately examined Katrina's eyes and started questioning her.

"Do you have a headache or pain in your neck?" He gently felt her head and then moved to her neck.

"No."

"Does any of this hurt?" He pushed and poked. "Do you have double vision?"

"Nope and nope," Katrina replied, sleepily.

"I don't think she has a concussion, but I'd like to keep her here for a few hours to keep an eye on her if that's okay." Slade glanced at Blaze.

"Absolutely." Blaze didn't even look at Slade but continued to stare down at the now sleeping Katrina.

"She's going to be fine," Slade reassured him. "She may have some scarring, but not too bad."

A red haze fell over his eyes as he looked at her bandaged arms. "Listen, I need to talk to Sloan for a minute."

"No problem." Slade nodded, busy cleaning up with Jill. "We're going to stay here with her."

Blaze leaned down and pressed his lips to her forehead, then stared for a second longer before turning and walking out of the room. He headed down the hallway opposite Sloan's office and out the door. Taking off in a run, he rounded the corner to see Sid's bike. With quick strides, he jumped on and took off, not even looking to see if traffic was coming.

Today this ended. Today people would die, and she would be safe.

Chapter 32

Katrina woke in a panic. Her eyes searched frantically before she sat straight up then felt the pain in her arms. With a hiss, she slowed her movements.

"Hey, easy." Jill stood from Slade's desk.

"Where's Blaze?" Katrina glanced around, not seeing him anywhere.

"He went to see Sloan," Jill replied, trying to get her to lie back down. "Come on, Katrina. Slade doesn't want you up yet."

Katrina was off the table and heading out the door. She knew Blaze wouldn't have left her to see Sloan. She knew exactly what he was doing: going after Breaker and her father. As she rushed down the hallway, with Jill following close behind cursing, she called upon help.

Checking the kitchen, she only saw Steve, who jumped when the door flew open. "Hey, how you…?"

She rushed back out and continued her search. Adam and Angelina were coming down the stairs.

"Where's Blaze?" Katrina met them at the bottom.

"What's going on?" Steve popped the last piece of his sandwich in his mouth.

"She's looking for Blaze, who said he was going to meet with Sloan." Jill frowned. "And she's supposed to be lying down."

"Why? What's going on?" Adam glanced away from Jill to Katrina.

"He's going after my father and I seriously doubt anyone's with him." She was proven right when the Warriors started to file out of Sloan's office. The only one missing was Blaze. She turned pleading eyes to Adam. "Please."

Adam thought for a minute, his eyes searching hers. "He just left with the DA, heading to six-fifty Melbourne Street."

"What in the hell are you doing up?" Slade called out after her, but she continued out the door and down the steps.

"Dammit, Katrina." Sloan's voice was next. "Wait a fucking minute."

She knew even a minute was too much. She didn't have a minute and knowing her father, neither did Blaze.

Aware she was being rushed, she called out. Within seconds, she was cut off from the Warriors by hundreds of birds. She turned to make sure her barrier was effective.

"Neat trick." Ronan's twang came from behind her.

Katrina ignored him, hearing Sloan shouting for her. "Are you going to stop me from going?" She knew Adam had filled them in on what was going on. "If you promise not to stop me, I will disperse the birds."

When Sloan was silent, she cursed. She knew it was better for them to come, but not necessary. Her father wanted her; she could use herself to get Blaze away and then hopefully he could save her. What a fucking mess.

"I know them, Sloan. I've been right when you've been wrong about the Drakes," Katrina shouted in frustration.

"Don't think that's going to swing him your way." Ronan was still staring at the birds.

"Shut it," Katrina growled, waiting for Sloan's answer.

"How do you know he's there, Katrina?" Sloan finally responded with a question.

"I just know, dammit." She didn't care if they believed her; she just needed him to agree to help and let her go. Men could be such a pain in the ass. Warriors were insufferable.

******

Blaze easily left the compound with no one the wiser. Shit was going to go down, and he didn't want to bring his brothers in. Fear of the past rode him hard, that and maybe he just wanted the sweet taste of revenge to be his own.

He pulled up to the courthouse and waited. He didn't have to wait long before the piece-of-shit Nico exited, heading for his car. With the ease of a panther, Blaze walked up and slid into the passenger seat at the same time Nico slid into the driver seat.

Blaze relished the fear pulsating from Nico at the intrusion.

"This is exactly what you're going to do." Blaze knew his eyes were flame-red. He also knew how fucking evil he looked, but he didn't give a shit. "You're going to drive out of this parking lot like we are old friends."

"What do you want?" Nico's hands shook as he started the car.

"Now why do dumb fucks who piss me off ask me that?" Blaze hissed. "Drive."

Once on the road, Blaze grabbed the wheel and maneuvered them to the side of the road. "What do you want?" Nico sounded scared, his tough DA antics long gone.

"You're going to take me to your boss." Blaze leaned toward him, his voice hard and expression fierce; he was not taking any bullshit.

"My boss?" Nico looked confused.

"Samuel Drake, asshole." Blaze slammed Nico's head against the steering wheel. "Does that help ring a fucking bell?"

"He's not my boss." Nico's nice, neat slicked-back hair was now hanging in his face.

Blaze slammed him again, harder this time. "Wrong answer."

"Okay!" Nico cried. "Okay, I'll take you."

"Fuck yeah, you will." Blaze sat back in the seat. "Now, wasn't that easy, Nico? Just do what I tell you and you might live through this. Though it's highly unlikely."

Blaze felt satisfaction in Nico's sissy sniffs as he whimpered in fear. He'd lied; Nico wasn't getting out of this alive.

"How much further?" Blaze asked, looking around.

Nico pulled down a side street. "It's the house at the end of the road."

"You make frequent visits, Nico?" Blaze ordered him to pull over behind a van, which Nico did quickly. "Don't fucking lie to me."

"I do." Nico wouldn't even look at him. "He threatened my

family, my wife and kids. I had to do what I did."

"Bullshit," Blaze hissed. "You could have come to us for protection, and you know it. The money is what put your family in danger, you piece of shit."

Nico didn't say anything, just whimpered pathetically.

"Do they have cameras?" Blaze asked, his eyes searching the area once again. "Do they have fucking cameras set up here?"

"No, not… not yet," Nico sputtered. "They just moved in since you burned their main place down."

Blaze smiled, no humor involved. "Okay, this is the end of the road for you, Nico."

"What?" Nico did look at him this time. "But you said if I listened to you, I'd live."

"I lied." Blaze punched Nico in the face, knocking him out instantly. He would let him live for the moment. "Pussy," Blaze spat in disgust. Getting out of the car, he pulled Nico out the passenger side by the hair. Popping the trunk, he shoved him inside then looked around and shifted. Rushing around, he climbed into the car and calmed himself.

Angling the rearview mirror, he looked at himself and grimaced. He hated to shift. Hated to see himself as someone he wasn't, especially this fucker. Slicking back his hair, he double-checked himself to make sure he was ready. After snapping the mirror back in place, he put the car in drive and pulled out, heading toward revenge.

The whole time he drove down the street, he remained vigilant, searching. It didn't even look like the fuckers were worried about anything, and that pissed him off. They would soon regret that. Once parked, he got out of the car and walked up the sidewalk.

"What the fuck do you want?" Blaze turned to see a dumb fuck glaring at him, trying to act like a badass.

"I need to see Samuel." Blaze kept his cool, calming his hand from shooting fire and setting the fucker ablaze.

"He's busy." The man smirked, not moving.

Blaze tried to think and act like Nico, but fuck, that wasn't easy. He turned to leave, but looked at his name patch. "Okay, I'll let him know that Stubs didn't feel that information on his daughter, Kat, was important enough to interrupt."

"Ah, wait." The asshole no longer sounded sure of himself. Blaze stopped and turned back around. "Come on, he should be done by now."

"Oh, good." Blaze followed the dick. "So how did you get the name Stubs? The ladies give you that name?"

"Watch it!" The man turned, his nostrils flaring with anger. "After you're done here, it will be nothing for me to slit your fucking throat."

"Sorry," Blaze said, trying to sound sincere. He must have done a good job because the man turned and led him into the house.

The first thing he saw was a woman lying on a pool table being fucked by Samuel Drake. Her tits bounced with each ram of his dick. Her moans and cries sounded like a bad porn flick. There were five members standing around with their dicks out jacking off, watching their president fuck the hell out of her.

Samuel looked his way and smiled, but then turned his attention back to the woman. "This is some fine pussy, boys." He grunted, then reached out with both hands, grabbing her heavy tits. "I'm going to fuck these next. Breaker, you can fuck her while I do that."

"Sure can, boss." Breaker rubbed his cock harder and faster. "I'll fuck her good."

"Boys, move out of the way so our good DA can get a clear view." Samuel grunted and laughed at the same time. "He likes watching. Don't ya, Nico?"

Blaze wasn't sure how Nico would have answered that so he kept quiet. His gaze roamed casually to check his situation just in case he had to fight himself out of there. There were girls in all different states of undress lying around, some sucking cock, others being felt up and fucked. His anger hit hard thinking of Katrina growing up in a place like this. White powder was lined up on tables in easy access to snort while needles lay around as if it were the norm.

He heard Samuel shout his release, making a big production of coming. The more Blaze saw, the angrier he became. To think of anyone, let alone Katrina, growing up with this sick fuck was enough to make him lose his shit.

"Goddamn, Breaker, that blow is some fucking good shit. Makes me horny as fuck." Samuel leaned down and snorted another line before walking toward Blaze.

"Only the best for you, boss," Breaker said, as he started to fuck the woman. She seemed to be enjoying it so Blaze wasn't too concerned for her.

"Almost good enough I might fuck you, Nico," Samuel said, then laughed. "Ah, man, I'm just fuckin' with ya. I have to be really fucked up to stick my dick in a man's ass. You want to take a turn with Tina? How about some snort?"

"I'm good, but thanks." Blaze was so close, all he had to do was reach out and snap his fucking neck, but he wouldn't, yet.

"How's that wife of yours?" Samuel put his arm around Blaze and walked him to the table next to the pool table and the fucking. "Now that's a fine piece of ass. I was kinda sorry you've been doing such a good job for us. I really wanted to get to know her better."

That put a new light on things with Nico. Blaze had thought he had been lying about threats to his family. He pushed that to the back of his mind; he'd deal with that later. "I've got some information on your daughter."

"Nico, I don't want information. I want her." Samuel was no longer the nice guy offering him sex and drugs. "Isn't that right, Breaker?"

"Fuck yeah," Breaker answered as he rammed into the woman repeatedly.

"Now, Nico, that's how you fuck a woman." Samuel watched with lust in his eyes. Then the sick fuck said something that almost had Blaze blowing his cover. "Kat sure will look mighty fine on that table, won't she, boys?"

Whistles and shouts filled the air. The motherfucker would put his own daughter in place of that whore. Well, Blaze knew for damn certain none of those fuckers would live for that to ever happen.

Blaze had purposely sat on the side of the table that allowed him to see everyone. He had already counted eleven fuckers who were going to die and six females who had better take cover. He had just enough bullets to finish them off.

"So what information do you have on Kat, Nico? Or should

I say, Warrior?" Samuel asked, finally taking his eyes off Breaker fucking their whore.

Blaze went for his gun, but was instantly stopped as silver chains fell on him. Fighting their hold, he looked up to see a fucker grinning down at him. They had set a trap and he had walked right fucking into it again. Fuck! This time he would come out on top—as soon as he got out of those fucking chains.

Samuel stood from the table and leaned in Blaze's face. "So glad to have you in my home since you torched my last one." Samuel let loose with his fist, punching Blaze in the face. "Damn, that felt good!"

Blaze kept his eyes on Samuel, not even acknowledging that he'd been hit.

"You Warriors didn't think you were the only one collecting information, did you? I knew the chance of you coming in as one of my men was high since you're a shifter. Actually, I didn't even think about Nico, good one. But as soon as Nico didn't take a snort or go for Tina's wet pussy, I knew it was you." Samuel punched him again.

"That all you got, old man?" Blaze shifted into himself, licking the blood from his own lip.

"Oh, aren't you in for a surprise." Samuel's eyes narrowed in wicked delight. "I think you've bitten off more than you can chew, boy."

Chapter 33

"Get rid of these fucking birds, Katrina, and you got a deal," Sloan shouted, his tone angrier than she had ever heard it.

"Don't say that then try to stop me," Katrina added with a frown.

"Katrina!" Sloan's yell had her immediately releasing the bird wall.

The Warriors watched as the birds flew up in the air and hovered, as if waiting for her next command.

"If one of those fuckers shits on me, I'm going to be pissed." Sid glared at her, then back to the birds.

"You and I are going to have a long talk after this is over," Sloan warned as he passed. They all ran to their bikes, leaving her behind.

"Come on." Ronan grabbed her hand, taking her toward a pickup truck.

Jumping in, Katrina held on as Ronan followed the Warriors, who seemed to know exactly where in the hell they were going. Ronan even followed them up on curbs to avoid traffic, taking out mailboxes while blaring his horn.

"So how in the hell do you do that with the birds?" Ronan asked as he took out another mailbox, then jumped the curb back onto the road.

"I don't know." Katrina held on tightly, watching the traffic light turn red. Then she squeezed her eyes shut when he blew right through it. Realizing they were still moving, she opened them and sighed in relief. "We just understand each other."

"So you're like a bird whisper?" Ronan glanced over at her with a grin.

"Something like that." Katrina kept her eyes on the road. This man was crazy behind the wheel. Then again, the Warriors weren't making it easy for them to follow.

Finally, they came to a skidding stop behind the Warriors in an abandoned lot. Katrina hopped out, running toward them as Sloan shouted orders.

"That won't work," Katrina said, listening intently. "All that is going to do is cause a shootout. Let me go in."

Sloan cursed, looking toward Adam. "Tell her!"

"What?" Panic rose to her throat, choking her. "Tell me what?"

"They got him." Adam glanced away from her. "And—"

That was all Katrina had to hear. She looked down the street knowing it was the house at the end, where Samuel Drake always set up house. Always at the end of a fucking road away from prying eyes. "Read me and don't make a move until I say so," she told Adam before taking a step.

"Just hold on a fucking minute." Sloan grabbed her arm, which she jerked away.

"No, you haven't listened to a word I've said about the Iron Drakes." Katrina looked at them all. "I know them. I am them, dammit!"

Sloan seethed, his nostrils flaring in anger and frustration. "What's your plan?"

"I walk in and—"

"No." Sloan shook his head. "Not alone you won't."

"If a Warrior goes in with me, they'll know more of you are out there. This has to be an element of surprise. Take out the ones outside and wait. Plus I won't be alone," Katrina said as ten large coyotes came out of the shadows and surrounded her.

Sloan cocked his eyebrow, then seemed to look at her differently. "Go on. I'm listening, not agreeing, but listening."

Damn. That was all she had, and her hesitation clued Sloan

in to that very fact.

******

Katrina walked down the street slowly to give the Warriors time to get in place and quietly take out the men she knew her father had stationed around. One thing about her father was he didn't defer from his routines. When her father saw her, he wouldn't even think of anything else; it would give the Warriors the upper hand. Plus, he didn't think anyone could outsmart him, but she *was* her father's daughter.

Katrina knew she had been spotted, but no one stopped her as she walked up the sidewalk to the front of the house. This told her that they had been given orders to let her enter the house without being stopped.

She reached out and opened the front door. She hoped it would be the last time she had to call upon Kat. She was going to need her for this. As her eyes adjusted, she realized she'd walked into one of her father's famous fuck fests.

"Hey, Dad," Katrina said as the coyotes formed a barrier between her and the Iron Drakes.

"Kat, what a pleasant surprise. We were just talking about you." If her father was shocked at seeing her waltz in, he hid it well.

"I see your fuck fest is still going strong and the drugs still flow freely." Katrina glanced around with a cocked eyebrow, seeing Tina lying naked on the pool table, her legs spread wide. "And Tina is still a slut."

"Now, Kat." Samuel frowned. "That's no way to talk about Tina."

Katrina gave a snort as she searched, trying not to show any signs of emotion for her father to feed from. Blaze sat cut and bleeding in a chair with silver chains across him.

Katrina's eyes shot to her father's. "You know that's a federal crime? He's a Warrior. What happened to your rule of keeping your noses clean where cops are concerned? Or is that just for the cops who are in your pocket and on your payroll?"

"Oh, baby girl, stop trying to act so tough. We both know you're crying inside seeing him like this. He is *your* Warrior, isn't he?" Samuel leaned down to look at Blaze. "She acted like this with her mother, you know. Trying to act all tough like it didn't bother her."

Katrina forced back her scream when her father stood up straight, then slammed his elbow across Blaze's already brutalized face. Then watched her closely.

"Damn, girl. They toughened you up some." Samuel's evil laugh filled the room, followed by the laughter of the Drakes standing around watching. "Why don't you come here and give your good old dad a hug?"

The coyotes surrounding her growled low as Samuel took a step toward her. They suddenly sat, then lay down, stretching out. Katrina tried to get them to get back up, but they remained on the floor, one even rolling on its side.

"I got powers too, girl." Samuel continued toward her. "I've gotten pretty good at them too. You may be able to block my power, but they can't."

She could feel Adam in her head but wanted them to wait. It wasn't time. Her eyes shifted to Blaze, who glared at her through the blood dripping down his face. She watched him struggle with the chains.

"Let him go." Katrina nodded toward Blaze, but still looked at her father. "You have what you want."

"You think I'm that goddamn stupid?" Her father turned into the lunatic she knew he was. He reached her, grabbing her by the throat and pushing her against the wall. "You better than anyone should know I'm not stupid, girl." His spit hit her in the face and she flinched away.

"Let her go!" Blaze's voice was even, without pain.

Samuel still held her neck, but turned toward Blaze. She could hear Adam in her head, but continued to hold them off. Blaze was defenseless, and she let them know as much. She had to get him loose first.

"Let her go?" Samuel laughed, squeezing her neck tighter.

She fought his hands, but his grip was too tight. "Let her go, he says."

The men laughed, leaning around like they were watching a show and enjoying it; their guns were also out as if expecting trouble.

"Oh, I'll let her go," Samuel said, then turned his attention back to Katrina. "As soon as she tells me how many Warriors are outside my house right now."

Katrina tried to speak, but he was squeezing too tightly. "None," she managed to gasp. "Just me."

"You lying bitch. Didn't I just tell you I wasn't stupid? I know these Warriors and I know they won't let one of their own go without a fight." He picked her up, still holding her throat. She grasped his hands, trying to take the pressure off. "You brought this down on my house and you're going to fucking pay dearly. What your mother went through is nothing compared to what I have planned for you."

Blaze's roar of outrage gave her courage. Letting go of his wrist, she slashed out her hand, her fingers slicing him across the face. His shocked expression turned to rage. Releasing one hand from her neck, he touched the wound and looked at the blood.

"You bitch," he snarled. Then he flung her across the room toward Breaker.

Before hitting the ground, she prayed that Adam, who was still reading her, caught on that they did not heal, just like her. His wound did not immediately close. Once she'd hit the ground, she slid, banging into the leg of the pool table. She was grabbed by the leg, dragged, and picked up by Breaker, who slammed her on the pool table.

She fought with everything she had, but he was too strong. She could hear Blaze's roar of rage, the laughter of the men, and her father's curses. Breaker grabbed her bandaged arm and squeezed, making her scream in agony.

"Stop!" her father commanded. Everyone went silent, and Breaker let go of her arm. Her father grabbed a nasty rag and held it to his face. "You will pay for this. Take care of her, Breaker, while I take care of this bastard." He removed the rag, the scratches red and angry. Blood oozed down his face as he nodded toward Blaze. Four men headed toward Blaze and her father.

Her eyes met Blaze's for a brief second, before his eyes shifted quickly toward the floor. Her gaze followed to see the coyotes starting to move. Her father's lack of concentration was releasing them and he hadn't realized it.

"I'll make sure she pays." Breaker grabbed Katrina's face, holding it still as he leaned down to lick her cheek. "And I can't wait."

"Get off me!" Katrina sneered at Breaker, still trying to kick her way free. She was not going down without a fight.

"You'll never touch me again. I'll kill myself first, you son of a bitch."

"You'll regret that, Kat." Breaker's hands tightened at his side. "I will make sure you will regret those words."

"Fuck you." Katrina spat in his face, her anger getting the best of her. "I'm not afraid of you."

Breaker reared back and smacked her across the cheek. "Well, I guess I'll have to make sure to change that," Breaker growled, and acted like he was going to smack her again, making her flinch. "Not scared, huh? Lying bitch."

"Better to be a lying bitch than my daddy's bitch like you are," Katrina said with a smirk. "How does it feel to bend over for Samuel Drake?"

"You're going to regret that little comment when I bend you over this pool table." Breaker threatened grabbing for her, the sound of Blaze breaking free stopped him.

Chapter 34

Blaze was going to spank her ass good once this was over, if they survived it. What the fuck did she think she was doing showing up there? Fear for her rushed through his body as she baited her father. She finally spotted him, but her eyes quickly shifted away.

Her father got up and leaned in his face. He saw his mouth moving, but paid no attention to what he was saying. His focus was Katrina and how in the hell he was going to get her out of there unhurt. The elbow to his face only pissed him off more.

Each time the bastard hit him, the more determined Blaze became. He wondered how in the fuck Katrina had known he was there and how she got away from the compound without any of the Warriors knowing, unless.... His eyes searched out the windows, but saw nothing. Fuck! He was helpless and she was in danger. The only comforting thing in this whole fucked-up mess was the coyotes in front of her, separating her from harm.

At least, until they lay down at her feet. He then remembered her warning about her father being able to control moods. Shit! He shook his head, trying to clear the dripping blood out of his vision. His hands were held immobile by the chains. One thing Blaze could take was a beating. What they were doing to him was nothing he hadn't had done before. He just needed to wait for that one chance to strike, but now with Katrina in the room, the waiting was done. He had to act fast.

Seeing Samuel push Katrina up against the wall had Blaze working his power. He needed to focus, but dammit, seeing the bastard's hands on her was sending him into a killing rage.

"Let her go!" he shouted as he watched him pick her up by the throat. To his pride and horror, Katrina slashed out, clawing him in the face.

Seeing her fly through the air then hit the floor hard before slamming into the pool table was more than he could take. No one was paying attention to him; instead, they were watching Katrina getting abused and enjoying it. Everyone would die for that. He glanced down to see the fire sparking from his hands in spite of the silver chains. The silver not only inhibited his movement, but dimmed his power. It was a fight, but he felt his power growing stronger.

He glanced over to see Katrina being dragged from under the pool table by Breaker, who slammed her on top of it. She fought but wasn't strong enough. The movement of the coyotes caught his attention; they were coming out of her father's control. His eyes met Katrina's briefly while her father screamed orders. Fire formed in his hands like an inferno when Breaker slapped Katrina across the face.

Breaker's inhuman scream sent him into action. With a roar of his own, his whole body shot into flames and the chains broke, scattering everywhere. Once free, he stood and controlled the fire. No way would he take them out with it. He wanted his fucking hands on them; maybe not all of them, but two of them would definitely die by his hands.

Chaos ensued as Warriors rushed in and the coyotes, he was sure on Katrina's command, took down Samuel Drake.

Reaching for the gun the dicks hadn't even searched him for, Blaze, who was a dead shot, ended the lives of the three bastards rushing him. He heard a cracking noise in time to see Breaker snap a pool cue in half and hold it to Katrina's throat. He used her body as a shield.

"Put the gun down," Breaker commanded. "Or this will go in her throat like butter."

When Blaze didn't move, Breaker pushed the stick in the side of Katrina's neck.

"Don't test me, Warrior."

Blaze dropped the gun, his eyes never leaving Breaker.

"Call them fucking things off." He pushed the stick deeper until Katrina did as he said.

Her father lay moaning and screaming as he rolled around.

"So this is how the badass Breaker takes care of business? Hiding behind a woman." Blaze glared at him. "You're as good as dead if that stick goes in any deeper."

No one moved, waiting to see what Breaker was going to do. He pulled the stick away from her neck and shoved her away, tossing the stick at her. "This should be fun." Breaker cracked his knuckles.

"I don't give a fuck what happens, he's mine and do not interfere," Blaze warned the other Warriors as he swiped blood from his face. "He's mine."

"No, fucker." Breaker rushed him. "You're mine!"

Both men roared as they collided, the force knocking them both off balance and out the window. Blaze turned, pulling the bastard underneath him. It was only a first-story fall, but Blaze never ended on the bottom with the enemy on top.

As they hit, he landed punches, one after another. His rage knew no limit. The memory of Breaker smacking Katrina played repeatedly in his mind. Picking Breaker up, he shoved him back, hard.

"Come on, fucker, give me a fight," Blaze taunted, wanting nothing more than to prolong this bastard's suffering. "I'll even give you a free shot."

Breaker wiped the blood from his face and quickly took a swing at Blaze, who didn't even block. He took the hit and smiled.

"You hit like a bitch!" he sneered, thrusting his foot out and kicking Breaker across the yard. "Let's see if you die like one too."

Breaker rolled to his feet, but remained bent over. Blaze was already healing from his wounds, which were almost closed, but Breaker's wounds bled freely, and Blaze knew he had broken ribs from the kick.

"Not healing very well, are you?" Blaze smirked, seeing Breaker's worried frown.

Breaker looked up, hate filling his eyes. "You know, Warrior. Whenever you look at Kat, whenever you stick your dick in her, know I was there first."

Blaze flew at him in a blur of fury. He was relentless with the beating he delivered to the bastard who'd dared lay a hand on what belonged to him. No one stopped him, no one dared. Before delivering the killing blow, Blaze stopped and leaned close so the last words Breaker would ever hear came from him and him alone.

"And I will make sure you are wiped from her memory, motherfucker." Blaze relished the fear reflected in the bastard's eyes before he took his head in a headlock and gave a final death twist. He dropped his dead body immediately and walked away, already forgotten. His eyes went straight to the window to see Katrina staring out. He headed her way, determined that she forget the bastard, starting immediately.

He reached the window they had busted through. His hand reached in to touch her battered face. "What in the hell were you thinking?"

Katrina squeezed her eyes shut; a single tear escaped. "I was thinking of saving you."

Careful of the broken window, Blaze pulled her close. "Remind me to bust your ass for this stunt later," he whispered, his eyes searching to make sure there was no danger, only to fall on her father, who lay whimpering on the ground.

The Warriors were searching the area, making sure everyone was dead and collecting the ones who weren't. Ronan glanced his way.

"Take her out." Blaze let go of Katrina and climbed in through the window.

"Blaze, no." Katrina held tight.

"You don't need to see this." Blaze looked down at her. "Trust me."

It took her a minute, but she gave in, looking tired of the fight. Ronan took her, leading her away and around her father.

"Kat, where are you going?" Samuel lay on his back, holding his side, which was bleeding profusely from all the bites and claw marks from the coyotes. "Kat! I'm your father. You can't leave me like this, goddammit! Kat!"

"Shut the fuck up." Blaze nudged his bleeding side with his boot. He waited until Katrina was out the door. He was proud that she had kept her emotions in check and let him handle the situation without a word.

"Kat is my fucking daughter," Samuel hissed, then began coughing, blood seeping out of the corner of his mouth. "The ungrateful bitch belongs to me."

Blaze knelt. Grabbing Samuel by the front of the shirt, he pulled him up, ignoring his howl of pain. "Where is your son?"

"What?" Samuel looked at him, surprised. "My son? My son is dead to me. Fucker up and took off, the coward."

For some reason Blaze believed him, but felt he needed to question further. Katrina's brother could be a threat to her, and that shit just wouldn't do. He planned to eradicate all threats directed toward Katrina, even if it took him forever. "Why did he take off?"

"Cause he's a fucking pussy, that's why." Samuel spat more blood. "He couldn't follow orders. He couldn't even bring Katrina in when he had her. No, the damn pussy kept the boys from bringing her in. Killed one of my men over her. She wouldn't listen and started fighting them, so they fought back and he killed Sami, then let her go."

Blaze gazed toward the door where Katrina had left, wondering if she knew any of this information. He felt Samuel grab his leg and looked down.

"Let me go and I swear you'll never hear from me again," Samuel pleaded, his eyes wide with pain.

Blaze just stared at the man he had much hatred for. "You're going to die today, Samuel Drake." Blaze narrowed his eyes. Then he looked up at the coyotes who had their heads cocked, but eyes on him. "Not by my hand, but by my doing. And you are going to die knowing that her name is not Kat, but Katrina soon-to-be Bateman. She does not belong to you, because she is mine. Now go to hell, where you belong."

Blaze stood and took a step backward. The coyotes took their eyes off him to stare behind him before growling down at Samuel.

"Fuck you!" Samuel screamed his rage. "She is nothing, you hear me. Just like her fucking mother. Nothing!"

Turning, Blaze saw Katrina staring at her father through the broken window. With a curse, he stepped in front of her father so she couldn't watch what was happening as the coyotes tore into him. He continued forward, drawing her eyes to him. She stepped back and he climbed out the window and took her into his arms.

"Will you ever listen?" he growled, putting one of her ears

against his chest and his hand over her other so she couldn't hear her father's dying curses of her.

******

Katrina held him tight, her body shivering as her emotions hit her at once. It was truly over.

"Why in the hell didn't you take her away from here?" Blaze bellowed at Ronan.

"Well, short of knocking her out, that wasn't happening." Ronan, who stood close, shrugged. "And I don't hit women."

"Jesus!" Blaze cursed, leading her away from the house. "And how in the fuck did she end up being here alone?" Blaze stopped in front of Sloan.

Katrina pulled away from him. "It was my plan, Blaze."

"Oh, is that so?" Blaze glared down at her, then back to Sloan.

"And she was right." Sloan nodded toward the wooded area around the house where Damon, Sid, and Jax were pulling dead Iron Drake members from the shadows. "He had this place staked out. He knew you were coming and wanted to make damn sure you stayed. If we had rushed in here, this ending would have been different."

Blaze still didn't look happy; he looked deadly with dried blood on his face, his hair plastered and sticky.

"As much as it pains me, her plan was better than ours and we should have listened to her from the start. If we had, today may not have happened," Sloan said, ignoring Katrina's grin. "And by the way, who in the fuck gave you permission to go out on this little adventure alone?"

"Don't even start with me," Blaze growled, pulling Katrina with him. "I'm getting her out of here now. I don't want to hear shit about what I did. I'm still pissed you all let her walk in here alone."

"She was not alone," Sloan responded as the blood-covered coyotes walked past them all and headed toward the woods. One stopped next to Katrina, then bowed its head before following the rest. "Holy shit, I need a fucking vacation. Fucking outlaw MCs, a wall of birds and coyotes… Jesus."

Katrina laughed at Sloan's words, then started to cry. Blaze picked her up and carried her down the sidewalk and out onto the street.

"You're safe, Katrina. You will always be safe with me," he vowed, holding her close.

"I heard what he said about my brother," Katrina said, her words muffled into his chest.

"I'll find him," Blaze promised, holding her tighter. "And if he's a threat, I will kill him."

"I remember now, I didn't at the time, but he's the reason I was able to get away that day." She looked up at him, her eyes swirling with confusion. "But why, when he did nothing to help our mother?"

"I don't know, Katrina." Blaze frowned, placing his chin on the top of her head. "I wish I did because I know this is going to haunt you, but I promise I will find your brother so you can ask him that question yourself. You will have closure, one day."

Katrina thought about what he said and was about to tell him no. She didn't need to know, but that would be a lie. He was her blood and as far as she knew, her last living relative. Even with everything that had happened, she realized how very lucky she was. The man holding her in his arms was the only family she would ever need; she was about to tell him just that, but a distant voice drew her attention.

"Help!" A muffled scream reached her ears.

"What was that?" Katrina looked up at Blaze, sniffling.

"Ah, what?" Blaze looked down at her, then glanced toward a car with a frown.

"I could have sworn I heard someone yell help." Katrina frowned then heard it again.

"Oh, that," Blaze said, but kept on walking. "The DA's in the trunk of the car."

"And you're leaving him in there." Katrina looked over his shoulder to see the car moving as loud thumps came from it.

"Yes," Blaze replied, then grinned down at her. "I am. I'll let Sloan or somebody know he's in there. Tomorrow."

As if Nico heard him, the screaming and thumping grew louder. Katrina shrugged and laid her head against Blaze's chest, deciding then and there that she wouldn't doubt him again. He was a man who could keep her safe and she was more than willing to let him. She was done being afraid and she was done being scared, but she was definitely ready to have someone to lean on. It felt so very right.

Chapter 35

The bar was busy, which was fine with Katrina. She liked to keep busy when she wasn't with Blaze. Things had settled into a nice routine since that day a week ago. Her face was finally healed and had healed quicker than before, which made Slade happy. He thought that maybe her continued feeding from Blaze would make her stronger. Looking toward the door again, she frowned. Blaze should have been there by now.

Tonight Jared and Tessa were announcing their news. Tessa had finally been cleared and was not in any danger of eating humans as Jared liked to joke. Glancing at her tables, Katrina noticed that the one with the light out had someone sitting in it. Grabbing a napkin, she rushed that way. She set the napkin down and looked up at the light.

"Can I get you a drink and a light bulb?" She grinned, then looked down to see Blaze staring at her. He grabbed her, quickly pulling her into his lap.

"Hey!" she squealed, then dropped a small kiss to his lips. "I didn't see you come in."

"I like sitting in the dark watching this sexy waitress I've had my eye on," he teased with a wink before taking her bottom lip with his teeth. "You think it's dark enough for me to fuck you without anyone seeing?"

"God, I wish." Katrina moaned as he deepened his kiss.

"Come on, let's get out of here." He started to slide out of the seat with her in his lap.

"No, we can't." Katrina pushed at him, stood, and straightened her clothes as she glanced around. "I'm working, plus Tessa and Jared are coming to surprise everyone. Didn't you notice that everyone is here?"

"Well, you can take a quick break." He stood and pulled her through the bar.

"Katrina?" Bobby shouted as they passed. "Your order is up."

"I got it, Bobby." Lisa grinned, watching Blaze pull Katrina out the back. "I'd say fuck the job too if a man like that was leading me somewhere."

Katrina smirked, hearing Lisa's remark, then tossed her a wave of thanks.

They stepped outside and Blaze stopped, looking around with a frown. "Okay, this isn't going to work." He walked further out, pulling her with him.

"What are we doing?" Katrina laughed, not really caring as long as she was with him. The snow was coming down hard and it was absolutely beautiful.

"There!" he said, then led her toward an open field next to the bar. Finally he stopped.

Katrina smiled, then looked up at the sky. Leaning her head back, she stuck out her tongue, catching the ice-cold snowflakes.

"You know, the first time I saw you do that, I think I loved you." Blaze's voice filled the silence.

Closing her mouth, she moved her head so she could look directly at him. "I got you beat." She touched his chest. "I knew I loved you the day you turned me."

"You are so beautiful. I don't know what I did to deserve your love, but I'll take it and I will cherish it and you." Blaze touched her face. "I'm really not good with words and shit."

Katrina chuckled. "You're doing pretty well, Warrior."

He knelt in front of her. "Katrina, I have never loved anyone in my life until you. I can be a bastard, and I won't always say the right things. I will make you mad, you may even hate me at times, but always know I will never let harm come to you again."

Katrina watched as he pulled a box out of his pocket and opened it. A beautiful diamond ring sparkled as the snowflakes fell on the stone. Her hand slapped over her mouth as she stared.

"Katrina, please say something." Blaze actually sounded nervous.

"What exactly are you asking me, Blaze?" She pulled her eyes away from the gorgeous ring to look him in the eye. "You know what, it doesn't matter. Yes! Whatever it is, absolutely yes!"

He took the ring out and placed it on her finger. Then he stood and took her in his arms for a kiss that could melt a mountain of snow. She heard the happy screams coming from the bar and knew she'd missed Tessa and Jared's surprise, but she didn't care. She was exactly where she wanted to be.

"Guys!" Steve's voice broke through their little reunion. "Hey, yo! You missed it! Come on! Tessa is a freaking vampire!"

"Can I kill him?" Blaze growled against her lips.

"No, you cannot," Katrina whispered against his.

"Dammit!"

"Play nice, Blaze." Katrina laughed when he growled, then carried her back to the bar.

"I don't do nice well." He put her down and held the door open, but they both noticed Ronan leaning against the wall with his hat pulled low over his eyes.

"Ronan," Blaze said.

"Blaze," Ronan countered.

"You lost?" Blaze frowned, wondering what he was doing outside.

"No, just watching to make sure a certain lady is being taken care of." Ronan tipped his hat up to look at Blaze.

"I'm fine, Ronan." Katrina smiled at him and pinched Blaze when he growled. "Thank you."

"Yeah, thanks, Ronan." Blaze added a glare to his sarcastic remark. He ushered Katrina inside with one last snarl at Ronan, who just smirked then lowered his head again. "Can I kill *him*?"

"No." Katrina turned and smiled up at him. "Jealous?"

"Yes," he answered. "You are mine, and I think you have a thing for cowboys."

"I do not, but if you decided to wear cowboy boots tonight, I wouldn't complain." She gave him a wink.

Blaze growled and pulled her into the shadows. It was a while before they made the party.

AUTHOR NOTE

Thank you so much for the support you have shown me over the years. I appreciate you all more than you will ever know. I know it's not reality to think I will make everyone happy with my stories, but know that with each word written you, the readers, are always in my thoughts.

A special thank you to my editor, Becky Johnson, who pushes me further than I could ever push myself. Donna Pemberton, the extra steps you go through to make sure the stories come out right is amazing, thank you. Donna Bossert, don't know how I even functioned in the writing world before you, thank you for every single thing you do. My awesome review team, thank you for letting me know what sucks and what works, you totally ROCK! The awesome Warriorettes, you are the best street team and I can't even express how much I appreciate each one of you. To my family, who I adore, thank you for always having my back. And again, the readers. Thank you so much! I've said it before and I will continue to say it….without you there is no story!

Blaze – The Protectors Series

COMING SOON

'The Protectors Series' Book #11 The Invisible Warrior

'Lee County Wolves' Book #3 Forbidden Desire

The Enforcer Book #2 Not Yet Titled

Find out more about me and the Warriors at

www.teresagabelman.com

https://www.facebook.com/pages/Teresa-Gabelman/191553587598342?ref=bookmarks

Printed in Great Britain
by Amazon